CARLY PHILLIPS

Hot Item

HQN™

ISBN 0-373-77122-3

HOT ITEM

www.HQNBooks.com

Printed in U.S.A.

Dear Reader,

I am so happy to bring you the last in THE HOT ZONE trilogy. *Hot Item* is Sophie's story, and she's ready for her happily ever after. She just doesn't know it yet. She also doesn't know that her perfect man is none other than an athlete. Riley Nash, football player, is everything Sophie isn't—he creates his own rules and doesn't believe in her form of organization. You know what they say—opposites attract. So read on to see what happens when they do! Thank you for joining me for the ride of Annabelle, Micki, Sophie and even Yank and Lola, and Spencer's stories. I've had a blast writing these books, and I love hearing from you. You can write me at carly@carlyphillips.com or P.O. Box 483, Purchase, NY 10577 or visit my home on the Web at www.carlyphillips.com.

Happy reading!

Best wishes,

Carly Phillips

To everyone at Harlequin—
Donna Hayes, Randall Toye, Dianne Moggy,
Katherine Orr, Marleah Stout and Tracy Farrell
for believing in me. And a special thank-you to
Brenda Chin for pushing me harder and making me
better (I hope!) with each book.

Hot
Item

PROLOGUE

YANK MORGAN LEANED back in his favorite chair and puffed on a Monte Cristo cigar. Damn, life was good. At least, as good as it could be with his three nieces sick with colds and too quiet for his peace of mind. He'd been caring for the girls since their parents died in a plane crash a little over a year ago and he'd done his best to maintain normalcy for them and for himself. Hence, his weekly poker night with the guys.

"Hey, Morgan. You folding or what?" Curly asked.

"Depends on your hand."

Curly glanced at his cards and rubbed his hand over his bald head, a sure sign the man's hand sucked. "What the hell. I'm in."

"Me, too." Spencer Atkins, Yank's friend and business rival, tossed his bet onto the pile of chips in the center of the table and pulled a long drag of his cigar.

"Better not inhale," a small female voice warned.

Yank frowned and turned to the doorway. His middle niece, Sophie, stood in her flannel nightgown and glared, arms folded across her chest.

"You're supposed to be resting," Yank said.

She shrugged. "My nose is stuffed. I want Lola," she said, speaking of his assistant and one-time lover, not that any of the girls knew that last part. Lola was the only female influence the girls had.

Yank didn't discourage their relationship. But the woman complicated his life to no end and reminded him of their once-hot affair. He had his hands full with three little women. He didn't need a fourth female making demands on his time and forcing him to give up the important things. Things like cigars and poker.

"Can I call her, Uncle Yank? Please?" Sophie asked.

"Yeah, can she call her?" Spencer asked, laughing. "As if you'd say no. It's no hardship having that beautiful woman around twenty-four/seven, is it, Morgan?"

Yank scowled. "Take some aspirin instead," he told his niece.

"Aspirin's no good for children. There's a new study out that shows it can cause something called Reye's syndrome. Lola would know that," Sophie said in an accusing tone.

He groaned. "You wanna call her, call her. Just make sure she knows I'm tied up with the boys."

Sophie rolled her eyes. "She knows. Everyone knows Tuesday night's poker night." Sophie ran over and kissed his cheek. "Thanks, Uncle Yank. I promise not to bother you again."

He hugged the little girl tight. "You never bother me."

She clasped her hands behind her back. "You

mean that?" she asked in a serious voice, one too old for her eleven years.

Losing parents did that to kids, Yank had learned. Annabelle, the oldest, had taken over the mother role whenever Lola wasn't around, bossing her sisters and making sure everyone behaved. Micki, the youngest, tagged along with him everywhere he went, never giving him time or space to breathe, obviously afraid if she did, he'd run away and never return. And Sophie lost herself in books as if she could escape into another world. But she also used the knowledge she learned to try to control everyone and everything around her.

Yank figured she thought if she orchestrated life, she wouldn't lose people around her the way she lost her parents. When had he turned into a damn shrink? he wondered. "Go," he said softly. "The sooner you call Lola, the sooner you'll get some sleep."

She nodded. "Okay." She ran out of the room and he heard her chattering on the phone from the kitchen.

"Sorry," he muttered. "Let's get back to business."

Spencer lifted his glass and took a sip of the whiskey Yank kept in the bar. "Son of a bitch. I'm out." With a scowl, he folded his hand. "I'll just have a smoke and watch Yank take the rest of you suckers for all you're worth."

A few hands later, Spencer reached for his cigar, then narrowed his gaze when he came up empty-handed. "Winning's not enough for you, Morgan? You have to stoop to stealing stogies for fun?"

Yank tossed his cards onto the table. "I take offense to the implication. I'm winnin' fair and square. And I didn't take your damn cigar. Maybe you're getting old and you forgot whether or not you lit one."

Curly rose to his feet. "Come on, boys. We don't need to fight amongst ourselves. Spence here can have my cigar. If my wife smells it on me she'll douse me with kerosene and light a match." He glanced down. "Hey, wait a second..."

Yank winced. "Yours is gone, too?" he asked, a sneaking suspicion dawning.

The other man nodded.

"Mel?" Yank turned to the fourth man.

"Mine's gone, too."

Yank groaned. "Sophia Francesca Jordan!" he bellowed. "Get in here now."

"You don't have to yell, Uncle Yank. I'm right here." Sophie's voice sounded from beneath the card table.

The little sneak. How had she gotten underneath there without them noticing? he wondered.

She tried to stand too soon and bumped her head. "Ouch!" Finally she stood in front of him, guilt written all over her little face. Her cheeks were pink and her blue eyes too wide and innocent.

"Give the boys back their cigars," Yank demanded.

Her eyes filled with tears. "But..."

"Don't tell me you didn't take them. What else would you be doing sneaking 'round under there?"

She shook her head. "I wasn't going to say that."

"What were you going to say?" Spencer asked in

a surprisingly kind voice considering he'd nearly strung Yank up alive for stealing his cigar. Faced with the midget culprit, his tone gentled as it always did around Sophie. He had a soft spot for the middle kid.

Sophie clasped her hands behind her long flannel nightgown. "The Surgeon General says smoking's bad for your health. It'll turn your lungs black and clog your arties."

"Arteries, doofus," Annabelle said, walking in from the doorway. "Sorry, Uncle Yank. I fell asleep and forgot to watch her. It won't happen again." She grabbed her sister's hand and pulled, trying to drag her from the room.

"Stop," Sophie whined. "I'm right and they all know it."

"It doesn't matter. They're guys and guys smoke," the third Musketeer chimed in, surprising them all by walking in from the kitchen. In her hand, Micki held the ashtray with all the men's cigars.

"Hey, it took a long time for me to collect those without them noticing," Sophie said.

"But they weren't yours to take." Annabelle walked around the room, handing each man a used cigar.

In all likelihood nobody got the right smoke and Yank cringed. "I think it's time to call it a night."

"If Lola had come, none of this would have happened," Annabelle said. "She'd have kept Sophie busy in the kitchen."

"If Lola had come, she'd be sprayin' Lysol around all our heads," Yank muttered.

"That's not nice, Uncle Yank." Micki smacked him on the shoulder with her little hand.

"See?" he said to his friends. "This is why I won't git married ever. I already got three little women telling me what to do."

Curly shook his head. "It's more like with three little girls, you couldn't find a woman in her right mind who would have you."

"Except Lola. But Yank's not bright enough to know a good thing when he's got one," Spencer said with a laugh.

"This from someone who's already got one divorce under his belt."

Sophie pulled the sleeve of Spencer's sweater. "Really? You were married? To who? When? How?"

"None of your business, little girl." He softened his words by patting her on the head.

"Like that'll satisfy her. Sophie needs to know all details about all things."

"What'd she look like? Why'd she leave? Or did you leave?"

Yank chuckled. At least she'd stopped harassing them about the cigars. Though given Sophie's inquisitive nature and need to control everything and everyone around her, he should probably lock up the Cubans. Heaven help the man who had to deal with her when she grew up.

CHAPTER ONE

"ACCORDING TO a reliable source, top sports agent Spencer Atkins, of the recently merged firm Athletes Only and its subsidiary PR firm The Hot Zone, is gay." Sophie Jordan groaned when she saw the line in New York City's most read gossip column.

How would the players Spencer represented react to the news? How would Spencer handle being outed? But most importantly, how in the world had this secret come out now, well over a month after she and her family had learned the news for the first time?

In the time since they'd learned the truth, Spencer's revelation had been put aside in favor of more pressing projects: the merger of Yank and Spencer's sports agencies and the all-important spin that "we're better and stronger than ever." Enough time had passed that even Sophie, who normally covered all bases, had dismissed the possibility of the story being leaked.

"Guess I thought wrong," she muttered. Sophie hated being wrong. It meant she'd miscalculated and the feeling sent her spiraling into an anxious frenzy, the only solution being to regain her precious control.

Problem was, she didn't see any way to find her center. Sophie, who shone behind the scenes, couldn't hide behind books or To Do lists now. She couldn't even push her sisters to the forefront of the storm and handle things in the background. Chaos reigned and she was the only one available to handle the media mess sure to follow.

Annabelle was home on maternity leave with her baby girl, Sydney, and Micki was on her honeymoon with Damian Fuller, her retired center fielder husband. Their receptionist had called in sick, the temp agency still hadn't sent anyone over to cover and the phones were ringing off the hook.

She glanced at the flashing switchboard behind the reception desk and imagined the many messages accumulating on voice mail, the reporters asking for confirmation of the story and the players they represented caught off guard by the news. She didn't want to believe they'd turn against Spencer because of his sexual orientation. Her family felt no differently about Spencer upon hearing the news. But knowing human nature, and athletes in particular, Sophie expected a difficult transition period anyway.

Anxiety and upheaval were things Sophie understood all too well. In the past few months, her life had been drastically changed by her sisters' marriages, followed by Uncle Yank and Lola's reunion. Lola had even taken over dealing with Uncle Yank's macular degeneration and postsurgical care for his broken hip.

Without someone else's issues to focus on, Sophie had been left at loose ends. Add to that the merger of Atkins and Associates and The Hot Zone, and life as she knew it had been blown to bits. Normal was nowhere to be found.

So yes, she could relate to the players being upset by the new status quo. They, like Sophie, would just need to adapt to the notion of change.

As if willing it could make it so. She shook her head. If adapting were simple, Sophie wouldn't be feeling so lost and out of control right now.

She glanced at her watch and realized it was already ten in the morning. Where in the world was the man of the day? Spencer always arrived at the office punctually at nine. It was one of the things she could count on in her suddenly crazy world.

His prompt nature and conservative ways were a part of what Sophie liked about him. She could relate to his methodical means of coping with life, which were much like her own. From the time she'd moved in with Uncle Yank, she and Spencer had had a father-daughter type of connection. He'd always given her the attention and respect that often got lost within her own family, thanks to her being in the middle of Annabelle, her vibrant older sister, and Micki, the younger sibling who seemed to fit right into Uncle Yank's athletic life.

"Ms. Jordan?"

Sophie glanced up to see a woman standing before her. She had to be in her early twenties, and by her tentative expression, definitely not wizened in the ways of business.

"Yes, I'm Sophie. Please tell me you're from the Helping Hands Temp Agency?"

The brunette nodded. "My first day actually. I'm Nicki Fielding."

"Nice to meet you." Sophie swallowed over her disappointment in being right since she could use an experienced receptionist. "As long as you can answer the phones, say 'no comment' until The Hot Zone is ready to issue a statement and take messages, you'll do just fine."

"No computer work?" the girl asked.

"Not today, you won't have time." Sophie lightly prodded her toward the front desk where the telephone still rang, the lines lighting up like fireflies, and prayed Raine would get over the flu soon.

"Okay, the main desk is covered," she said aloud. "Now I can move on to the next order of business."

Spencer. Just where was he?

She dialed his home number, but his answering machine picked up immediately. She tried his cell phone next but it went right to voice mail. She pursed her lips. It wasn't like him not to check in if he was going to be late. Had the media leak sent him temporarily underground?

She worried about how he'd handle the public and the press and about his mental state. After all, he'd kept this secret for a lifetime. He'd always been vague about his prior marriage. She remembered asking him about it when she was a little girl. She'd never received a straight reply and now Sophie understood why. He must be in a panic now.

Sophie knew she had to find him and soon. In addition to being someone she looked up to and respected, he was a close friend of the family and had been for years, even before the merger. He had never let business rivalry affect his friendship with Uncle Yank and he had been there for Lola when she'd thought things were over with Yank for good. It was time the family returned the favor even if Sophie was the only family member around to do it.

She looked forward to the challenge and not just because helping Spencer spin his life story to the press would give Sophie something to think about besides being alone and uncertain of what turn her life would take next. Although she had to admit the diversion had merit.

No, Spencer Atkins was a good man with a good heart. He'd weather this "coming out" with Sophie's help, while she'd do her best to represent the absent Hot Zone family members. He deserved nothing less.

SPENCER ATKINS DESERVED a swift kick in the ass, Riley Nash thought and tossed the newspaper across the den in disgust. What had started as a mention in a gossip column had escalated to the back page of all the major New York newspapers.

Big-time sports agent Spencer Atkins was gay. Who knew? Not his only son, that's for sure.

Riley shook his head. What a sham his life had been. He'd always known who his biological father was even though he'd been adopted by Senator Harlan Nash of Brandon, Mississippi. A right-wing conservative with aspirations of living in the White House. A man whose constituents wouldn't be happy to know that the senator's wife had once been married to a gay sports agent—and that Senator Nash had raised the man's son.

Riley groaned and ran a hand through his hair. Spencer Atkins and his mother had parted ways while his mother was pregnant. She'd met Harlan Nash while she was going through her divorce and from what Riley understood, it'd been caring at first sight for Anne, love at first sight for Harlan. He'd married Riley's mother knowing she was pregnant with another man's child and raised him like his own. Harlan could be controlling and dictatorial with his staff and on occasion with his family, but no one could fault him for his goals, his drive…or for his heart. Over the years, his mother had grown to love her husband deeply.

Having grown up in Mississippi, Riley wasn't fond of his stepfather's politics or of the political climate in his hometown. The recent polls had proved it was anti gay marriage. But he loved Harlan Nash and wasn't about to see him hurt by something that was beyond his control.

Riley's mother, Anne, had always suggested he tuck the knowledge of Spencer's parentage away and do nothing with it, but Riley had been curious. Even more so when he'd realized what his real dad did for a living. A natural athlete from day one, Riley desperately craved the man's approval and acknowledgment and he'd tried hard to get it.

As a kid, Riley thought once Spencer saw his son's talent in his chosen field, Spencer would reach out to him. Yet despite being a junior-high and high-school quarterback, despite countless trophies, awards, write-ups in the local papers, nothing about Riley had ever captured Spencer Atkins's attention. He never answered Riley's letters or returned his calls.

Still, he'd had his biological father in mind while he'd played QB for Boston College and won the Heisman. With no reply to his request that Spencer represent him, Riley had been the first-round draft pick, with Yank Morgan as his agent. Still nothing from his old man. He'd taken that silence as the final slap.

Once Riley had accepted that the man would never publicly acknowledge him as his son, he'd told himself he didn't care. If the man didn't want anything from Riley, Riley didn't need a damn thing from him. He no longer worried about what other people thought of him and had carried the same attitude over into his life, doing things his way.

Riley had started his career with Cincinnati and hoped to end it where he played now, with the New York Giants. He was a good enough player to get away with coloring outside the lines, something his coaches and his agent accepted and understood because as much as he looked out for number one, he looked out for his team as well.

Looking back at the path he'd chosen and the reasons behind it, Riley realized it was a damn good thing he loved his profession. Otherwise he'd have wasted his life pursuing a football career just so he could get the attention of a man who wanted nothing to do with him.

As today's headlines proved, Riley didn't know a damn thing about who Spencer Atkins was or what he wanted. He only knew what Atkins wanted the world to see. So in addition to "absent, disinterested parent," Atkins could now add "fake" to his impressive résumé.

"Way to go, Pop," Riley muttered under his breath.

"Did you say something?" Julia, a beautiful redhead who'd spent the night in his bed, strode in from the other room.

He'd been so caught off guard by the news in the paper, he'd all but forgotten Julia was waiting in the bedroom.

Coming up beside him, she wrapped her arms around his neck and pressed a kiss against his cheek. "What's going on? Why didn't you come back to bed?" She eased her body into his lap.

"Nothing important." He turned to kiss her full on the lips, running his hand over her breasts. His body responded immediately, assuring him he was nothing like the old man.

The old man he only knew about from stories his

mother had told him when he was a kid. They'd broken up because they were incompatible, she'd said. They'd wanted different things out of life. Those once vague words began to make more sense now. Had his mother known about Spencer all along? Had she found out during their marriage? Or was she discovering the truth now over her morning coffee, along with the rest of the world?

Suddenly, Julia rose to her feet. "Your mind's somewhere else," she chided softly.

"Yeah." He glanced down, unable to deny the obvious.

"Well, I really need to get back to the hotel anyway. My plane leaves at noon."

Julia was a flight attendant who traveled the world and sometimes called Riley when she was in New York. Sometimes not. The arrangement worked well since Riley had an irregular schedule, thanks to his joint-custody arrangement with his ex-wife.

His thirteen-year-old daughter, Elizabeth, came first on his list of priorities. Yet another way he was nothing like the man who hadn't raised him.

He followed Julia back into the bedroom.

She strode over to the bed, unaffectedly naked and began picking up her clothes. "Did I tell you Jacques asked me to marry him?" She casually tossed the news his way.

He raised an eyebrow, not surprised the words didn't elicit a reaction one way or another. He enjoyed Julia but he wasn't in love with her.

"Then how come I don't see a ring?" he asked lightly.

She shrugged. "I told him I'd think about it." She pulled her shirt over her head, the spandex molding to her near perfect curves. "I'm getting tired of the traveling, the hotel rooms. It's lonely. I could give up my career and not look back," she admitted.

Riley nodded. "I hear you. There comes a time everyone has to make choices." He paused and met her gaze. "I take it this is…goodbye, then?"

She nodded. "I couldn't say yes without telling you. And besides I thought we deserved one last time together." She treated him to a smile.

An easy parting, he thought thankfully. He'd been blessed that way. Even his short marriage to Lisa had ended amicably and they'd never argued over custody or money, mainly because as the mother of his child, he'd denied her nothing and even increased her monthly payments as his career had soared. Just a case of marrying too young and expecting too little.

Similar to his own parents, or so he'd always thought. Once again he caught himself wondering about Spencer Atkins. Had Spencer's marriage been a ruse? An attempt to live a so-called normal life? Had Riley been conceived out of love as he'd been told by his mother or as the unfortunate result of a lie on the part of his father?

So many questions. He wished he didn't give a damn, but Riley could no longer deny his curiosity.

And if he wanted to know more, so would the reporters who'd gotten wind of this story. They'd dig and dig deep. They'd find the marriage certificate that bore the names of Spencer Atkins and his mother and they'd discover that she'd had a child.

In no time the scandal would reach his stepfather, who was running for the United States Senate as a representative of the great state of Mississippi. A lifetime's worth of hard work and dedication, and aspirations of living in the White House would go down the drain. Riley wouldn't let that happen.

Of course he'd be a liar if he didn't admit some self-interest in the matter, too. If the press found out the relationship between Riley and Atkins, Riley's life in the locker room would be a living hell. The guys would question his masculinity and not even his marriage and kid would save him. Like father, like son the guys would say. Riley could hold his own with his teammates and he knew the scandal would blow over with time, but his teenage daughter didn't need the hassle from the fallout.

Riley shook his head at the irony. A lifetime of wishing the man would acknowledge him and now it was the last thing he wanted.

His best option was to reach Spencer before the media did and convince him not to talk. Which shouldn't be a stretch for a man who'd made silence an art form. Frustration filled Riley over the need to turn to Spencer Atkins for anything, but he reminded himself that it wasn't his own needs driving him. He'd be making the effort for his parents and his daughter.

The time had come for father and son to meet face-to-face at last.

THREE DAYS HAD PASSED and Spencer was officially MIA. Sophie paced her office, wearing a path in the plush carpeting, which she'd discovered was twenty-five steps from the window overlooking the East River to the bathroom in the far corner. Back and forth, back and forth, but no matter how far she walked, the reality never changed. The football draft was three weeks away and Spencer Atkins had taken off for parts unknown.

John Cashman, this year's Heisman winner and almost newly signed client, was calling hourly to speak with Spencer or Yank. Yank's cruise made him unavailable and the younger agents weren't appeasing Cashman with their answers.

Sophie's palms sweated over the athlete's last threat. If he didn't speak to Spencer by the end of the week, he'd sign with the Cambias Agency, their number one competition.

Uncle Yank and Spencer inspired loyalty and cared about their clients' future, while Cambias only saw dollar signs in his bank account. But a young, healthy, starry-eyed kid who'd never been injured wouldn't appreciate the experience Spencer and Uncle Yank brought to the table. And at the moment, Cashman wasn't listening to anything Sophie or the other agents had to say.

The dog she was babysitting stared from the place she'd adopted as her own. Noodle, Uncle Yank's Labradoodle, carelessly lounged on the client-designated chair. When not rolling over onto her back for a belly rub, she licked herself in unmentionable places. Sophie didn't mind watching the dog, but animals really weren't her thing.

Which was why she steered clear of any personal relationships with professional athletes, she thought, giving herself her first real laugh of the day. A laugh she desperately needed. With the recent marriages, honeymoons and pregnancy, Sophie was in charge here at the office and she'd never felt so alone. It was a state she'd judiciously avoided since her parents' deaths. She'd also avoided feeling as lost and scared as she had when she'd lost her mother and father by maintaining firm control over life.

Some called her anal. She figured she was smart. And being smart, she couldn't let chaos seep into the agency, despite all that was going on.

Yesterday she'd received a handwritten note from Spencer, postmarked from New York. "Laying low. Back in time for draft." As if that would pacify John Cashman.

She walked over to the chalkboard she kept with everyone's schedules marked on it. All active clients on the sports side were divided among the agency representatives. She'd doled out the PR to the new people she and her sisters had hired in the past few months, opting to leave the handling of Spencer's situation for herself.

So far she'd avoided the media because she wasn't ready to give a statement without talking to the man in question, which was one less thing to deal with, at least for now.

But the draft players represented by Yank and Spencer were antsy.

She picked up the phone and buzzed Spencer's personal secretary, a woman named Frannie who'd worked for him for years. Frannie ran Spencer's life.

"Frannie, this is Sophie. Can you bring me a list of all the places Spencer has vacationed in the past few years along with the phone numbers of any relatives he regularly speaks to?"

"Not a problem, but I don't think he'd contact those people or go to any place that the press could easily find him."

Sophie sighed. "I know you're right but I have to do something. Otherwise I'll lose my mind. How's it going with Cashman?"

"I told him Spencer was due to call, but we just didn't know when, and as soon as we heard from him, he'd hear from us. And I made him promise not to do something stupid in the meantime."

Sophie tried to breathe steadily so she didn't get light-headed and pass out, something she was known to do on occasion. "I don't trust him or Cambias but it's the best we've got for now. Thanks, Frannie."

"Hang in there, honey. I'll get those names to you as soon as I can." Frannie disconnected.

No sooner had Sophie hung up the phone when someone knocked on her door. Obviously her secretary wasn't sitting at her desk to intercept him. Lori did her work but enjoyed her coffee breaks more.

"Come in," Sophie called out, hoping this was good news for a change.

She turned to greet her visitor and knew immediately she was in deep trouble. He had a black leather jacket slung over his wide shoulders, razor stubble on his handsome face and a reputation that preceded him. Although Sophie and The Hot Zone had never handled Riley Nash's publicity, he'd been a client of her uncle's too long for her not to know him.

He made his presence known each time he came to the office. He oozed raw male sexuality. And her body responded to it, despite her brain's warnings to ignore the man. Normally her body listened to whatever Sophie's analytical mind dictated but not when it came to Riley Nash.

As partners in The Hot Zone, Sophie and her siblings shared equal responsibility, but as sisters they had an understanding. Micki handled the difficult athletes and Annabelle the jocks, which was how they'd ended up paired with Damian Fuller and Brandon Vaughn, respectively. Sophie took care of the more refined aspects of the business. She booked photo shoots, galas and large charity events. Things that she could control.

Sophie didn't do jocks. Not in any sense of the word. So the fact that she drooled at the sight of her uncle's star football client really ticked her off. She hated that this cocky jock could affect her on a purely elemental level when the other men who came and went from these offices didn't even make her blink. Riley Nash blew her precious control to hell and back.

She desired him badly and he knew it. He also knew the attraction flustered her and he took shameless advantage, going out of his way to seek her out and push her buttons. And just when she didn't think the sexual tension between them could soar much higher, he'd stop by her office for a visit and up the ante between them. That he'd show up here now, mid-crisis, was a move she hadn't anticipated and sure as hell didn't appreciate.

Drawing a deep breath, she leaned against the desk and resisted the urge to check her hair and makeup. "Let me guess. You charmed your way past my secretary?" she asked him.

"If she'd been at her desk, I'm sure I would have." He strode forward, full of cocky male attitude. "Nobody was outside to stop me."

She sighed. This day was just getting better and better.

He stepped beside her, standing so close his warm scent penetrated her pores and she grew damp in places he never failed to remind her existed. She no longer tried to convince herself that her reaction was normal for a woman who'd been sexually deprived for well over a year. Her sudden increase in temperature and spike in arousal had everything to do with Riley Nash.

"So what can I do for you?" she asked him.

He grinned. "Depends on what you're offering, sweet thing."

Each time he spoke, he confirmed her notion that he was the embodiment of every jock nightmare she'd ever had. Raunchy, sexist, impossible to control. It didn't matter. The man's mere existence turned her into a drooling idiot.

She looked him up and down, trying to appear as if he didn't faze her one bit. "Turn down the wattage on that smile, big boy. I'm busy and don't have time to indulge your flirting today." She glanced at her watch and tapped on the dial. "Well? What can I do for you?"

His smile withered. "I need to see Atkins."

"Yank's your agent," she reminded him as if he were dense.

"This is personal not professional."

His words took her by surprise. As far as Sophie knew, Riley had no dealings with Spencer Atkins or his former agency. Come to think of it, he hadn't been to the office since the merger. "I didn't realize you two knew one another."

"And I didn't realize I had to answer to you before I could see my…before I could see Spencer." He clenched his jaw tight, obviously withholding information.

Sophie was in no mood to push him for answers

or bait him today. She had enough on her plate. "Look, it's been a long day." It was as much of an apology as she was willing to offer him.

He glanced at his watch and chuckled, his light brown eyes dancing with flecks of gold. "It's only ten in the morning."

"Exactly," she said wryly.

He met her gaze and the connection she couldn't deny sparked to life between them. She wished it was purely sexual, but something about the man captured her so completely, she often wondered what more existed beneath the jock exterior. Something had to for her to be so drawn to him. She just wasn't the type to be hooked by something as insubstantial and superficial as sex appeal.

"So what's got you all riled up so early, if not my dazzling presence?" he asked.

"Let's just say you could see Spencer if I knew where he was." The admission was a huge one. She was *trusting* Riley's discretion.

He lowered himself onto the corner of her desk and nodded slowly. "I guess if I were Atkins, I'd be laying low, too."

"I take it you've seen the articles." Not only had the papers picked up on the gossip column entry and turned it into front page headlines, but they'd noted Spencer's sudden disappearance from his usual lunch and dinner haunts.

Riley nodded.

"But that doesn't mean he ran away," she said defensively. "How about you leave your number and I call you once I reach him?"

He tipped his head to one side. "No can do."

"Well, you can't stick around here waiting who knows how long just to have a personal word with—"

"My father."

"What?"

Riley winced at his admission, then ran a hand through his hair and took a deep breath. "What guarantee do I have that you'll keep that information confidential?"

"My word." She tried not to show how affronted she was by Riley's lack of faith considering she'd just divulged sensitive business information herself.

"I'd prefer something more tangible." Riley reached into his pocket and pulled out a small wallet, thumbed through some bills and then lifted a folded check from inside.

Without warning, he looked up and met her stare and she discovered he was just as hot when he wasn't deliberately turning on the charm. His gaze simmered with heat that had nothing to do with sex, but suddenly Sophie couldn't think of anything else. Those big hands wrapped around the check had her imagining all sorts of other things he could do with them—to her.

He grabbed a pen and began to fill out the empty spaces on the check, all business.

"What are you doing?" she asked.

"I'm hiring you." His head was still bent over as he wrote.

His sandy-colored hair was shaggy, long and as
sexy as the man himself.

"That way I can divulge all my personal secrets
and you're bound to keep things confidential."

She wasn't sure she wanted to hear them and her
mouth grew dry. "I'm not a lawyer."

"No, but you're a publicist and if I hire you and tell
you things about my life and career, you won't go
spilling the information to the press without my permission. True?" He cocked an eyebrow in certainty.

She nodded. "True."

"Then consider yourself hired."

Sophie accepted the check with trembling hands.
She'd just entered into a business agreement that was
bound to give her deeper insight into Riley Nash. And
that shift in their dynamic could very well increase her
desire for the man. As if her life wasn't complicated
enough, Riley had just joined her for the ride.

CHAPTER TWO

AT SOPHIE'S OBVIOUS attempt to feign composure and pretend his hiring her didn't send her into a tailspin, Riley bit the inside of his cheek to keep from laughing aloud.

She folded the check in half. "You could have just trusted me instead of insisting we enter into some ridiculous employment contract." Her tone held a trace of hurt over his lack of faith.

Maybe she had a point. Hiring her probably made little sense, but he hadn't been able to think of another way to guarantee his secret remained private.

"I don't know you well enough to trust you, but we could remedy that," he said in a deliberately suggestive tone, his words meant to explain as well as to tease.

Whenever he stopped by The Hot Zone offices, he could never resist coming to see the blue-eyed blonde. He enjoyed their sparring and liked trying to figure her out. Sophie Jordan presented an intriguing mess of contradictions, her inherent control and conservative facade so at odds with the simmering heat he saw in her eyes.

He inhaled deeply. As usual her luscious scent evoked images of hot bodies in tangled sheets.

"So now that I represent you, what comes next?" she asked warily.

He understood her discomfort. He and Sophie shared an unusual relationship that consisted mostly of a sexual dynamic neither understood.

For Riley, Sophie was the antithesis of every woman he was normally drawn to. Riley liked his women *real*. He enjoyed tousled hair he could mess up with his hands and he preferred to see a woman's cleavage, not guess at what her breasts looked like beneath a prim silk blouse. His agent's niece might be a knockout in the classical sense, but with her hair pulled into a tight knot and her prissy suit, she wasn't his type. Yet she never failed to brighten his day.

He couldn't say he did the same for her. Sophie had a distinct inability to deal with the sexual tension between them. Two minutes in his presence and she'd lose her composure, changing from Grace Kelly cool to downright flustered. A pink flush tinged her cheeks whenever he was near.

Today, however, she seemed more tense than usual and something suddenly urged him to be sensitive to what was going on in that head of hers and respect the boundaries she'd raised. Another anomaly, Riley thought. He always respected women but when it came to Sophie, he wondered what she was thinking.

Feeling.

Desiring.

He inhaled deeply. Unbidden, he was treated to visions of eating strawberries and champagne directly off her porcelain skin. His groin tightened with a hard-on he hadn't felt the likes of in years. Not a good way to respect her feelings, Riley thought.

She picked up the pen he'd discarded and began to tap it against the desk. "Okay, if you aren't going to explain, I have a few things to say first. And now that you've hired me, I have the right to speak my mind."

"Lack of a professional relationship has never stopped you before," he reminded her with a wink.

Her cheeks burned brighter. "But now I have the satisfaction of knowing you're paying me to tell you the way things are going to be." A Cheshire-cat grin tilted her lips as she enjoyed what she perceived as the upper hand.

She'd soon learn he rarely gave up control. Doing things his way was the only means of assuring himself that nobody would hurt him the same way his real father had.

"So what's going on in there?" He lightly tapped her head.

She swallowed hard. "I've known Spencer practically my whole life and he's never mentioned having a son. Never mind one who's the top quarterback in the NFL."

He folded his arms across his chest. He hated the subject, never mind that he'd opened this Pandora's box. "So?"

"So considering the news currently circulating, forgive me if I question your story, as well as your motives for wanting to see Spencer."

He wasn't surprised she had the guts to stand up to him. After all, she was one of the top publicists in a male-dominated market.

He raised an eyebrow. "The man was just outed. Do you really think I'd pick this particular time to announce my relationship to Atkins unless it was true?"

She paused, then slowly nodded, acknowledging his point.

Although she accepted his argument, he couldn't ignore how she'd leaped to Spencer's defense. "So what are you? Atkins's protector?"

She squared her shoulders. "Don't underestimate me because I'm a woman, Nash. We're like family around here. What affects one of us affects us all."

How nice that Atkins had family here when he'd so deliberately ignored his own. Her words shouldn't have hurt but they did. They sliced like a knife inside Riley's chest. Unfortunately they didn't diminish the need for him to talk to the old man.

Since the Atkins and Hot Zone merger, Riley had done all his agency business over the phone. He hadn't wanted to risk running into his father. Now that was exactly what he wished to do.

He needed to reach Atkins and ensure the man's silence, as he'd promised his mother when she'd called in a panic earlier. Which meant he also needed Sophie and whatever connections she had.

He had no choice but to spill his guts. "Whether or not he's ever acknowledged the fact, I am Spencer Atkins's son. Actually, I'm just another of his dirty little secrets, but this secret affects more than just him. I need to talk to him as soon as possible."

Sophie's expression softened. "I would tell him if I could. Unfortunately, Spencer has been out of touch for three days. And while we're sharing secrets, I should add if we don't get in touch with him soon, the agency will lose the first-round pick in the football draft." She expelled a frustrated breath. "So can you help me?"

Apparently she needed him, too, putting them on more equal ground. The notion eased the vise squeezing his chest. "I haven't been in contact with Spencer in the past few days, either." He deliberately left out his lack of a relationship with the older man up until now. "But I can make some calls and see if anyone in my family has any ideas about where he might go." Starting with his mother, Riley thought. It may have been years since she and Spencer had spoken, but maybe she remembered some relatives or someplace he liked to hide out.

"Feel free." Sophie gestured to the phone on her desk.

He strode over and sat down. A howl sounded loud and shrill in his ears at the same time he jumped off something warm and soft. He glanced down. A white curly-haired mutt glared at him from Sophie's desk chair.

Sophie laughed, a light, carefree sound, so opposite from her normally uptight voice he was astounded. It made him want to see her loosen up in every way.

"Something funny?" he asked.

She shook her head. "I just didn't realize Noodle had switched seats."

"Better to sit on the dog than on dog—"

She cleared her throat, cutting him off.

"Sorry. Didn't mean to offend your delicate sensibilities." This time *he* chuckled. "How do I get an outside line? Need to dial nine?"

She shook her head. "Just pick up the phone and press any free line."

Resigned, Riley dialed his mother and had mixed feelings when she wasn't home to take his call. On the one hand he was grateful he wouldn't have to upset her by discussing Spencer again, and on the other hand he was aggravated he'd have to spend more time on this search.

"Hi, Frannie. Come on in." Sophie's voice interrupted his thoughts as an older woman with gray hair walked into the room, a piece of paper in hand.

"Spencer has two sisters and a niece who live in Florida," the other woman said.

Sophie nodded. She knew he had family in Fort Lauderdale.

"He's always calling them and sometimes he goes there to visit. Number's on the paper here." Frannie waved the yellow sheath in her hand. "He also owns a time-share in Aruba but it's rented now, so I can't see him going there. Then again if we knew whether or not he took his passport…"

Sophie shook her head. "No way of knowing that. Let's start with family." She glanced at Riley through half-lowered lashes.

"Oh my! I didn't realize you had company. I should have knocked."

"That's okay. This is an emergency. Besides, Mr. Nash is a client of Uncle Yank's." She paused. "He's also a client of mine and we can trust him."

Frannie smiled. "Okay then. I'll be at my desk if you need me, though I have to warn you about something."

Sophie raised an eyebrow.

"Spencer's sisters are eccentric, to quote his words."

"Whatever that means, but I'll keep it in mind. Thanks."

"They're also not answering the phone and there's no machine to record a message. Oh, and John Cashman called. Again."

"This isn't happening." With a groan, Sophie flung herself into the nearest chair, more flustered than he'd ever seen before. "Maybe Spencer's sisters are on vacation, but that doesn't mean Spencer couldn't be there anyway and not taking calls."

Frannie shook her head. "They don't travel. Like I said, eccentric. But you're right. That doesn't rule out the possibility that Spencer went to his sisters' until the heat here in New York dies down."

So he had run off, Riley thought. He didn't blame

the man for wanting to avoid the scandal, but he hated to think his father was a coward.

"Frannie, do you have an address for his sisters?" Sophie asked.

She nodded. "On the paper." She handed Sophie the page. "Just buzz me if you need me."

"Will do and thanks again," Sophie said, gratitude evident in her tone.

Once the other woman had let herself out and shut the door, Sophie glanced at the paper before turning to Riley. Her eyes seemed wider, a mixture of concern and hope in their blue depths.

"If Spencer's sisters don't answer the phone, it looks like I'm headed for Fort Lauderdale. I need to talk to Spencer in person and figure out a game plan."

Her intentions were too vague, Riley thought. He glanced at the ceiling, avoiding her gaze while he took time to think. If he let her go to Florida alone and she didn't find Spencer, no harm done. If she did find the old man, Riley needed to know whether she would convince Atkins to spill his guts to the media in a sympathy play. If so, he might reveal more than the truth about his sexual orientation, and that might include Riley's parentage.

"Once you find Spencer, all you want is for him to get in touch with his clients?" Riley asked.

"In part. I want to save the potential clients and calm his current ones."

Apparently the frenzy surrounding this story went deep. They didn't have time for a long conversation on how other athletes were handling the news, but Riley was curious. Personally, he had no problem with anyone's sexual orientation. He just wished it wasn't *his* biological father who'd come out. During his stepfather's election year, no less.

Sophie had begun pacing the floor of her office. He glanced at her face and realized she was counting her steps. "Why the hell are you doing that?"

"Twenty-four, twenty-five." She stopped at a closed door. "Routine gives me comfort," she explained.

Anal and compulsive, he thought, and didn't have to wonder how she'd handle his fly-by-the-seat-of-his-pants approach to life. Not well.

"Will you let me know how you make out in the Sunshine State?" he asked.

She nodded. "Not a problem." She rubbed her hands together in anticipation. "I can't wait to do some damage control. I need him to issue a statement in response to all this media coverage. In my experience it's always better to have a client's version of events sent out to the media first, forcing other people to respond. In this case we can't do that, but if he replies with the truth before the reporters start digging and speculating, his reputation will come out stronger in the end."

"Whoa." She hadn't mentioned a press release earlier.

Ignoring him, she strode to the desk and began punching in the numbers on the page Frannie had given her. She waited, phone hugged tight against her ear as the phone rang and rang on the other end.

She hung up the receiver and shot him a frustrated glance. "I need to book a flight for tomorrow morning. At least I'll feel I'm *doing* something."

Riley closed his eyes tight, his choices narrowing. If Sophie convinced Spencer to issue an honest statement and he revealed his connection to Riley, all hell could break loose in the conservative red state of Mississippi. After all, she'd said it was better to trump the media before they dug up the dirt and Spencer might choose to do just that.

He had to be by her side when she found his old man.

Once again she picked up the phone, this time hitting the intercom button. "Frannie, book me a seat on the first flight to Fort Lauderdale tomorrow morning."

He rubbed his hands over his burning eyes before focusing on Sophie. She looked as upset as he felt at the moment.

He could only imagine how she'd take his next announcement. "Make that two seats," he said loud enough for the woman on the other end of the speaker phone to hear.

BY LUNCHTIME, Sophie still hadn't reached Spencer's sisters by phone. She desperately needed air. It wasn't enough that Spencer was missing and her world was collapsing in chaos, but she had Riley Nash joining in her search. She didn't know how she'd focus on finding Spencer with the biggest distraction of all hanging around. The sexiest distraction.

She headed for the nearest café around the corner

from the office where Cindy James, a friend and publicist at The Hot Zone, was supposed to meet her. It was a blessedly warm day for March in New York City and she was glad they'd chosen someplace with outdoor tables where she could enjoy the fresh air. Sophie ordered a Diet Coke while she waited and then breathed in deeply, allowing herself the illusion that all was well.

"Hello, Sophia," a masculine voice said with a hint of a Spanish accent.

One that would be sexy if not for the man who possessed the self-assured tone. She eyed the handsome Dominican man, with his designer suit and too-welcoming smile, warily.

"Hello, Miguel," she said to her uncle and Spencer's number-one adversary. "What brings you to this neck of the woods?" The Cambias Agency was in the Bronx, close to where former President Bill Clinton had taken his new offices shortly after leaving the White House.

"May I?" He gestured to the empty seat.

To say no would be rude. "Of course."

He joined her, sitting directly across the small table, where his gaze lingered on hers. When she'd met him at industry events, he'd always been polite and solicitous. Even so, he made her uncomfortable. Miguel Cambias always had an agenda, which made trust something she refused to give.

"I visited your offices to show support for my colleague," he said, obviously referring to Spencer. "The gossip about him in the paper is unfortunate."

Sophie raised an eyebrow, wondering if he'd come to show support or to revel in his opponent's misfortune. "I didn't think you read Liz Smith," she said of the well-known New York gossip columnist.

"My secretary does, as do most people who want to keep up with the pulse of this town. Besides, the story is headline news. Surely you already know that."

She did. She'd just been hoping that he'd slip with more information, like whether his clients were calling about the news, or worse, whether Spencer's clients were inquiring about other representation. Not wanting to let on that she was concerned, she couldn't ask.

"Since my secretary told you where to find me, you must also know Spencer's taken the day off. I'll be sure to relay your concern next time I see him."

Miguel placed his hand over hers. "This can't be easy for you or your uncle. I know how close you all are."

Sophie slid her hand from beneath his and waved it dismissively through the air. "It's not a problem for us or for Athletes Only. I can assure you of that."

He glanced over her shoulder. "I think your lunch date is here."

He rose from his seat at the same time Sophie looked up to see Cindy standing behind her, silently waiting for an opportunity to interrupt. Sophie shot her friend a grateful look. Her timing couldn't have been better. She had no desire to continue talking to Cambias and try to decipher his intent.

"Cindy, I'd like you to meet Miguel Cambias. Miguel, this is Cindy James. She's a publicist at The Hot Zone," Sophie said.

"I'm surprised we haven't met before." His eyes sparkled with definite interest.

"I recently moved here from L.A." A blush spread over Cindy's freckled cheeks.

Even to a casual observer, it was obvious the interest between these two was mutual.

"It's wonderful to meet a coworker of Sophia's." Ever the gentleman, he pulled out the chair. "Especially such a beautiful one."

Cindy took her seat but not before Cambias's gaze raked over Cindy's modellike curves and curly red hair, which hung down to the middle of her back.

From the glimmer in his dark eyes, it appeared that Miguel liked what he saw. "May I offer a word of advice?" he shifted his attention to Sophie, his eyes gleaming with hidden knowledge that made Sophie nervous.

"Can I stop you?" she asked easily.

He laughed. "There are people who don't take other's sexual orientation lightly. You should have Spencer talk to his important clients before someone else does."

His tone was friendly. His words were not. Sophie understood the hidden implication. Spencer's nervous clients were up for grabs. She had to find the man and soon.

"I appreciate the advice." She forced a smile.

"If I can do anything, please let me know. In case you misplaced my number—" He reached into his breast pocket and pulled out a business card, handing it to Sophie. "And even if you didn't, if your beautiful friend is interested in meeting for drinks, she can take the card instead."

He winked at Cindy before leaving and Sophie's friend nearly swooned. Sophie had seen Miguel have this effect on women at many charity events. The Spanish accent and his Antonio Banderas looks were enough to lure any unsuspecting female into his clutches. Which Sophie supposed might not be a bad thing for a woman who wasn't his professional competition.

As soon as Miguel was out of earshot, Cindy leaned forward. "So? Is he one of the good guys?" Blatant curiosity shimmered on her friend's face.

Sophie sighed. Cambias wasn't someone Sophie would touch with a ten-foot pole, but she had an inherent bias against the man. For all she knew, outside of business the man was a saint.

"I honestly don't know. But I do think he had an ulterior motive for coming here today." She just wished she knew what it was.

"I'll be careful."

Sophie slid the business card toward Cindy, who snatched it up and placed it in her purse.

"What do you say we double-date? That way you can try and figure out what he wants," Cindy suggested.

Sophie shook her head. "When it comes to Miguel

Cambias, you're on your own. Just don't divulge any secrets," Sophie said, laughing.

She wasn't worried. Cindy's ethics were solid and she wasn't privy to anything on the sports-agency side of the business. Besides, Sophie had other problems to deal with. "I'm going to need you to hold down the fort for a while."

"Where are you going to be?" Cindy asked.

"Florida." With Riley Nash.

RILEY THREW some clothes together in a duffel bag. He grabbed the shaving kit he always kept packed, since he traveled often during the season, and tossed it in as well. Then he picked up the phone.

He wasn't looking forward to informing his daughter he'd have to cancel their day tomorrow, but since she was in school he'd have to let his ex-wife know. Lisa would relay the message to Elizabeth about the change in plans and Riley would call her from Florida.

Lizzie, as he'd called her since she was a baby, lived with her mother and stepfather in Scarsdale, a ritzy suburb outside of New York City. Riley had chosen an apartment in Manhattan, so he could be nearby.

Lisa, Ted and Riley had managed to co-parent fairly well, at least until the teenage years had kicked in. Now they disagreed on how to handle Elizabeth, how to give her things without spoiling her and how to discipline her over her declining school grades.

Add attention deficit disorder to the mix and they really had their hands full, Riley thought.

He didn't think Elizabeth would mind him canceling since he saw her a couple of times a week and weekends when she wasn't busy with her friends. She was probably sick of him by now, he thought with a smirk, and would be glad he'd had a change of plans.

Scratch that. Even if she was relieved that she didn't have to hang with her father, she'd act as if she'd been slighted and wronged just so she could pick a fight and piss him off. His sweet baby had woken up one morning and morphed into the very thing a parent dreaded most: a hormonal teenage girl.

He dialed and a familiar female voice answered on the first ring. "Hello?"

"Hi, Lisa."

"Hi, Riley," she said. "How's the man of leisure?"

He didn't take offense. She'd never recognized that he worked out as hard on the off season, if not harder, never taking good health or good shape for granted. "I'm fine but I have to take an unexpected business trip."

Lisa didn't know Spencer Atkins was his father and if he hadn't revealed the secret during their brief marriage, he sure as hell wasn't about to spill his guts now. "Can you tell Lizzie I'm sorry and I'll make it up to her?"

"You can tell her yourself since she's home with a stomach virus. We would've called you today and canceled anyway. She's going to need to rest tomorrow, too. Hang on. Elizabeth," she screamed, probably over the blare of music from his daughter's bedroom. "Your father's on the phone."

"Hello?" a miserable-sounding Elizabeth said after picking up another receiver.

"Hi, Lizzie baby, how are you doing?"

She groaned. "I've been barfing my guts up all morning," she said on a whine.

"Aww, jeez. I'm sorry. But I'm sure you'll be back to your old self in no time."

"Yeah."

"Well, at least I don't feel as bad telling you I have to be out of town this weekend."

"But…but…" A huge pause followed. "You said we could have PF Chang's. You promised!"

He couldn't help it. He burst out laughing. "Honey, if you could eat Chinese food anytime soon, I'd make a point to stay home. Don't pick a fight just to have an argument. I'll take you out for dinner as soon as I get back. I promise. I'll even bring you back a surprise."

She remained silent, a deliberate, guilt-inducing silence.

"I'll call you and see how you're feeling, okay?" Not expecting a reply, he added, "Be good and remember when you start to eat, do it in small doses and do it smart."

More silence followed. The kid had made guilt into an art form, Riley thought. "Feel better, baby."

"I'm not a baby," she muttered.

Maybe not but he'd gotten a reply out of her, which had been his goal. He chuckled and heard the click in his ear, indicating she'd hung up.

"You spoil her," Lisa said just as he'd been about to put down the phone.

"I didn't realize you'd stayed on the extension."

"Let's just say I was curious how you'd handle her."

A quick glance at the clock told him he had to get moving or risk missing his flight, but he couldn't let this pass. "I don't need you eavesdropping on me," he said through gritted teeth.

"If you upset her, she's just going to take it out on Ted and me," she said.

Ted had been Elizabeth's stepfather for the last seven years. For someone who wasn't interested in sports, he was a nice enough guy. Unfortunately he also had a kid from a prior marriage and he was much stricter than Riley. He didn't approve of the gifts and extras Riley bought his daughter, which probably explained Lisa's listening in. But it didn't excuse it.

"I've got to run, but do me a favor? Have some faith in me or soon we'll be at each other's throats."

Lisa cleared her throat. "I'm sorry I listened in. But—"

"I've got to go."

"Just one more quick thing. Do *not* bring her home any expensive gifts from this trip," Lisa said.

He rolled his eyes. "Bye." He chose to ignore her warning. Elizabeth was his daughter and he'd buy her anything he damn well pleased.

CHAPTER THREE

SOPHIE'S HEAD POUNDED as she exited the cab at the airport. The pain in her temple had nothing to do with Spencer and everything to do with her traveling companion.

She had enough on her mind without having to deal with the constant distraction Riley would provide and she'd called him in a last-minute attempt to discourage him from joining her, but the man insisted on being there the minute she found his father. Assuming she even tracked Spencer down. Sophie had her doubts.

She'd tossed and turned all night, sleepless over the thought of being so close to Riley on the flight and on their trip. She was too attracted to him for it to be healthy, Sophie thought.

Athletes, she thought with frustration. She'd avoided dating them for years, leaving the bold, brash kind of guy for Annabelle, who'd always known how to handle them. Riley Nash had a string of women following him everywhere he went and unlike Annabelle, Sophie wouldn't know how to compete.

As the middle sibling, she created her own sense of order and followed a path she herself dictated. She could attract a man's attention and hold it, but she'd only do that for the right sort of man. A man she could understand and control. Accountants, executives, people who understood schedules and did the expected. Riley was the lone bullet in Russian roulette. She never knew when to expect him to hit or what would happen when he did.

She glanced at her watch once more. Just because she didn't see him now didn't mean he wasn't here. They'd agreed to meet at the gate. Sophie passed through security quickly and easily. She had the routine down pat. She wore slip-on shoes, no belt or heavy jewelry that might beep when she passed through the metal detectors and slow her trip. Before she even neared the scanners she methodically pulled out her laptop and cell phone, then slipped off her jacket as well.

She settled into a chair by the gate an hour prior to takeoff just as the airlines always instructed. By the time they called for first-class preboarding, Riley still hadn't arrived. Sophie's stomach cramped.

Frustrated and annoyed by his lack of consideration, she gathered her things and settled into her seat on the plane. Telling herself she didn't care that he'd stood her up, she pulled out her travel-size pillow and placed it behind her head, settling in for the two-and-a-half-hour flight.

Seconds before the cabin doors closed, Riley

made his entrance. Oblivious to how late he was, he strode onto the plane. As if on cue, a female flight attendant ushered him to his seat as if he was a visiting dignitary. The rest of the women attendants then fawned over the handsome football star, asking for his autograph and fluffing his pillow and covering his legs with a blanket. Even the pilots took time out of the cockpit to meet him.

Riley Nash didn't have to worry about following the rules other people lived by, and with each favor bestowed upon him, Sophie would bet he lost more of the manners and sense of courtesy others deserved. All he had to do was charm everyone around him and all was forgiven.

She couldn't forget that easily. All this scene did was reinforce what Sophie already knew: a man like Riley flirted as easily as a candy man bestowed treats to children. All the times he'd sought Sophie out at the office, it had been to feed his ego, not because he had some kind of interest in her. And she admitted to herself now, that had been the little hope she'd held on to deep in her heart. That the great Riley Nash had some secret crush on her the same way she had on him.

Fat chance. His flirting with the flight attendants showed her that all the times he'd come on to her, it'd been an act. Just Riley Nash, football star, looking for more attention. Well, he wouldn't receive any more special treatment from her, she decided, and after takeoff, Sophie buried herself in a book and outwardly ignored her traveling companion.

Inwardly, she was completely aware of him. Once again, it didn't matter that her emotions were bruised or that her mind warned her to steer clear. Every feminine instinct she possessed was on high alert. Riley's body was big and snug in the next seat and his arm constantly brushed against hers, disturbing her peace. More than once she glanced over to see if he'd noticed the sparks and heat she felt so strongly. Not a flicker of emotion showed in his expression. There was not a hint of a reaction to touching her, damn the man.

And she damned herself for wanting anything from him at all. She shut her book and closed her eyes but the simmering awareness remained, made more potent by his alluring cologne. She sighed and shifted in her seat, trying to get more comfortable.

"Can I get you anything to drink?" a female voice asked.

The flight attendant's question was a welcome distraction. "Red wine, please," she said.

"Another Scotch, thanks." Riley winked at the woman who flushed pink.

"Be right back," she promised, placing a hand on his shoulder and letting it linger before striding down the aisle.

"Oh, brother," Sophie muttered, unable to control her reaction.

He glanced over. "What are the chances that this drink'll take some of the starch out of your shorts?" he asked, his Southern accent coming through.

"Excuse me?"

He turned toward her, his arm leaning against hers, his amazing eyes studying her through thick lashes. "You've been sitting there like a prima donna from the minute I got on this flight. You haven't said two words to me, including hello, and your pretty little nose is so high in the air I'm surprised you don't have altitude sickness. Drop the attitude and we might have some fun on this trip."

She opened her mouth then closed it again. She ought to be offended by his words, but she knew he had a point. She'd been a bitch from the get-go and not just because she was uptight about Spencer being gone.

She hated to admit it but she was hurt by the realization that she was nothing special to Riley Nash. And the sad fact was, if he *did* corner her and turn that potent sex appeal her way, she'd be a goner for sure.

She looked at his freshly shaven face and imagined how her hand would feel caressing his skin. "Do you really think my nose is cute?" she heard herself ask and almost cringed.

He chuckled, flashing one dimple in his cheek. "Cuter than your personality at the moment. Elizabeth with PMS is more pleasant than you've been and, trust me, that's saying a lot."

She swallowed. "Who's Elizabeth?"

He paused a beat. Then another. Finally he said, "My thirteen-year-old daughter."

Sophie breathed out a sigh, promising herself it wasn't one of relief that he'd been referring to a daughter and not a girlfriend. She racked her brain in an attempt to remember what, if anything, she knew about Riley's past and surprisingly she came up blank.

Like father like son, she thought. She didn't know much about Spencer's past, either.

Riley was her uncle's client and her sexual nemesis and verbal sparring partner, but he was an enigma. An athlete she'd always opted to stay away from, mostly because he shattered the illusion of control she held on to. The illusion that allowed her to function without worrying about either the people she loved leaving her or the important things in her life falling apart.

"Here you go." The flight attendant returned. She placed their drinks on their tables, pausing by Riley's aisle seat. "Can I get you anything else?" The woman barely offered Sophie a glance and when it came to Riley, she wasn't talking about food or drink.

"No thanks, but I'll be sure and ring your bell if I think of anything," Riley said in that sexy voice of his.

The flight attendant smiled and headed to the row behind them.

Sophie tried to relax and took a long sip of her red wine, savoring the flavor when suddenly the flight turned bumpy, the plane jostling in the air.

Riley laughed. "Isn't that the way? As soon as they serve drinks, the turbulence starts." He lifted his cup and took a large sip to lower the amount so that it wouldn't slosh over the top.

Sophie did the same with her wine, more for fortification than need. Riley wore a short-sleeve T-shirt that showcased his muscular forearms and tanned skin. Obviously he'd been on vacation recently, she thought as she admired him all the way down to his gold Rolex watch and long, tanned, ringless fingers.

His dark lashes fringed his eyes, which looked more hazel than brown today. But he was the same man who easily tossed out sexual innuendo and caused her hormones to go wild. She just couldn't reconcile this sexy, carefree man with one who had responsibilities as a parent.

Parents were warm and loving, soft and caring. At least those were the fuzzy memories Sophie had of her mother and father before the plane crash took them from her for good.

"So how'd you become a father?" she asked, steering her mind off the ever-painful topic.

"The way most people do." He shot her an amused look. "You do know about the birds and the bees?" He nudged her elbow with his.

A heated flush burned her cheeks. "I meant I didn't know you were a father."

"Whew. I'd hate to think I needed to teach you the facts of life," he said, still grinning. "Though I suppose that could be fun."

This conversation was definitely getting out of hand. Her hands trembled and she placed her wine on the tray, still holding on to the cup because of the turbulence.

She bent over, searching for her MP3 player and headphones just as the plane bounced once more. She grabbed for her cup and missed, knocking over the lightweight plastic, causing the red liquid to spill. The wine traveled across the tray, onto her lap, and splattered on her white shirt.

"Damn!" She tried to blot the mess with paper napkins, but it wasn't working. She needed the bathroom to clean up.

As if anticipating her next move, Riley stood so she could exit the row and head back to the restrooms. His coloring was ruddy as he tried without success not to laugh at her.

So far, this wasn't a flight she wanted to remember and she just hoped it wasn't an omen for their quest to find Spencer. Holding on to the seat tops to steady herself, she walked quickly down the aisle toward the lavatories. Thank God one of them was vacant and she let herself inside.

"Wait."

At the sound of Riley's voice, she paused, giving him time to place his foot inside, preventing her from closing the door.

She looked at his sexy face and her heart rate picked up speed. "What do you think you're doing?"

"Joining you." A hint of a challenge tinged his voice and a teasing smile curved his lips.

"No!" She summoned outrage when she was really intrigued.

"Come on, sugar. I want to help you." He leaned a broad arm against the small opening.

This wasn't the first time she'd heard a hint of

a Southern accent and she wondered where he was raised, but inquisition and conversation could come later.

She licked her too-dry lips. "Thanks but I can handle cleaning up all by myself."

"So you clean and I'll watch. It'll give me a chance to talk to you in private."

She panicked, not from fear but from the overwhelming desire to get up close and personal with this man who was everything she normally avoided.

Sophie dated men who were safe. Men who didn't flirt with every woman they met. Men who weren't demanding. Men who didn't put their feet into her personal space and insist they get their way. Yet, though it galled her to admit it, there was something inherently arousing about his dominance.

"There's no room in here." She gestured to the small space behind her in a last feeble attempt to do the right thing.

The safe, expected thing.

He pushed the door open farther with his knee and wedged his big body inside, forcing her to step back. Then she heard a loud click as the lock slid into place and the dim light went on overhead ensuring the sign outside the door read Occupied.

They were completely alone and very, very close.

RILEY DIDN'T KNOW what had gotten into him. One minute he'd been ignoring Sophie and her pissy attitude and the next he was enjoying making her squirm. She couldn't handle the sexual banter without blushing a hot shade of red, which only made him want to push her buttons even more.

She was cute when she was mad but when piqued by jealousy, like when she hadn't been sure who Elizabeth was, Sophie was downright sexy. He'd followed her into the small bathroom to…what?

"I'm not joining the mile-high club with you." She glared at him, but those wide blue eyes flashed with definite interest, contradicting her words.

"And here I thought you were already a member," he said.

No way had she ever had sex anywhere but a bedroom. He'd bet his Super Bowl ring on it. Suddenly the thought of initiating her to sex in different places and positions held great appeal. He had a damn hard-on to prove it.

Shit.

This wasn't the first time his impulsive behavior had gotten him into trouble. Like the time he'd been caught making out with the teaching assistant in the janitor's room in college. The difference was, the T.A. had been older and willing.

Sophie, for all her N.Y.C. chic, was definitely a lady in every sense of the term. It was part of what drew him to her, Riley knew. The lure of someone different, someone special.

She deserved better than a quickie in the sky, no matter how much fun it might be. To distract himself, he reached over and pulled some paper towels from the holder, dampened them and began to blot her shirt where the wine had stained.

He gritted his teeth, determined to ignore her full breasts and pointed nipples. Perfectly rounded breasts and hardened tips just made for a man to suckle and tease. He tried to focus instead on her flat belly, where the liquid had concentrated.

She grabbed his wrist, stopping him. "Seriously, Riley. What are you doing in here?"

He groaned. Good question. One he was still trying to sort through himself. No way would he admit he'd just followed her on impulse. "Since we're going to be spending time together, I thought we could come to an understanding."

She shifted in an obvious attempt to get more comfortable in the cramped space, but her thighs came in direct contact with his and the flame burned hotter. Her sweet sugary scent, more refined and classy than most women's, sent his already heightened senses soaring.

Sophie drew in a startled breath, an admission that the awareness between them definitely wasn't one-sided. Yet she sighed in clear annoyance.

"Just what did I do to piss you off so badly?" he asked.

"You were *late*." She said the word as if he'd committed a cardinal sin.

She turned toward the mirror and he followed her stare so she was unable to look there without seeing his shocked expression. "That's it?" he asked. "I arrived a few minutes late and you're holding it against me?"

"It was rude! We agreed to meet before the flight. You left me wondering if you were even going to make it in time." Her voice quivered and she glanced the opposite way, this time toward the safety of the empty wall. "I told you routine gives me comfort." She spoke the last words softly.

A quiet admission of weakness, Riley thought.

Aw, hell. He hadn't meant to alarm her. He'd forgotten how seriously Sophie took life. Even with the dim lighting in the restroom, he could see her cheeks had turned pink and she'd sucked her lower lip into her mouth, embarrassed at admitting her neuroses aloud.

"Hey," he said, softly. "I said I'd be here."

"And I was supposed to take your word for it? The minutes ticked by and boarding had begun—"

"Were the cabin doors closed?"

She shook her head.

"Well then, there was still plenty of time for me to arrive."

"I don't work that way. I don't think that way. I plan ahead. And right now I need to find Spencer before my whole place of business falls apart. I have Cambias sniffing around and no sign of Spencer. He said he'd be in by nine on Monday and he wasn't. You said you'd meet me at the gate," she said, the implication clear.

He'd let her down. The thought didn't sit well with him. Not a normal reaction for a man who did his own thing on his own schedule and answered to no one.

Most people accepted his behavior.

Sophie wasn't most people.

She folded her arms across her chest, as if that would provide a barrier between him and her emotions. Between them.

As if.

He placed a hand beneath her chin and turned her face toward him. Her skin was softer than anything he'd touched before and his gut churned with the sudden desire to kiss her lips and see if that pink pout felt as seductive as it looked. If her mouth tasted like the sweet heaven he imagined.

He shook his head to redirect his thoughts. He and Sophie had a mutual goal. To find his father and smooth over the mess created by the media. Not to create another one at thirty thousand feet.

To that end, they needed each other. "Look, I'm just not used to answering to anyone except Lizzie."

Sophie blinked, probably as startled by his semi-apology as he was.

"That's what you call your daughter, Elizabeth?" she said.

He nodded, the old familiar pride welling inside him. Lizzie was Riley's whole world and he'd do right by her in ways his biological parent had never done by him. He'd be there for her and she'd know her daddy loved her.

"Lizzie's thirteen going on eighteen. She has attitude up the wazoo and some discipline problems at school, but she's smart and special and gorgeous. And I'm going to have to buy a shotgun to keep the hormonal idiots away," he said, awed as always by the young lady his daughter was becoming.

Sophie laughed, a light, airy, more relaxed sound than he'd heard from her since boarding.

"I take it you have some firsthand experience with being one of those hormonal idiots?" she asked.

"You know what they say. Boys'll be boys."

She inclined her head. "So what do you suggest we do to make this arrangement work?" she asked, turning the conversation back to them.

He leaned against the counter, thinking about what would help them get along for the duration of the trip. "How about we begin by understanding each other a little more? I'll start. Atkins is my long-lost father and though I have my reasons for needing to talk to him, I doubt he'll be happy to see me." Riley offered the difficult admission as a peace offering.

A flash of understanding flickered in her eyes along with the steely resolve he'd seen before. "I respect your privacy, but you hired me to help you. Besides, before I can bring you to Spencer, I'm going to need to know those reasons. We're like—"

"Family. I know." When used along with Spencer Atkins, the word *family* tasted sour in his mouth.

He paused, wondering how much more detail to reveal now and decided the lavatory wasn't the place for long-winded explanations. "I'll fill you in. Just not here."

She nodded. "Fair enough. I suppose you're looking for an admission of my own? A quid pro quo toward understanding? Well, fine," she said before he could reply. "I'm a pro at handling other people's crises, but not when everything around me is falling apart. If Spencer doesn't turn up soon, my entire life's going to crash and burn." She blinked once, then blinked again.

He thought she was fighting tears, but she covered it so well he couldn't be certain. He admired that strength.

All Riley knew for sure was that for Sophie routine provided comfort and Atkins's disappearance had thrown her carefully structured life into disarray.

They had that in common, he thought. He'd been thrown for a loop, too. His sudden inexplicable desire to take care of her threw him. For the first time, other than Lizzie, it wasn't all about him, and those feelings for Sophie messed with his carefree philosophy on life, and made him very, very nervous.

Still, he couldn't stop the words that came next. "I'll try harder not to screw up your schedule," he said, hoping he could handle answering to someone, even on a short-term basis.

"Thanks." She offered a smile and something inside him lightened with the knowledge that he'd eased her burden.

"And I'll try not to be such an uptight pain in the ass," she said, taking him by surprise.

He hadn't expected her to know herself so well or to admit as much to him. Drawn by need and a compulsion he couldn't explain, Riley reached out and pulled at the binding holding her bun in place. She gasped in surprise as strands of honey-colored hair fell around her face in waves, softening her features, making her appear infinitely more touchable.

More human.

More kissable.

She moistened her lips and he sucked in a sharp breath. Right now he was definitely one of those hormonal idiots they'd just discussed. He leaned in so they were almost cheek to cheek and he inhaled her fragrant scent.

Together they generated enough heat in the small space to steam the mirror, set off the smoke alarm and send the flight attendants barging in.

"Ladies and gentlemen, the captain has turned on the Fasten Seat Belt sign. Please take your seats as soon as possible." The flight attendant's voice broke into his thoughts.

He saw in her expression the moment she realized that she'd almost kissed Riley Nash at thirty thousand feet. Her eyes opened wide and she jerked away. Her knees came in contact with the toilet bowl and she sat on the closed seat with a thud.

He chuckled and held out his hand to help her up. "Tell you what. I'll leave first and you can sneak out after me."

"You're a true gentleman, Nash." Her voice held more than a hint of sarcasm, but her eyes held a wealth of gratitude.

He decided not to remind her that people had probably already seen him follow her into the bathroom or had likely already come to their own conclusions about what the two of them were doing in here. She had enough on her mind and Riley's presence on this trip probably wasn't helping her keep things in her life running smoothly.

But he couldn't change the strength of their attraction nor, he admitted, did he want to.

CINDY THOUGHT she knew what frazzled meant. Coming from a family that consisted of herself and her father and the employees of his California seaside restaurant, she'd grown up harried and working practically from birth. She'd gone to UCLA and hadn't moved East until her father had passed away last year. It had been tragic. An employee had stolen money from the register after hours and set a fire to cover his tracks. Frank James, "Jimmy" to his friends, had tried to save his restaurant and prized possessions before the firefighters arrived. He'd died of smoke inhalation inside the restaurant he'd adored.

After she'd survived that loss, Cindy thought she could handle anything. But The Hot Zone offices without the Jordan sisters, and Athletes Only without Spencer or Yank, was the equivalent of utter chaos. She and several others had been forced to work on a Saturday just to begin to deal with all that was going on and going wrong.

"And why did I agree to watch this dog?"

She'd just returned from a long walk with Noodle. One made longer by the dog's desire to sniff, wander and *not* do business when told. She stepped off the elevator feeling out of sorts and almost out of options.

"Ms. James?"

"Yes?" Cindy turned to the temp who'd been working for the past couple of days.

Even if Raine, their normal receptionist, returned from her serious bout of the flu, the office could still use the manpower Nicki Fielding provided. Cindy had no doubt Sophie would agree.

"You have messages." Nicki held out a stack of pink papers.

Cindy pushed the notes into her suit jacket pocket.

"Ms. Jordan called from Florida. I told her everything here was fine, which is true. Sort of. I mean the reporters are still hanging around," Nicki whispered, gesturing to the group who'd perched themselves on the sofa, hoping for an interview from anyone here. "I just keep telling them 'No Comment,'" she said, looking to Cindy for approval.

"You're doing great." She smiled at the young girl.

"I'm trying." Her brown eyes were huge. "I don't think Ms. Jordan thinks I'm that qualified."

Cindy shook her head. "It's just crisis time around here. We'll all come through this fine. You're being a huge help, I promise."

The dog pulled on the leash and she groaned. "Go, you little pain in the—" Cindy leaned down, released the catch and the dog bolted, likely for the safety of Yank's office, where Sophie said she could find the pooch if she went missing.

"If you need me, I'll be in my office returning calls." Cindy patted the papers in her bulging pocket and walked past the reporters, head held high, looking straight ahead before they could begin to toss out questions.

Cindy shut her door behind her, leaned against it and sighed. She couldn't wait to hand this place back to Sophie. When she opened her eyes, she stared in shock. The most beautiful red roses sat on her desk.

"What the...?" She bent close and sniffed the glorious petals, breathing in their floral scent. As she pulled out the card, she realized the vase wasn't a typical glass holder from a florist but etched Baccarat crystal.

"Red beauties for a redheaded beauty. Have dinner with me. Miguel." Cindy read the card and shivered.

She'd been living in New York for a little over six months and although she'd made friends, she hadn't dated anyone special. She hadn't met anyone who seriously interested her. Until she'd laid eyes on Miguel Cambias. His dark eyes and naturally dark skin, so different from many of the surfers and actors she'd met in California, caused goose bumps to prickle up and down her arms.

But his business card had burned a hole in her pocket and she'd left it untouched in her desk drawer ever since. Loyalty was important to her. She'd learned it from her small band of "family" back home, a group related by love not blood.

She worked for The Hot Zone. She enjoyed her job and she appreciated all three Jordan sisters and the familylike atmosphere they brought to the firm. For Cindy, this place was similar to her father's tiny restaurant and she didn't want to lose the inroads she'd made.

She slowly opened her desk drawer and stared at the business card tucked safely away. She also didn't want to make a mistake and spend forever wondering what if. Fingering the business card, she turned it over and over in her hand. Sophie hadn't asked her not to see Miguel. She'd just suggested Cindy be careful.

With those words in mind, Cindy picked up the phone. After all, what harm could come from one little dinner? she wondered.

CHAPTER FOUR

INDIGNITY SURROUNDED Sophie. When she'd headed out of the lavatory a short while after Riley, the people seated in the immediate area had applauded. Now as they waited for their luggage to arrive on the conveyor belt, she stood next to Riley and was forced to accept another very uncomfortable situation. Her panties were damp with desire and he was the cause.

So much for not doing athletes. So much for not doing *this* athlete. Much to her dismay, her fears had just been realized. If not for the plane's descent and the pilot's order to return to their seats, she'd have probably been initiated into the mile-high club and enjoyed every minute.

She rubbed her aching temples at the thought. Because in all probability, Riley could have just as easily substituted one of the flight attendants for her. The thought stung and stayed with her, hanging over her shoulders like a bag of rocks.

Sophie had a business to save and her uncle's partner to find. She needed to focus and she needed a plan. Instead, she'd been distracted by the athlete who thought with his—

"Which one's yours?" Riley asked.

She glanced at the luggage slowly coming around on the belt and pointed to the black bag with the hot pink string that identified the suitcase as hers.

Riley hefted the bag as if it weighed nothing, then grabbed an older-looking duffel before turning her way. "We're good to go?"

She nodded. "I arranged for a rental car. All we have to do is check in over there." She pointed to a large green neon sign. "A bus will take us to the lot with the car and we can be on our way."

"Sounds good. Any idea where we're going?"

"I printed out directions from MapQuest on the Internet. We should be all set."

Half an hour later, they were settled in the rental car on their way to Spencer's sisters' in Fort Lauderdale. Sophie shifted restlessly in her seat, the air-conditioning doing nothing to cool off the heat surging through her body. The tingling awareness reminded her of what had transpired between them in the bathroom of the airplane.

Still she tried for normal conversation. "So what do you know about Spencer's Florida family?" Sophie wanted to enter the situation as prepared as possible.

"Not a damn thing." A muscle ticked in Riley's jaw.

Obviously she'd hit a nerve.

"What about you? You're the one who said he's like family. What do you know about his sisters?"

"About as much as you."

"In my experience, in Atkins's world, family loyalty runs one way only."

Sophie didn't reply, because she wondered if Riley didn't have a point. For all the years she and her sisters had known Spencer Atkins and for all the holidays he'd spent with her family, Sophie now understood they didn't know the man at all.

She heard the anger in Riley's voice and saw the rigid way he held his body as he drove. She studied his strong profile and could only imagine the tension brewing inside him.

"I guess we're on this fishing expedition together." She reached out and covered his fingers with hers.

He jerked in surprise but didn't move his hand away. She didn't have to wonder if his skin tingled as much as hers, if he was as affected as she. One glance at his lap answered that question. He wanted her, all right.

"We're here. If you can tear your gaze away from my—"

"Okay!" She cut him off before he could phrase the words that would make her blush even more.

She scrambled out of the car and preceded him up the walk leading to a small patio home. The entire community was comprised of similarly styled houses painted in pastel pinks, yellows and blues. A warm breeze blew around her. There was a serenity to the community that Sophie wasn't feeling at the moment and she hoped they'd find Spencer quickly so they could be on their way.

Riley jogged up beside her. "You know there's nothing wrong with two people being attracted to one another."

"There is when one of those people flirts with anyone in a skirt, which means the other one could be any woman for all it mattered. Oh, and especially when the two people are all wrong for one another."

He chuckled, a masculine sound that said *I know better*. She hated that he found her feelings amusing.

Without warning, he tangled his fingers in her unruly, humidity-messed hair. The light tugging sensation was stimulating. She trembled despite her internal warnings to protect herself from his charm.

His lips turned upward in a grin. "You're mistaken—not about the flirting, because I do enjoy that."

She stiffened.

"But you're by no means any woman. You're unique, Sophie Jordan." His voice deepened to a husky rasp. "And as for being wrong for each other, well, that depends whether you're looking for sex or commitment, sweetheart."

His words should have been like a bucket of cold water dumped over her. Instead the word *sex* reverberated inside her head. She also couldn't help the pleasure she felt in knowing he'd considered her unique. When in her life had she been that?

But Riley had said she was special and at the idea of sex with him—sweaty bodies, hands everywhere and this big, gorgeous man filling her completely—she trembled all over.

Who cared if he was an athlete? Sophie thought.

She did. Or she should. Just like she should care that her business hinged on finding the man who might be inside this house. Shaking off thoughts of sex *for now,* she leveled Riley with what she hoped was her fiercest glare.

"Let's see who's home." She strode up the steps and knocked. She'd figure out later what to do about this man who had her quivering and practically jumping him in the front yard.

Suddenly the door opened a crack. "Who's there?" a female voice asked.

"Sophie Jordan. I—"

"Sophie Jordan who?" a female voice asked.

"Sophie Jordan, Spencer's business partner and longtime friend."

"Phooey. I was hoping you'd have a fun name we could play with. Like *Ben.*"

Sophie narrowed her gaze. "Ben? Why Ben?"

The door still didn't open enough for her to see who was on the other side. "Because you'd say Ben who? And I'd say Ben there, done that."

She shot Riley a glance over her shoulder and whispered, "Frannie said they were eccentric."

Riley rolled his eyes. Just what he needed. A set of weirdo aunts in addition to a gay father who wouldn't acknowledge his existence.

"Can we talk face-to-face?" Sophie asked. Her voice held no trace of her anxiety.

She hid her worries well, but he understood her

concerns and would do his best to help ease them. That didn't mean he wouldn't enjoy his time with her while they were together. She was too easy to tease and, man, he enjoyed it when she blushed. All in all she was a distraction from the problems he was here to deal with and he knew he provided the same diversion for her.

Although he'd talked himself out of acting on his desire in the airplane bathroom earlier, there was no way he'd be able to keep his hands off her for long. If she looked at him with those blue eyes filled with yearning one more time, he'd say to hell with his good intentions—as long as she understood it would be just sex.

Suddenly the door opened wide, cutting off his thoughts. A woman with bright red hair, clashing hot-pink lipstick and 1970s blue eye shadow stared back and Riley had a sinking hunch he could count her among his long-lost relatives.

"Sophie, darling, I'm Darla Atkins, Spencer's older sister. Of course you'd never know it by looking at me. Florida holds the secret to the fountain of youth. All this humidity provides moisture for the skin," she said. "I'm so happy you're here. Spencer has told us so much about you and your sisters."

But from what Sophie had said, Riley knew that Spencer hadn't told the Jordan sisters anything in return.

Darla pulled Sophie into an embrace that she welcomed awkwardly, patting the older woman on the back before stepping away and putting distance between them.

"And who is this handsome fellow?" Darla's focus drifted past Sophie to Riley.

"Riley is—"

"Your paramour, of course! No need to explain. He's such a handsome hunk, you're a lucky woman, but then he's a fortunate man to have such a beauty as you on his arm. Spencer's filled me in on your accomplishments over the years. I know how bright you are. He's proud of all three of you girls." She paused, as if debating what to say next. "But he always thought you were special," the other woman said, lowering her voice.

Riley tried not to laugh at her sudden whisper. It wasn't as if Annabelle or Micki was anywhere near to hear the comparison.

Sophie reached out and grasped the other woman's hand. "Thank you," she said softly, her heart and all of her emotions bared in those two small words.

For the first time in years, he softened toward his biological father and all because of how he'd treated Sophie. Spencer's instincts had been on target. He'd been right to single her out and give her the attention she obviously craved.

But warring with his unexpected admiration was an old childhood jealousy because Sophie and her sisters had received the love and approval Riley had always sought and failed to achieve. He forcibly reminded himself he was no longer that needy child, and it helped to ease his flash of pain.

"He's not my paramour," Sophie said in her haughtiest tone, her pert nose in the air.

Maybe it was her vehement denial. Or maybe it was how appalled she sounded by the notion of being linked to him, as if their recent truce and the lingering sexual tension didn't exist. Riley's ego, wounded first by Spencer's lack of acknowledgment and then by Sophie's blatant disregard, took over.

He stepped forward and slung his arm around her shoulders, pulling her close. "Now, honey, didn't we talk about you getting over this shyness? Of course we're lovers and Ms. Atkins obviously has no issues with our relationship, so why hide it?"

Sophie turned her head to him, shooting daggers at him with her eyes. "Riley…" Her voice held a warning edge.

He raised an eyebrow, silently challenging her to deny the heat where their bodies touched and the pulse-pounding desire thrumming through them even at that moment.

Spencer's sister, meanwhile, watched avidly.

"Ms. Atkins," Sophie began.

She shook her head. "Darla, please."

Sophie smiled. "Darla. Riley needs—"

"I need to speak to you," he said, cutting off any details Sophie might have let slip.

Why tell the chatterbox that he was Spencer's son when they were looking to keep the news quiet? In case

Sophie didn't get his drift, he squeezed her waist, hoping she took his cue to remain silent about the truth.

He glanced at her delicate profile. Although she continued to scowl, no doubt still unhappy about his pronouncement that they were a couple, she kept her mouth shut tight and he exhaled in relief.

"Come in, come in." Darla led them into the house.

Riley noticed she didn't comment on their need to speak to Spencer.

Was his father here? Riley's gut cramped at the notion of finally coming face-to-face with the man who'd avoided him all his life.

Riley held on to Sophie, long enough to whisper in her ear, "Just when are you going to ask her if the old man's here?"

"I thought I'd finesse the situation. If Spencer isn't here, and she doesn't know that he's missing, I don't want to worry her."

"What did you say?" Darla asked.

"Nothing," Sophie replied, and pulled Riley along.

Together they entered a small kitchen with red-and-black wallpaper, modern appliances and homey clutter all over the place. The place was well lived in, Riley thought. Unlike his mother and stepfather's home, which was an old estate on acres of land with servants to keep things immaculate and clean. The contrast was striking and yet Riley liked the warmth he sensed in this house. He wouldn't be surprised if Spencer had decided to hide out here until the scandal blew over.

Following Sophie's lead, Riley settled into a chair at the kitchen table, letting Sophie direct the conversation. They declined the offer of drinks and snacks, and they made small talk until Darla finally asked, "So what are you doing in Florida?"

The question didn't bode well for their search, Riley thought.

"When was the last time you spoke with your brother?" Sophie asked, instead of replying directly to the other woman's question.

"Oh, that Spencer's an erratic one. Sometimes he calls daily, sometimes more often and when he's busy during draft season, we don't hear from him for weeks on end."

"We?" Riley asked out of curiosity.

"My sister, Rose, lives here, too. She's at the market. It's grocery day and this is her week, which is a good thing because my sciatica is acting up and I don't think I'd be able to bend and put things into the cart easily. Unless of course I wink at that cutie they hired. He might be willing to help me," she mused.

"Isn't that jailbait?" he whispered to Sophie.

She nudged him in the ribs.

"It's hard to find a man over seventy with all his hair and his own teeth. Ian's got both." Darla glanced at Riley, a twinkle in her eyes.

This was a smart cookie, Riley thought. He wouldn't be surprised if she was talking in circles on purpose to distract them.

"Draft season's coming up," Riley said, picking up

on her thread of conversation. "Does that mean you haven't heard from Spencer lately?"

"He checks in," she said vaguely.

"He took a sudden vacation but didn't say where he was going," Sophie said. "We were hoping you'd know where to find him."

Darla leaned forward in her chair. "Why didn't you just call and ask me?"

Sophie blinked. "We did. Often. Nobody answered."

"Oh, that Rose. She's got herself a new boyfriend and doesn't answer call waiting when she's talking on the phone. I always tell her she's such a chatterbox. Nobody enjoys hearing incessant nonsense." She sniffed as if she were above such things.

Riley did his best not to laugh.

"Well, we're hoping Spencer will call tonight seeing as it's my birthday and all, so you may get lucky yet."

"Happy birthday," they both said as if on cue.

"Thank you," the redhead said, beaming.

Riley glanced at Sophie but couldn't tell whether she was buying Darla's story. For Riley, the jury was still out.

Darla rose from her seat. "Now you'll stay here for as long as you're in Florida. Spencer would never forgive me if I didn't treat family right."

The woman had no idea how right on the mark she actually was with that particular word, Riley thought. He tried not to wince while Sophie immediately reached out to him in understanding, her hand covering his thigh. He wondered if she realized how intimate the gesture was or how often she'd touched him in the past few hours, mostly when she was looking out for him or protecting his feelings.

He liked it. A lot.

"We don't want to cause any trouble, so we'll stay in a hotel," Sophie said.

Darla shook her head. "Nonsense." She waved the suggestion away with her hand. "Didn't Spencer tell you this is sort of like a retirement community, only better because we don't rent, we own it all. Spencer bought the land years ago and helped us develop it. Rose's daughter, Amy, runs the place and lives in one of the homes. You'll meet her soon enough. Luckily one of our patio homes that we normally lease is empty. The place is clean, fumigated and immaculate. You two will be quite comfortable."

Had she come up for air? Riley wasn't certain. He couldn't focus on anything except the notion that he and Sophie would be sharing a patio home. She continued to prattle on, giving him no time to digest the information now or even decide how he felt about them living together for the duration of their stay in the Sunshine State.

One night or a week, it didn't matter. With the sparks flying between them, he knew damn well he wasn't leaving Florida without sleeping with Sophie Jordan.

FEELING LIKE A FOOL, Spencer crouched in the bushes outside his sister's patio home. Thanks to an open kitchen window, he was able to listen to Darla's chatter and Sophie's concern. She hid it well, but knowing Sophie, she was climbing the walls trying to handle all the publicity herself without the help of her sisters. Spencer had left her in a bind and for that he felt badly.

But he wasn't ready to face the world with his secret exposed. He might as well walk through Central Park bare assed, as Yank would say. In any other profession, his clients would be shocked but they'd understand that his private life didn't have anything to do with his professional one. Any other profession wasn't the world of sports.

Most athletes were macho men who had neither the time nor patience to understand anything outside their world. He wouldn't be surprised if some of them had a phobia about homosexuals. Still, he hoped he wouldn't lose more than one or two clients. He'd be home in time for the football draft, but he needed a plan before he returned. Then he'd see how evolved they actually were.

He glanced at his sister's house and frowned. He wished Darla hadn't insinuated he'd call her later, giving Sophie a reason to stick around. Instead, his well-meaning, ever-talkative sister had offered the use of an empty unit in the neighborhood so Sophie would remain here. The worst part of it all was that Sophie hadn't flown down here alone.

The door to the house opened wide, interrupting his thoughts. Sophie stepped outside followed by Riley, *Spencer's son.*

He broke into a sweat, the realization of all he had to answer for in his life overwhelming him. He understood that in Riley's eyes, Spencer didn't deserve a damn thing. He'd planned it that way, looking out for Riley behind the scenes. Yet now that Spencer's reality was public knowledge, he thought maybe his son deserved to understand his absent father's choices. But the same truth that had sent him underground would probably cause his son to turn away in disgust.

He wondered why Riley had come looking for him now.

Why had he hooked up with Sophie in his quest?

And, he also wondered, why did they look so at ease together?

Spencer squinted against the sun and stared at their retreating backs. Was that Sophie slipping her hand into Riley's?

Holy moly, were they involved?

If they weren't, they should be. The idea settled in Spencer's brain and remained. Sophie, the sister with the intellect he admired and the warmth his son would appreciate. She was strict and would crack the whip, taming Riley's wild side while giving him a run for his money.

Spencer knew he had nerve, planning anything for the child he'd never publicly acknowledged, but it wouldn't be the first time he had looked out for his son behind the scenes, and it wouldn't be the last.

"Psst!"

Spencer looked up. His sister, Darla, opened the kitchen window and called to him.

"They're gone. You can come back inside now."

Spencer waited until the rental car pulled away from the curb before standing, then stretching his old legs until the cramping subsided. "This hide-and-seek stuff is for the young," he muttered, smoothing the wrinkles out of his pants.

He walked into the house and joined his sister.

"You're only as old as you feel and right now you're feeling sorry for yourself. For no good reason, either," Darla said.

Spencer scowled. "Would you rather I go home and do a tell-all interview? Embarrass my only son and disgust my clients?"

Darla shook her head. "I think you underestimate those who care about you."

He burst out laughing. "You care. You, Rose and Amy." He mentally added Yank, Lola and the girls to the list. "But if you think my clients care about anything more than their next paycheck and their status in the sports world, you're wrong. To them, a gay agent would be an embarrassment and I damn well know it. I need time."

Darla started for the door.

"Where are you going?" Spencer asked.

"To pick out my outfit for my birthday party tonight."

He hated what he had to tell her next. "I can't be there."

"Because Sophie and Riley will be?" Darla delivered a challenging stare.

Spencer massaged the sore muscles in the back of his neck. "I hate like hell to miss it, but I'm not ready to deal with them."

"Coward."

"Maybe."

"He looks like you," Darla said. "He has your eyes."

"He has my good looks, doesn't he?" Spencer asked.

His sister rolled her eyes. "I wouldn't go that far."

Spencer grinned. He couldn't control his pride in the man his son had become and he couldn't help but hope that one day Riley would feel the same pride in him.

And maybe the 49ers would win the Super Bowl.

"Just make sure you find a way to keep those two together," Spencer said.

Because if his coming out accomplished nothing else, maybe it would help his son settle down.

CHAPTER FIVE

SOPHIE ADJUSTED her seat belt and glanced at Riley's taut expression. His jaw had been locked tight ever since they'd left Darla's house and started the short drive to the patio home as instructed by Spencer's nutty sister.

"I don't believe a word Darla said." Sophie broke the silence first, figuring if it were up to Riley, he'd remain mute.

Riley nodded in agreement. "I don't, either."

Sophie wondered what Darla really knew about Spencer's disappearance and how hard it would be to find out. The other woman liked to ramble but Sophie had seen hints that she wasn't as flighty as she appeared.

In the meantime, she and Riley would have to spend time in sunny Florida living under one roof and they needed to set some ground rules. "You never should have told Darla we were lovers." Sophie had counted the minutes until they were alone so she could call him on that whopper.

"Does the idea bother you that much?" He placed his arm behind her head and glanced over, searing her with his sexy gaze. "Or is it the fact that I turn you on that's driving you crazy?"

Stars spun in front of her eyes and she blinked, trying to focus on anything but his accurate words. "Why didn't you tell Darla who you were?" she asked, changing the subject to one *he* wouldn't like as much.

"I'd think that was obvious. Darla didn't strike me as the silent type. I need to ask Spencer to keep the news of my parentage quiet."

He'd never before told her why he needed to speak with Spencer and he clammed up again about why he wanted his relationship to Spencer to remain under wraps. As he gripped his hands tighter around the wheel, she decided now wasn't the time to ask. Later, when they were settled, she'd question him more. At the moment, she was more worried about the feelings this trip had to be stirring up inside him.

The fact that she cared about his emotions at a time when hers were being tested told her too much about her growing feelings for this man, and that they weren't just sexual. It would be so much easier if they were.

He drove along a circular road, their path marked by frequent speed bumps. "You were hoping that Darla would recognize you, weren't you?" Sophie asked.

"Hell, no." But a muscle twitched in his jaw, proof that she'd come too close to the truth.

Spencer's sister had been so enthusiastic about Sophie and how Spencer felt about her, yet she'd been painfully oblivious to who Riley really was.

Sophie inched closer, bumping her knee on the center divider. "Come on. Riley's just not all that common a name and I bet that you were wondering if she'd know who you were."

He let out a frustrated groan. "Do me a favor? Find someone else's life to dissect."

Though his lips tipped upward in a sexy grin, softening his words, he'd hit a nerve anyway. Her uncle always complained about how she tried to run his life and her sisters joked about how they were glad that their marriages gave them a break from her constant prodding.

She wasn't a silent middle child. Instead, her compulsive nature was a sore spot and she'd hate to think her personality would drive Riley away. Not that she wanted him…well, she *wanted* him, she just didn't want to want him. But she certainly had no desire to turn him off. Not when he turned her on so much.

She groaned. Her thoughts were a jumble and Sophie realized the time had come to think through what she wanted to do about this uncontrollable attraction to Riley Nash, especially now that they'd be under one roof. As soon as she had some alone time, she'd weigh the pros and cons of her alternatives— the way Sophie always made a decision. Though not spontaneous, the method worked.

A sunny yellow-colored house caught her eye. "I think this is the place," Sophie said.

Riley turned into the short cobblestoned driveway

and parked the car. "Darla said Rose's daughter would meet us here."

"That'd be your cousin Amy." The words slipped out before she could censor them.

"Anyone ever say you can be a real pain?" Riley asked.

Well, hell. She obviously wasn't going to change, so if he didn't like it, he could lump it, as her uncle would say. "On occasion."

Sophie had many faults, but she prided herself on knowing both her strengths and weaknesses. Though she'd promised herself to work on her more compulsive tendencies—like trying to control others' lives along with her own—some habits were hard to break. And her married sisters assured her that the right man would love her for who she was. All of her, faults included. That man couldn't possibly be Riley Nash.

Not in the long term, but you're only in Florida for a few days. A little voice in her head teased her with possibilities, but he stopped the car at the curb before she could ponder further.

No sooner had they stepped onto the curb than a pretty brunette pulled up in a golf cart. She jumped out to greet them, a wide smile on her face.

"You must be Sophie." Without warning, Amy pulled Sophie into a hug, just as Darla had.

Sophie stiffened. Though she considered herself a warm person with her family, she wasn't overly affectionate with people she didn't know well. She kept her reserve and her distance until she learned whether or not she could trust them. Spencer's sister and niece held no such qualms about strangers and they breached Sophie's personal space without thought.

She stepped back and immediately felt the press of Riley's hand into her back. He understood, she realized, and she relaxed into his touch. Obviously she hadn't pushed him too far. The thought pleased her much more than it should.

The fact was, she was way beyond attracted to him. The man could have her with the snap of his fingers and it was time she dealt with the fact. Besides, she had enough chaos in her life without adding fighting with herself over Riley. Obviously there was something mutual going on between them.

So what if he flirted with every woman on the planet? Sophie didn't want a lifelong commitment with a brash athlete who liked to do things his own way and ignore the rules. That didn't mean she couldn't sleep with him though.

Just to get him out of her system, she assured herself. Besides, ever since his earlier comment about them being lovers, she couldn't shake the notion from her mind. She couldn't turn off her body's response to his voice or his touch.

Sophie trembled. She'd never had such persistent thoughts like these about any man. But then Riley Nash wasn't just any man. He never had been.

"And you're Riley." Amy walked up to Riley and perused his face.

Riley stared back, attempting not to squirm and trying not to think of this woman as his cousin, but Sophie had put the words out there and he found himself studying her for resemblances. He immediately detected similarities in their eye color, or maybe he just thought he should.

How did Sophie expect him to walk away with his pride and his emotions intact if she insisted on labeling these people in a way that indicated they ought to mean something to him? They didn't. Not any more than he meant anything to them.

Amy shaded her eyes from the sun with one hand. "You've got your father's eyes."

Riley stiffened. Apparently he should never underestimate these Florida relatives. "You know who I am?"

Amy nodded. "Of course. My mother keeps a scrapbook of all your accomplishments. She knows Uncle Spencer will want to have it one day."

Riley snorted in disbelief. But he couldn't dispel the pleasurable warmth her words caused. Someone on this side of the family kept tabs on him. It just wasn't Spencer.

"I take it Aunt Darla pretended not to know you?" Amy asked.

"I don't know if she was pretending or not. She just didn't acknowledge me as anyone other than a visiting guest." He squared his shoulders, trying not to let this woman's prying eyes get to him. He sure as hell didn't want her pity.

Without warning, Amy reached out and touched

his arm. "Aunt Darla and Uncle Spencer are thick as thieves, as my mother likes to say. I would guess she thought she was doing what Spencer would want her to do. Although personally I think it stinks that he's never publicly recognized you all these years."

Riley flushed hot. His entire life he'd lived with the notion that he was an embarrassment to his real father. To have it verbalized was mortifying. To have Sophie hear it bothered him even more.

"I'm sure it's small consolation, but my uncle Spencer is proud of you. He talks about your accomplishments all the time," Amy said.

"I doubt it. Did you know he was gay?" He forced himself to ask.

Amy shook her head. "But now that I do, if I had to venture a guess, I'd bet he thought he was protecting you by keeping his distance, as ignorant and misguided as that might be."

"I'd rather save this conversation for Spencer."

Amy clasped her hands in front of her. "Aunt Darla told me you came down here hoping you'd find him."

Sophie nodded. "Have you heard from him lately?"

"Not since the story hit the papers, poor Uncle Spencer."

"This can't be easy for him," Sophie said. "Do you know whether your mother or aunt have heard from him?"

Riley wouldn't be surprised if they caught Darla in a lie to protect her brother, but Amy shook her head.

"Not that I know of. But today is my aunt Darla's

birthday and we're having a big bash out by the pool tonight. If Uncle Spencer's going to show up at all, it would be for his sister's party. I really hope you'll join us. It's always fun for the residents and trust me when I say it's a sight to see."

"What are you, the cruise director?" Riley asked. He couldn't picture this young, vibrant woman spending her days with wackos like his aunt Darla.

Amy laughed. "A pretty good comparison. I schedule the activities and entertainment, I break up the occasional squabbles among the residents and I get free room and board. It's not a bad life."

"Are there any other young people here?" Sophie asked, giving voice to his thoughts.

"Enough. We aren't a retirement place with specific rules about age. We're a happy mix. I'm a social worker, but I hate being confined to an office all day, so this kind of job is perfect for me. So can I count on seeing you tonight?"

"We'd be happy to come." Sophie answered for them both before Riley could even think it over.

"That's great! You'll get to meet my mother and hopefully Uncle Spencer will show up or at least call by then. And now we know where to find you if he does," Amy said, a satisfied smile on her face. "Oh, FYI, it's a luau theme and bathing suits are required. If you didn't bring the right clothes, there's a mall not fifteen minutes from here where you can pick up something to wear."

"Yippee," Riley drolly.

Sophie shot him a glare. "We'll be fine," she assured her.

Amy laughed. "Okay then, let me show you the house."

His newfound cousin walked off with Sophie, chatting as she led them inside. The two women had developed an easy rapport, which was surprising to Riley since he'd thought Sophie would break in two, she'd been so stiff when Amy had pulled her into a tight hug.

From the day he'd met Sophie, Riley had realized her uptight persona was every bit as much a part of her as his carefree one was to him. Over his years as Yank's client, Riley had learned a good amount about each of his agent's nieces. Sophie was the one who'd dealt with the loss of her parents by erecting a self-protective shield that she wore like armor and that few people could pierce.

He'd seen firsthand what happened to her when someone disrupted that sense of well-being she clung to for security. This trip to Florida was an attempt to set her world right once more. How ironic that it seemed destined to turn his upside down.

As they stepped inside, Amy dove right into the grand tour. The one-story house had an easy flow and, from the front door, he could see straight out to the backyard and small pool. She walked them around, from the kitchen with a breakfast nook for two, to the small den with a big-screen television, to the large master bedroom which had screen doors leading directly to the pool and hot tub beyond.

Riley could definitely spend some time here getting to know Sophie while waiting for his father to surface, he decided, unable to suppress the thought that had been the only thing keeping him sane. Being alone with Sophie gave him a sense of belonging he lacked down here among his very distant relatives. Not to mention the fact that sex with a willing Sophie, a Sophie who let down her guard, held tremendous appeal. After all, they were both consenting adults and understood the concept of no promises made, none to keep.

Sophie paused in the living room and turned to Amy. "Between your job and this party tonight you've got your hands full here. You don't need to worry about entertaining guests. Riley and I can easily stay in a hotel."

Riley wondered if her objection had anything to do with the master bedroom and king-size bed. Personally, the idea of staying here had begun to grow on him.

"Don't be silly." Amy waved away her objection. "What good would an empty unit do? Of course you'll stay here."

"Why isn't this place rented?" Riley asked.

"A married couple lived here until last month. They decided to move north to Jupiter where things are less crowded than in Fort Lauderdale."

"Why haven't you rerented it?" Riley asked. The

home had been kept up, the furnishings clean and modern. He was sure it would garner a profit.

"We will. But for now, it's yours. So enjoy."

"As long as you're sure."

Amy nodded. "I am."

"Then we're happy to take you up on your offer," Sophie said.

As she turned to Riley, her eyes darkened with the smoldering heat he'd seen in the airplane earlier.

"I'm certain we'll enjoy it." Sophie's words were for Amy, but Riley understood the underlying meaning was meant for him alone and the temperature in the small house suddenly soared, sweat rising beneath his shirt.

Amy smiled in approval, then let herself out, leaving them alone. Before either of them could address anything personal, Riley wanted the necessities out of the way.

"Guess we need to go shopping for luau attire?" Riley asked.

"It's not like I brought a bathing suit. Did you?"

He shook his head, then thought of Sophie in a string bikini. She'd be one hot item and when the night was over, there'd be no keeping his hands off her. From the dreamy look in her eyes, she was thinking the exact same thing.

SOPHIE HAD HIT the mall like a professional shopper. First she'd dispatched Riley to the men's department in Bloomingdale's so she didn't have the pressure of his intense stare following her everywhere she went. She'd been too much aware of him already. Then she'd chosen swimwear based on the styles and brands she knew would fit. Unfortunately, that had left her with one-piece suits, which worked fine in New York but around Riley seemed bland. At the last second, she'd pulled a daring, skimpy bikini off the rack before paying for her purchases.

Now, she laid her choices on the bed, her heart pounding hard inside her chest. Which one to wear? she wondered, wishing she had her sisters around to call for advice.

"You're on your own, Sophie girl," she muttered aloud. How ironic that she could deal with organizing an event for hundreds more easily than she could handle this.

Drawing a deep breath, she glanced at the array of bathing suits laid out before her. "Eenie meeney miney mo," she said, and reached for the one her gut told her would appeal most to Riley.

RILEY SAT in the pink-and-white living room waiting for Sophie to finish getting ready. He'd given her the master bedroom so she could dress in private and he'd taken one of the other rooms, consoling himself with the idea that, come tonight, no way would he be going to one of those smaller rooms.

Unfortunately, he might be all swagger and no substance. Sophie hadn't given him a glimmer of hope to count on, he realized, thinking back to earlier in the day. Riley normally hated shopping with women. He disliked waiting for them to sort through racks of clothing and then try on more things than anyone could possibly buy or wear in this lifetime. He loathed sitting on a couch outside a dressing room while the same woman paraded herself in front of him in an obvious attempt to entice him with her body and coax him out of his cash. Yet after Amy had left, he'd actually looked forward to taking Sophie to the mall.

When she'd insisted he go shopping for himself and meet up with her later, he'd been disappointed. And when he'd returned to find she'd already chosen a few items and paid for them without modeling them for him first, he'd felt absurdly cheated.

Of course, he preferred to stew about missing out on seeing Sophie in various bathing suits than to deal with the things Amy had said.

Spencer was proud of him? What gave the man the right to be proud of anything having to do with Riley Nash? He ground his teeth.

"I'm ready," Sophie announced, her voice a welcome break from his thoughts.

He turned around and his breath caught in his chest. If pushed, he'd have guessed she would pick a one-piece bathing suit that left everything to his overactive imagination.

He'd have been dead wrong.

"You look amazing," he said, once he'd caught his breath.

"Thank you." She stepped forward on endlessly long legs no longer covered by classy-looking skirts or slacks.

He suddenly envisioned her locking those limbs around his back, pulling him deeper and deeper inside her. The skimpy bikini bottoms and small top were nothing more than a joke meant to test a man's restraint.

And he was definitely being tested. He broke into a sweat and the fun come-on lines that normally spilled out so easily failed him now. He was afraid to dig too deeply into why she had such an intense effect on him, afraid he might find he was starting to care too much. He didn't want to put himself in a position of being rejected.

He'd promised himself he'd never give another person that kind of power over him again—the kind his biological father had. Sophie tugged at his heart-strings—a definite reason to limit his dealings with her to a short-term affair, before their different personalities drove her away.

"Are you ready?" she asked, wrapping a skirt around her waist.

He gestured to his Polo swim trunks and T-shirt. "This is as good as it gets."

Sophie looked him over and had to admit he looked darned good to her. "I think you can hold your own with the older set." She hoped her jokes covered her nervousness and insecurity, because the suit and sarong covered very little.

He strode up beside her, his body heat overpowering, his scent arousing. "The question is, can I hold my own with you?" he asked, his breath warm and minty against her cheek.

Sophie drew on every last bit of courage she possessed. "I'd like to see you try."

His eyes darkened as he took in the challenge she'd tossed his way. "Baby, I hope you know what you're getting yourself into."

She swallowed hard, but looked up with steely resolve. "I do." Because once Sophie made up her mind about something—or someone—she stuck with her decisions and she never looked back.

For years she'd been drawn to a man she thought was a flirt and a playboy, a jock and a rebel. In the past couple of hours, she'd learned that he'd been ignored by his biological father and survived the pain. That he had a daughter and a heart.

She'd already been so far gone by the time she'd walked off the plane, that at this point, she knew more than enough about him to allow herself to indulge in an affair. She knew more than enough to know she was in big, big trouble. But despite her normal caution, she was past caring.

She held on to that thought and to Riley's big, warm hand as they walked toward the pool area. She was well aware of what would happen when they returned to the house later, but for now they shared more than just mutual desire.

They shared the need to find his father.

As SOPHIE AND RILEY passed through the gate leading to the pool, torches lit their way and music floated through the balmy air. Limbo music. The sound brought Sophie back to her youth and the birthday parties Uncle Yank and Lola had thrown for her as a child.

"I'm not surprised Darla and company have planned some games," Sophie said, laughing.

"You're enjoying this."

"You sound surprised." She turned his way.

He cocked an eyebrow. "I shouldn't be? I'd have bet you'd be—"

"Too uptight to let loose and have fun?" she asked, knowing exactly what he thought of her. She had to admit she hadn't given him much reason to think otherwise.

"Your free spirit is something I definitely want to see firsthand." He winked and kept walking.

A free spirit, she was not. She glanced down at her string bikini and acknowledged that tonight she was not the same woman from their flight down. She couldn't afford to be if she wanted this time with Riley. But the fact that Riley made her want to shed some of her inhibitions was yet another reason to fear whatever was happening between them.

She glanced over the crowded pool, admiring the way the older crowd was enjoying life. "Let's just say that when I'm eligible for a senior-citizen discount, I hope that I'm as happy with life as Darla seems to be," she said as she rushed to keep pace with Riley.

"Fair enough," he said.

As they reached the pool, the party was in full swing. Chubby Checker's "Limbo Rock" blasted on loudspeakers while the guests mingled. Older men with bald heads or graying hair danced around the pool deck, grabbing any willing partner while the braver ones ducked beneath the limbo stick.

But what really made the party guests stand out was their attire or lack of it. The women displayed their assets in bikinis reminiscent of the movie *Calendar Girls* and their male counterparts wore Speedos in varying colors.

Riley shuddered. "I may never have a good night's sleep again."

She couldn't help but laugh. "I know what you mean." She'd much prefer Riley in his swim trunks to the tight Speedos. Who was she kidding? She'd prefer Riley *out* of his bathing suit, a wish that might come true later tonight. Her mouth grew dry with anticipation.

"Well, at least nobody here is one of *your* relatives," he muttered.

Sophie paused, realizing that what for her was an amusing way to pass time until she found Spencer, was a life-changing event for Riley. She didn't know anything about how he'd grown up or what the parents who had raised him were like, but he obviously wasn't comfortable with the idea that this wild geriatric set comprised his family and their friends.

Unfortunately for her, she wanted to understand and help him deal with whatever emotions were eating away at him. "Riley—" She reached out and touched his arm. Warmth tingled straight to her toes. "These people are no reflection on you."

He turned and stared at the place where her hand had made contact with his skin. "You don't need to worry about me. I'm fine," he bit out.

She heard the rebuke, swallowed hard and removed her hand.

Instead of walking away in search of his father as she'd expected, he immediately grabbed her hand and laced his fingers inside hers. His thumb caressed the center of her palm and the massaging sensation was oddly erotic, definitely a way to tease and send her pulse rate soaring.

She heard his silent apology for snapping at her and she understood how deeply Spencer's abandonment had hurt him. She wished she could ease his pain as much as she wished her heart wasn't already engaged with this man.

"Do you see Spencer?" He surveyed the crowded pool area.

"To find Spencer I'd have to mix with the crowd, and frankly I'd rather not look at anyone that closely," she said, deliberately changing the subject.

He chuckled, relaxing a bit. Her hand still in his,

he pulled her toward the center of activity, the make-shift bar on the side of the pool.

"I'm so glad you two made it." Darla greeted them with a frozen drink in her hand. She bent to take a sip but, instead of the straw, her lips hit the umbrella and she giggled like a young girl. She was dressed like one, too. "Piña colada anyone?" Darla asked.

"No thanks," Sophie said.

"Margarita? Daiquiri? Tom Collins?" She offered the drinks, trailing off with a loud hiccup.

"No, thank you. Darla, have you heard from Spencer?" Sophie asked, undeterred.

"Well, if you two aren't having a drink, that doesn't mean I can't have another. Rose is tending bar. Come meet my sister. Oh, Rose!" Darla called in her high-pitched voice.

Sophie shot Riley a glance. Darla was avoiding the subject and Sophie would bet she knew exactly where her brother was.

"Rose, this is Sophie Jordan and Riley." She didn't use his last name and Rose didn't ask for it.

Sophie tried not to wince. Instead she glanced behind the bar where a bleached-platinum-blonde blended drinks, an oversize floppy straw hat on her head.

Sophie leaned closer to Riley. "Were you hoping for normal?" she whispered.

He shook his head. "I've accepted that in this family, there is no such thing."

This family, not *my* family, Sophie thought. Well,

if they were her long-lost relatives, she couldn't say how she would react. "I take it your mother and step-father aren't—"

"Oddballs? No. They're as conservative as they come. Mom's a member of the Daughters of the Confederacy and my father's a personal friend of Rush Limbaugh. Enough said?"

She nodded and tried to absorb the opposite worlds that surrounded him now.

"So good to meet you," Rose said. "My daughter Amy told me all about you." She glanced at Riley and winked.

Sophie wished Darla and Rose would outright acknowledge him as Amy had. Rose's subtle winks and Darla's pretense had to hurt. Almost like reliving Spencer's rejection, she thought sadly.

"Good to meet you, too." Riley leaned one arm on the bar. "Have either of you beautiful ladies heard from your brother?" Riley asked, turning on the charm.

"Ooh, he's more handsome in person. Than in his pictures, I mean," Rose said, stammering over her faux pas.

Sophie couldn't stand it anymore. She hated how they were following some ridiculous mandate of Spencer's that she couldn't understand. She resented how they were sacrificing Riley's feelings for their brother's agenda.

When she finally got her hands on Spencer, she'd throttle him, but in the meantime she'd settle for taking on his sisters. "I've had it," Sophie said loudly.

Darla turned her way. "Did you say something, dear?"

"Yes." She perched her hands on her hips. "We've both asked you a question and you're ignoring us. Have you seen Spencer?"

Darla blinked and Sophie realized she wore fake eyelashes. "Seen him? No, no. I can't say I've seen him this evening. Rose?"

The other woman shook her head.

Sophie wanted to grind her teeth in frustration. "I guess we'll check in again in the morning before we leave."

"Oh dear! You've only just arrived. I'd hate to see you go," Darla said with meaning.

It was probably the first honest thing she'd said all night. Sophie shook her head, oddly disappointed in these people. "If Spencer shows up, I hope you'll let us know."

"They will," Riley said. "After all, why would they keep that information from *us?*" Riley asked, then without waiting for a reply, he pulled Sophie away from the two older women to a corner of the pool deck where they could be alone.

"I'm sorry," she said, not really sure what for.

He treated her to a grim smile. "That means a lot coming from Spencer's favorite Jordan sister."

She glanced down at the concrete, unable to meet his gaze. "Actually I'm sorry for that, too."

He lifted her chin with his hand. "It's not as if you knew about me. Unlike them."

"Isn't that part of the problem? That Spencer denied his only son?" She drew a deep breath. "I don't understand Spencer. From what I know of him he's a good, kind man. To deny you goes against everything I believed about him. It goes against everything *I* believe in."

And right now she believed in Riley. In what she and Riley could share tonight. She wanted only to stop dancing around their feelings and act on them.

"I vote we go back to the house." She voted they go to bed, but she couldn't bring herself to make the proposition out loud.

Instead she leaned up on her toes and touched her lips to his, letting her actions speak for her. She had no doubt Riley was as smart as she gave him credit for being and that soon enough she'd be in his bed.

CHAPTER SIX

RILEY SUCKED IN a deep breath, afraid to move, afraid if he blinked he'd discover he was dreaming. Because Sophie had touched her lips to his, giving him a green light.

Did she know how much he needed her? The desire between them was obvious. Mutual. The need was something else. She'd become an anchor in his suddenly turbulent life and, at the moment, he didn't know where he'd be without her.

He clenched his hand into a fist at his side and held his emotions in check. Testing what she was offering, he parted his lips.

Sophie responded, tasting slowly at first, grazing his lower lip before finally touching her tongue to his. She tasted minty yet sweet, and felt soft yet hot, all at the same time. His dreams held nothing on the reality of kissing this woman. A woman who loved to be in control of everyone and everything in her life, yet whose body shook with tremors that told him she was barely hanging on to that control now.

Riley felt the same way. His body shook with desire, and with the difficulty of holding back, but he respected how difficult this overture must be for her and didn't want to drive her away. Yet in its simplicity, this was both the most innocent and yet the hottest kiss he'd ever had, bringing everything to life inside him, including things he'd never felt before. Heaven help him when he thrust inside her body for the first time.

A warm, humid breeze blew around them and he couldn't resist uncurling his fist and burying his hand in the soft curls of her hair. The weather teased her normally controlled hair much the way he teased her, he thought, unable to control a laugh.

"Something funny?" She stepped back, looking completely ruffled and thoroughly kissed.

"Just that I finally broke through your composure and I enjoyed it even more than I thought I would." He paused to study her. "And so did you."

"Cocky man."

He shrugged. "Arrogant, too. Now let's blow this joint." In case his meaning wasn't clear, he held out his hand.

She slipped her fingers inside his and they started for the exit. He wove his way through the partially naked older people at the party, doing his best not to gawk. They reached the gate just as they heard a shriek followed by a loud splash.

Riley turned toward the pool.

A bald man waved from the deep end. "Come join

me, Darla!" His toupee floated beside him like a dead rat. His Speedo rose to the top next.

Sophie burst out laughing. "I wish I had my camera. Nobody would believe this."

"If my stepfather was here he'd disown me for sure," Riley muttered.

Sophie raised an eyebrow, curiosity written all over her intelligent face.

"Ever hear of Senator Harlan Nash?" he asked her. It was a rhetorical question, really. The man had made a name for himself with his right-wing conservative views and his close friendship with the current Republican president.

"No wonder you don't want Spencer to acknowledge you now," she murmured. "Let's get out of here," she said, sympathy on her face. But the twinkle in her blue eyes told him sympathy was the last thing he'd be receiving from her when *they* took off their clothes.

BACK AT THE HOUSE, Sophie trembled with desire. She'd been with other men but never one with the ability to reach past her walls. Never one who'd come to mean something to her so quickly. One day of watching him grapple with his family issues, and she wanted to help him figure things out. Of course focusing on Riley meant she didn't have to deal with her own life: phone messages from the chaos at The Hot Zone and Athletes Only, calls from reporters asking for Spencer, and their Heisman-winning client-to-be still hanging by a thread.

But it was Riley she wanted to focus on now. She'd thrown all caution aside and she intended to enjoy it. Living for the moment wasn't Sophie's M.O., but with Riley it felt so right.

He dimmed the lights in the bedroom, casting a sexy, muted glow, then strode toward her. Wearing nothing but bathing trunks, he presented a powerful presence, all tanned muscle and gorgeous male.

He cornered her by the bed, sexual heat emanating from him in waves. Sophie's legs shook and she lowered herself to the edge of the mattress.

"You're beautiful," he said, the sound of his voice taking her off guard.

She glanced up. "I don't need a come-on line. I'm already here," she said wryly.

"It's not a line, Sophie. You're beautiful. You must hear that all the time."

"Actually Annabelle's the beautiful one, Micki's the athletic one and I'm the smart one." She laughed self-consciously, but the labels had been given—nobody really knew by whom—and they'd stuck.

As a result, Sophie always relied on her intellect, even with men.

Riley stroked her cheek with his hand. "Whoever said that didn't know you very well."

A lump rose to her throat. "It's pretty obvious which sister is an analytical pain in the butt," she said, forcing out a laugh.

"It's also pretty damn obvious which sister is beautiful inside and out. You care about people, even arrogant SOBs like me." A sexy smile curved his mouth.

"Who said I care?"

Without warning, he bent his head and captured her lips in a hot, searing kiss. With no preliminaries, he thrust his tongue deep into her mouth. A tingling sensation took hold of her body and she leaned her head back, giving him complete access to whatever he wanted. His silken tongue swept inside, learning every part of her and then started over again.

She curled her hands around the comforter and held on. His mouth worked magic, arousing her in every way. Her breasts grew hot and heavy, and her nipples hardened into tight aching peaks. Dampness gathered between her thighs, leaving her a trembling mess by the time he was through.

"You did," Riley said when he finally lifted his head.

"I did what?" She couldn't think over the loud beating of her heart.

"That kiss just said you cared."

Sophie laughed, but she knew just how to wipe that smug look off his face. "I didn't know you needed a woman to care in order to have sex."

"With most women I don't."

Good thing she was sitting or she'd have passed out. "Just how many women have there been?" She closed her eyes, mortified that she'd even asked.

He chuckled low and deep. "Enough, but not as many as you obviously think." His tone grew serious.

Oddly, she believed him and she was glad. She

was so far gone, so enthralled with this man, she didn't want to think about other women. And she definitely didn't want to talk anymore.

Neither did he. He stepped forward and nudged her legs apart until he'd moved between her thighs. He knelt down, then ran his fingers over her calves.

"Soft yet muscular," he said.

"That's because I shave and I run."

He chuckled, then trailed a moist path with his tongue, from her knee up the inside of her thigh. Her flesh tingled and she was sure her skin quivered at the intimate touch.

He reached her bathing-suit bottom and paused. "I wonder...with all that control of yours, have you ever really let a man *know* you?"

She swallowed hard. "Probably as well as you've let any woman know you."

Riley had heard plenty from her uncle about her legendary need to control. He'd seen it on the plane. Viewed the depth to which she needed comfort, routine and the expected. And he doubted she let any man have the upper hand.

He tipped his head back and laughed. That's what he enjoyed about Sophie. She gave as good as she got. "Touché."

"I'm so glad—"

He silenced her with a finger as he slipped his hand inside her bathing suit to reach the secrets hidden there.

With his finger pressed on her damp folds, he

rubbed light circles and watched as her eyes dilated and she struggled for control.

"I mean it, Sophie. I want to know you. I want to know how you come."

She tried to clamp her legs closed, but his hand was already where he needed it to be and he knew she was only causing an increase in ecstasy.

"Unfair," she murmured.

"If we're going to do this, we're also going to be honest." He was pushing her emotionally, pressing her harder. He didn't know why, only that Sophie brought out a raw, primitive need to protect and defend, to take care of her. Precisely because she'd always acted as if she didn't need anybody, he wanted to take control and show her just how good it could be.

He released his intimate hold only long enough to ease her bottoms down her legs. Despite her annoyance with his topic of conversation, sexually he had her enthralled and she helped him by lifting her hips, giving him a view of heaven. His cock was hard as a rock, his body screaming for release. With any other woman, release would be enough, but not with Sophie.

While she eased back against the pillows, he kicked off his shorts and joined her on the bed, surprised and pleased to find she'd removed her bikini top as well.

He took in her full breasts and dusky nipples and drew a shuddering breath. "Oh darlin', you are something."

She blushed. "There it is again. That hint of a Southern accent," she said with a pleased smile.

"You like it?"

She grinned. "What can I say? You've got a lot to like," she said, her attention settling on his solid erection.

"Glad the feeling's mutual."

"Mmm." She reached for him, but he playfully slapped her hand away. If she touched him now it'd be over before it started.

"Now quit changing the subject." He eased beside her naked body and brushed a long, lingering kiss over her lips. "What makes you come?" he asked her again as he slipped his finger deep and deeper inside her.

She let out a moan and her hips writhed in restless motion, clenching around him.

"It feels good, but you don't come this way, do you? You need to be on top."

Her hips stopped moving, her breathy noises ceased.

Score one for him, he thought, pleased he knew her so well. "Baby, I'm gonna change that."

"Nobody has before." Her eyes flashed with the challenge.

"Luckily for you, I'm not nobody," he said, bringing his mouth down hard on hers.

Her entire body was as silky smooth as it looked and she smelled as delicious as he'd imagined. As for preliminaries, apparently they'd had all they were going to get—this time. She was hungry for him, too, matching him kiss for kiss, touch for eager touch.

As he'd expected, she attempted to take control, hooking her leg around his and straddling him between her thighs. Fortunately for her, he was stronger and able to flip them until she lay flat on her back.

"You don't play fair," she said.

"You'll thank me for it later." He reached out, cupping her breast in his hand, feeling her distended nipple press into his palm. He fleshed out the weight and feel, all the while making sure he aroused her further with every caress, every touch.

She fought him at first, her eyes open and wary, but eventually pleasure outweighed her determination and her eyelashes fluttered shut. He took it as a sign of trust and leaned down, drawing one nipple into his mouth.

She gasped aloud, but when he began a steady flicking with his tongue, she relaxed into the sensations. Ignoring his own body's need, he focused on hers. Never neglecting her breasts—first one, then the other—he cupped her feminine mound in his hand, determined to bring her to release and to be right there with her.

Her hips jerked upward and she whimpered, her desire for increased pressure obvious.

He slid upward so he could see her face. "I hear you," he whispered softly in her ear, and ground his hand harder.

Her breaths came in shallow gasps and he saw she was close. He could make her come this way or he could be inside her when she did.

No contest.

He lifted himself over her and reached for the condom he'd put on the dresser earlier. She opened her eyes at the crinkling sound. Blue eyes he found way too sexy and welcoming.

She bent one leg and he said, "Don't even try it, babe."

"What, you think you're a mind reader?"

"Are you telling me you weren't about to try and flip on top?"

A telltale pink flush tinged her cheeks.

"Sophie, Sophie," he said, poising himself over her. "Did I not promise you that you'd thank me?"

He kissed her at the same time he entered her in a smooth, damp thrust. As he slid deep inside, he realized he should probably be thanking her. Nobody had ever felt this good.

She picked up his rhythm quickly. Each time he pumped harder, she clenched her muscles, wrapping him in moist, intense heat. Each thrust brought him higher and higher still. He had to trust he was keeping his word and she was moving closer, too, because he was beyond thought, beyond reason. Beyond stopping.

Suddenly his world exploded in bright light and an ecstasy unlike any he'd ever known.

RILEY KNEW HER too well. Sophie's body still pounded with the aftermath of a release she'd had no control over. He hadn't moved from on top of her, his breath warm against her neck. He'd played on her biggest weakness and then proceeded to break down all her barriers until he'd called the shots. Making her vulnerable. To him.

"Damn you," she muttered, doing all she could to hold back tears. She hadn't cried since her first time and that had been because of the pain.

He rolled off and propped his head against one arm. "I didn't mean to hurt you," he said, brushing her tangled hair from her face.

She shook her head. "You didn't. It's just…"

"You always cry after sex?"

The word *sex* did it. She smacked him in the arm but, before she could speak or explain, he spoke.

"It wasn't just sex." He paused. "But I don't want to talk about what *it* was."

In a stupid way and because she was coming to know Riley, she understood. He had walls. So did she.

"That's fine. I don't want to explain the tears, either. Just don't say you proved yourself correct and we'll be fine."

He grinned and something inside her righted itself again.

They were two complicated people at a complicated time in their lives. She didn't need a man to make her life complete—she never had. But for some reason it was important that she matter to Riley.

"Ready for round two?" he asked with a seductive twinkle in his eyes.

Her body heated up all over again, but the jarring

ring of the telephone interrupted her before she could reply.

She shot him a curious glance. "Nobody I know has this phone number."

"Me neither. Elizabeth has my cell, that's all." He gestured to the pile of personal things on the nightstand.

She shrugged and answered the phone. "Hello?"

"Sophie? This is Amy."

"Hi, Amy. What can I do for you?"

"I'm sorry to bother you but I need your help."

The panic in her voice called to Sophie's take-charge instincts and she sat up in bed. "Of course. What's wrong?"

"I can't believe this. I really can't. My mother's in jail."

"What?" Sophie asked, stunned.

Riley nudged her arm. "What's going on? Did Spencer surface?"

She shook her head and held up one finger, silently asking him to wait. "What do you mean Rose is in jail? Where's Darla?"

Amy let out a groan. "Right there with her. I never made it to the party because I had an awful migraine, so I was laid up in bed. Next thing I know, the phone rings and it's Mom asking me to bail them out." Amy proceeded to tell Sophie the gory details of what led to the arrest.

Sophie alternated between holding in peals of laughter and exclaims of shocked disbelief. "So you're on your way to the station?"

"Actually I can barely lift my head to drive. That's why I'm calling. Can you please go bail them out for me?"

"Of course. Hang on while I find a pen and paper." She wandered the room naked in search of her purse, completely aware of Riley's intense eyes following her every movement, and even more aware of her body's response to the man.

Finally she found what she needed and grabbed the phone once more. "Just give me the information and we'll get on it right away." She jotted everything down, including Amy's phone number, and promised to call when they had the women safely on their way home.

"So what happened?" Riley asked once she'd hung up.

She realized she was about to further distance him from Spencer's side of the family. "Are you sure you want to know?"

He shook his head. "No, but lay it on me anyway. Fully armed is fully prepared." He folded his arms across his chest and waited.

She wondered if he realized what an impressive sight he presented—completely naked, muscled, tanned and so sexy he took her breath away. Which, she admitted, had been the problem since the day they'd met. He flustered her to the point where she didn't know how to handle anything around her. He took away the control that made her life comfortable and manageable. And making love with him hadn't diluted his impact as she'd hoped. If anything, she'd only fallen harder for this frustrating, sexy, totally inappropriate man.

"Well?"

She sighed, drawn back to the present. "Apparently, after Myron—that's the man with the toupee—jumped into the pool, Darla joined him."

Riley raised an eyebrow but said nothing.

"Things got really loud and rowdy, and thanks to the noise, someone called the police. By that time, Darla was standing on the diving board ready to cannonball." Sophie paused. She really didn't want to continue this part of the story.

"Go on," Riley said through clenched teeth.

Sophie closed her eyes and said, "She was naked."

"Oh gross," he muttered.

"Anyway, she was skinny-dipping and Rose got upset and went in after her to pull her out. She claimed all she really wanted to do was get her sister wrapped in a towel and sobered up."

"But?"

"But when she jumped in after her, her bathing-suit top fell off and that's when the cops arrived and arrested them for indecent exposure," Sophie finally finished, and opened her eyes to see how Riley had taken the news.

Not well if his flushed cheeks were any indication. "And the Florida cops have never heard of issuing a warning to a bunch of stupid people?" he asked.

Sophie winced. She'd thought the same thing.

"Apparently it wasn't the first time." Before he could work himself up further, she reached for his hand. "I've got to go bail them out. Amy can't do it because she's laid up with a migraine and can't move. Why don't you wait here—"

Riley groaned. "I'm coming with you," he said, obviously resigned to his fate.

RILEY HAD SEEN his share of precincts. He'd bailed high-school and college buddies out of county jails after juvenile pranks and drunken brawls. But he'd never had to rescue a relative from their own blatant stupidity.

A relative he couldn't afford to claim as his, yet he also couldn't ignore the sense of responsibility he felt for the older women. Blood was one hell of a motivator, he thought as he entered the police station with Sophie by his side.

Sophie. Now there was another complication in his life. He'd hoped having sex with her would finally get her out of his system. After all, that was the way it usually worked. Sex, some good times, some more sex and Riley and his woman of the moment went their separate ways. Once his marriage had ended, he'd never had the desire to stay in a long-term relationship and he'd never thought to give another one a try.

Thanks to a few psych classes in college and a couple of sessions with a shrink, he also knew why. Spencer had rejected him despite his best efforts to prove himself and as a result, deep down, the great Riley Nash believed he wasn't worthy of love and acceptance.

"What can I do for you folks?" the desk sergeant asked as they approached.

"We'd like to post bail," Sophie said.

"For Darla Atkins and her sister, Rose." Riley realized they didn't know what last name Rose went by.

The burly man behind the metal desk leaned back in his chair. "A dollar short and a few minutes late," he said, laughing. "Somebody beat you to it."

"Who?" Sophie asked.

But even before he turned around, Riley already knew. His stomach clenched and nausea washed over him, but he straightened his shoulders as he turned to see his father.

"The ladies should be out in a few minutes," the man behind the desk said. "You realize we had to teach them a lesson, Mr. Atkins."

Spencer nodded. "Just don't count on it sticking, Joe."

"You've got your hands full with those two," the younger man conceded, then turned his attention back to the ringing phone and the paperwork on his desk.

Riley stared at Spencer, acutely aware of Sophie standing behind him. After days of worry, he had no doubt she wanted to hug Spencer and then give him hell for causing her such concern. Instead she stood back, giving him time and space with his old man.

He turned to him now. Instead of demanding

answers to a litany of questions as he'd always imagined he'd wish to do, Riley found he just wanted to speak his mind and get the hell out. "So tell me how it is you sort out your priorities," Riley said, speaking without polite preliminaries. "You've always ignored me, but how the hell do you justify taking off on your business and leaving Sophie to handle your mess?"

Riley held up a hand to forestall Spencer from answering before he finished. "Yet you show up now to bail your rowdy sisters out of jail as if you haven't been MIA for days?" Riley shook his head in disgust.

Spencer bowed his head. "I don't expect you to understand." He shoved his hands into the pockets of his expensive trousers.

"Riley, let's give him a chance to explain," Sophie said, softly. She reached out and placed a comforting hand on his shoulder.

Too bad he was past being comforted.

"You and I have a lot to talk about," Spencer said to Riley. "Too much to cover right now."

Riley stared into hazel eyes so like his own they unnerved him. "Don't worry. I don't expect anything from you. Not anymore. So give whatever time you have right now to Sophie. Just one *favor* though." He forced out the word for his mother and stepfather's sake.

"Anything."

Riley scowled, but stepped closer so no one would hear. "Since you never bothered to claim or acknowledge me when I needed you to, don't bother doing it now. My mother, *father* and his campaign will thank you."

The color drained from Spencer's face. Riley forced back the wave of guilt. After all, he wasn't the one who'd denied the relationship for years.

"I can see where having a gay father would be an embarrassment."

Riley shook his head. "You've got it wrong. I could care less. But Harlan's my father and he's spent his life preparing for a run for Washington. The fact is that his constituency is solid right wing and I'm only looking to protect him."

Something suspiciously like pride flashed in Spencer's eyes. "He raised you well."

Riley inclined his head.

"Then he not only has my gratitude but my promise. I won't interfere with his campaign in any way."

In other words, Spencer wouldn't publicly claim Riley as his son and that's all he needed from this man.

He glanced at Sophie. "I'll meet you outside."

Her eyes were damp as she nodded.

Riley walked out the door, knowing he'd gotten what he came for. Neither his life nor his stepfather's life would change in any way. But instead of the relief and satisfaction he expected, Riley only felt a bone-deep emptiness.

CHAPTER SEVEN

SOPHIE LOOKED at the man she'd known all her life. Suddenly Spencer's hair seemed grayer, the grooves in his face deeper.

"I don't know you at all," she said, the disappointment growing inside her.

He'd always treated her differently than her sisters, with more affection and respect, as if he'd sensed how much she'd needed his attention. But in light of all she'd learned in the past few days, she no longer took pride in his special treatment. Not after the pain she'd heard in Riley's voice and seen in his eyes.

"You know me better than most," Spencer said, his voice grim.

"That's not saying much, now is it?" Within the offices of Athletes Only and at home among family, nobody held back any punches. Sophie wasn't about to do so now. "As far as work goes, I need you home if you still want a business to return to." She filled him in on the details and problems he'd left behind. "Now for the rest. Keeping your sexual preferences private is one thing. Denying your only son is another. *How could you?*"

He paused, as if searching for a way to explain. "It's all part and parcel of the same thing. Do you think that boy deserved my baggage? The news was bound to come out someday. Don't you think he deserves to be known for his achievements and not his father's issues?"

"You're saying you denied him in order to spare him potential embarrassment?" She shook her head in disbelief.

"Didn't he just admit as much by asking me not to acknowledge him now?"

"He did no such thing!" Sophie pounded her fist on a metal desk, her frustration mounting. "If you'd done right by him all along, this wouldn't be an issue. His stepfather would have worked his way around any pitfalls as Riley grew up. Instead you left a bombshell for them all to deal with whenever it might explode. You set Riley up as a boy who wasn't worthy of his father's love and now he's a man who thinks he never will be. He's standing by the only family he's known and that's admirable, but at what expense?" She blew out a puff of air, knowing that anything she said couldn't change the past.

"I did what I thought was best. That's what parents do for their children. Someday you'll see that for yourself."

She doubted she'd have that chance given her hangups, but that wasn't her concern right now. "I can't imagine what it's been like to keep your secrets," she said, softening her tone. "But I hope you'll find a way to fix things, if not for yourself then for Riley."

"The best thing I can do is to give him what he asked for. Nothing."

Sophie swallowed hard. "I disagree. Statistics show that children need their parents."

His hand cupped her shoulder in the fatherly way he'd always done. "Statistics aren't emotions. That's something else you need to learn for yourself."

She opened her mouth to speak, but Darla and Rose interrupted them, the commotion they caused disrupting the entire precinct. Both women wore wet bikinis covered by towels. Their makeup ran beneath their eyes and their hair was matted around their heads.

Sophie sighed. Riley might want to deny this part of the family, but they were vibrant and chaotic, independent and refreshing, much like Riley himself. And something told her that he needed them if he was ever going to release the hold he kept on his heart.

LEAVING SPENCER with the convicts, Riley and Sophie drove home in silence. Either she knew better than to ask questions about how he was feeling or she was equally disturbed herself. Either way, they'd gotten what they came for, Riley thought. It was time to go home.

But not before he finished the night with Sophie.

She entered the house ahead of him and immediately headed for the kitchen and pulled a bottle of chilled wine from the fridge.

"I noticed this in here earlier." She scrounged around for a corkscrew and opened the bottle like a pro. "I don't know about you, but I could definitely use a drink."

"Make mine a double."

She laughed and held out his filled glass. "To…" She trailed off.

"To us," he said, unable to think of anything he'd rather drink to.

She clinked her glass against his. "To us." In her eyes he saw longing and desire.

What he didn't see was a woman who'd demand more than he could give and that surprised him. Then again everything about Sophie shocked and pleased him. He never knew what to expect next except an innate understanding of him, something nobody had had before.

She took an extra long sip of her drink.

"That rough a night?"

She swallowed another. "I told Spencer off," she said, looking down into her glass. "I let him know he was dead wrong in the choices he'd made regarding you." She swirled the liquid around and around. "I said I didn't know him at all."

He paused, his glass at his lips, and swallowed the dry white wine. "Why?"

"Why what?"

"You and Spencer have a special relationship. He means a lot to you, yet you let him have it. Why?"

She raised soft eyes, revealing too much. "Because you've come to mean something to me, too."

He reached out and lifted the glass from her hands, placing it on the counter. Then lacing their fingers, he pulled her close.

"Sophie?"

"Yes?"

"Thanks."

Her smile warmed him straight to his toes. After meeting Spencer, he thought he'd never be warm again. She wrapped her arms around his neck and pulled him close, pressing her lips against his.

He groaned and, cupping her face in his hands, he tilted her head and deepened the kiss. He needed this. He needed her.

He thrust his tongue inside her mouth and she moaned aloud, her small hips gyrating against him, seeking relief he knew he could give. Relief he needed, as well.

Unable to wait, he lifted her into his arms and headed for the bedroom.

"I knew when I met you that you were the kind of guy to sweep a girl off her feet."

"Only the right girl," he said, nuzzling her neck in part to inhale her fragrant scent and in part to stop any further talking.

Sophie shut her eyes and savored the moment. They'd found Spencer, which took a huge weight off her shoulders, and she was alone with Riley, which made everything right in her world at this moment.

He lay her down on the bed and settled his body over hers, kissing her hard, as if he couldn't get enough. She returned each nip and lick, each touch and move.

But this time when they removed their clothes and he tried to press himself on top of her, she was ready. Oh, she knew he could give intense pleasure, but this time *she* wanted to be in control.

Pushing him onto his back, she grabbed his hand and placed that arm above him so his fingers gripped the post on the headboard, then she secured the other hand. "I'm trusting you not to move those hands," she said, eyeing him warily.

"And if I do?" His eyes sparkled with sizzling defiance.

She shook her head. "Don't make me have to tie you up, Mr. Nash."

He laughed. "Now that would definitely be something worth trying. For tonight though, I promise to be good, but only because I already proved myself right." He winked.

She didn't care what the reason was. She had him at her mercy. Her body tightened at the thought and, without further talk, she straddled his thighs.

He stood thick and erect and she bent her head, taking him into her mouth. He tasted salty and male as she moved her lips up and down over his hardened member. His hips bucked and he grew impossibly harder.

Suddenly he lifted her, pulling her over him. "Another minute and I'll explode, and something tells me you'd rather I be inside you when I come." Arousal and need darkened his face and beckoned to her. He quickly reached for protection, then sheathed himself and stared, waiting for *her* to take control.

Once again, he understood her. Words wouldn't come, so she spoke with her body instead. Poising herself over him, she slid down hard at the same time he pushed up and into her.

He filled her completely and her breath caught in her throat, the emotion of the moment taking her by surprise. Then his hands wrapped around her waist.

"Ride me," he said, his words a command she couldn't deny.

She closed her eyes and rocked her body against his, a movement guaranteed to bring her to orgasm. Except this time when she did, not only did he come along for the ride but so, she feared, did her heart.

THE MORNING ARRIVED too quickly, especially when the persistent ring of the doorbell woke Riley from a deep sleep. Considering the events of the night before, he wasn't surprised he'd slept so soundly. He was, however, surprised he'd stayed in bed with Sophie.

He usually preferred to sleep alone.

Since she was no longer beside him and her side of the bed was cold, he figured she was handling the door. He took a few minutes to pull on his jeans, brush his teeth and splash cold water on his face before seeing which of his relatives had decided to pay them an early-morning visit. His money was on Amy.

He was wrong. As he stepped out of the bedroom, he heard Darla's distinctive voice coming from the kitchen.

"I'm just so embarrassed. I came to apologize and of course to thank you for trying to bail us out."

"People make mistakes," Sophie said. "And of course we came to help. You don't need to thank us."

Riley could envision Sophie patting Darla's hand and reassuring her. Instead of joining them, he hung back.

"Some people make more mistakes than others. In our family it seems to be genetic."

"Lay off the alcohol, stop throwing parties and you and Rose should be fine," Sophie said, laughing. "I think the police just wanted to teach you a lesson."

"There were *hookers* in the tank with us," his aunt said dramatically.

Riley bit the inside of his cheek.

"But when I spoke of mistakes, I wasn't talking about last night's," Darla said. "I was talking about Riley."

He froze, every muscle in his body taut.

"No child is a mistake," Sophie said to Darla, her voice frosty.

Despite everything, he smiled. This feisty woman had come to his defense again.

"Oh my! I didn't mean that at all. Goodness, what you must think of me. Then again I haven't given you much reason to think anything good—"

Darla was rambling again, Riley thought. But she wasn't condemning him for being born.

He stepped into the kitchen, joining Sophie and sparing her from having to deal with Darla alone.

"Why don't you tell us what you meant?" he said, with more patience and warmth than he was feeling.

Darla forced a smile. She didn't look well this morning. In fact she looked hungover and embarrassed, but she'd cleaned up since last night and without the heavy makeup, he realized she was a very attractive woman.

"I shouldn't have pretended not to know who you were yesterday. That's what I meant when I mentioned making mistakes." She glanced down.

Sophie took that moment to slip her hand into his. The silent but sweet gesture of caring and support filled him with gratitude.

He glanced at his aunt. "Go on. Please," he said gently. "I'd really like to understand."

Darla swallowed hard. "Well, your father was always somewhat of…an individual. He did things his own way."

Sophie chuckled. "Like father like son, apparently."

"It would seem so." The older woman eased herself into one of the kitchen chairs and gripped the armrests. "Except in Spencer's case, he was an athlete, a guy who loved everything masculine and sports oriented—including other men. It just wasn't an accepted thing back then." She shook her head. "So he did what I suspect many gay people did. He tried not to be what he really was."

"And that's when he met my mother?"

Darla nodded. "Rose and I hoped he could make it work. *He* hoped he could make it work. He loved her, he really did."

"He just couldn't be in love with her," Sophie murmured.

"Exactly. This isn't my story to tell, but that's exactly why I pretended not to know who you were yesterday. It's what Spencer always did and I thought it wasn't my place to change things."

"Amy did," Riley said.

"Amy's smarter than I am. Anyway, that's behind us now. I want to know you, Riley. I want us to try to be some sort of family."

Riley stepped closer to this strange but obviously loving woman. "I am not angry with you. I couldn't be. You didn't put this whole thing in motion, like you said. But…"

She glanced up. "What?"

He hated to hurt her, but what choice did he have? "But things have to go on as they always were." They couldn't have the relationship she wanted.

No family barbecues, no bailing her out of jail, no getting to know each other. He went on to explain about his mother and stepfather, the family who'd raised him and the career aspirations that couldn't possibly accommodate these wacky, eccentric, unconventional people related to Riley by blood.

Darla nodded. Then she said all the right things and claimed to understand. But when she left, her shoulders were slumped and her eyes damp. He'd disappointed her in a soul-deep way, something Riley understood all too well.

He turned to Sophie. "How the hell did I become the bad guy?" He'd only requested they maintain the status quo, something *her* brother had put into place.

She touched his arm. "Hey. Everyone involved here understands the idea of protecting family. Look how Darla just protected Spencer. She won't hold this against you."

"I don't care if she does." The words slipped out before he could censor them.

"Forgive me if I don't believe you. Still, you did what you had to do," she said with complete understanding.

"And now we can leave. I'll see about a flight home."

"I already did. There's nothing until tomorrow. I booked us an early flight in the morning." She shrugged. "It's the best I could do."

He paced the kitchen, uncomfortable in this house and in his own skin. "I can't spend the day here wondering if any of the family is going to show up," he said, more to himself than to Sophie.

"If it helps, Spencer's already left. He went standby and was able to take the earliest flight to New York."

He exhaled hard. At least he wouldn't have to run into his father.

"I could be persuaded to walk Worth Avenue," Sophie said of the ritzy street in Palm Beach lined with exclusive shops.

He laughed. "I'd rather play strip poker with Darla and Rose." The pathetic thing was, they'd probably be more than willing. "As long as we're in Florida, let's go to the beach."

"Buy me a piña colada and I could be persuaded— after I check in at the office." Sophie grinned, a sinful smile full of sex and promise.

After last night, he knew she would make good. "Darlin', I'll buy you anything you want." Because with Sophie, he knew he could put this entire father mess out of his head while she drove him out of his mind.

WAVES RUSHED against the shore and water lapped at his feet. They'd driven to Fort Lauderdale, to a beach by one of the bigger hotels. Abandoning their shoes, they walked along the edge of the water, hand in hand.

"I am loving this," Sophie murmured.

Curling his toes into the damp sand, he had to agree. "Which part of this?" he asked, curious about what made Sophie tick.

"The relaxing part." She closed her eyes and bent down, feeling the cool water between her fingers.

Her lips lifted in a smile, the euphoria on her face nearly orgasmic and Riley's body tightened with the knowledge that he'd had her. And he needed to have her again.

She stood, hands on her hips, her jeans rolled up above her calves. "Spencer's home and holding down the fort at the agency, and Cindy's assured me things on the PR side are under control. I have twenty-four hours to do absolutely nothing. I suddenly feel free." Arms out at her sides, she spun around, much like a child in a playground.

He stood back and watched, enjoying the moment.

She stopped spinning and stood in front of him, out of breath and laughing. "As much as I hate to admit you were right, the beach was an excellent idea."

He grinned. "I'm always right." Thanks to her, Riley had put the confrontation with Spencer behind him and was also beginning to unwind.

A speedboat passed by them, the motion of the boat causing large waves in its wake.

"Look." Riley pointed up into the sky where people were floating in the air above the water. "Parasailing. There's nothing like it."

Sophie shaded her eyes from the sun and studied the person nearly in the clouds.

"What are you thinking?" he asked.

"Just that I've never done anything so daring."

Riley glanced from the sandy beach up to the clear blue sky. "No time like the present to start." They'd passed the rental area when they'd entered the beach.

"Oh no." She shook her head, the curls she'd let go natural today blowing around her. "It's one thing

to want to do it. It's another to actually go up there."
She shuddered at the thought.

But he could see the temptation in her eyes, the
desire to try and the building determination in her expression. He stepped around her and pulled her into
his arms the way he'd been dying to all day.

He snuggled his face in the crook of her neck and
inhaled deeply, the scent of beach and her fruity
shampoo assaulting his senses. "They have tandem
parasailing. You wouldn't have to be alone."

The thought of rising above the clouds with
Sophie snuggled close to his body had other parts of
him rising as well. "What do you say?"

"Well…"

He sensed her hesitation came from the fear of
being out of control. "I'll keep my arms tight around
you, like this." As he drew her even closer, his groin
pressed up against her and he swallowed a groan. "I
promise to keep you safe."

She let out a soft laugh. "If safe feels anything like
this, I'm not sure I can trust you," she murmured.
"But what the hell. Take me on an adventure."

He hadn't thought she'd take him up on his suggestion. She wasn't anything like the uptight woman
he'd originally pegged her to be, her ability to
surprise without bounds.

He glanced at her cuffed jeans. She wore a swimsuit
underneath, but for now she was wading without a
care. A far cry from the conservative woman in The
Hot Zone offices. And one he liked a whole lot more.

An hour and a half later, they were on a boat in the ocean, being buckled and harnessed, Riley strapped in behind Sophie for parasailing. Sophie had taken up over half an hour questioning the owner of the company about his safety record, licenses and asking for details about the water sport and what kept them in the air.

He'd folded his arms across his chest and let her go at it. His only contribution was to shoot the poor man a pitying look.

Riley was coming to understand that for Sophie to give up control, she needed to compensate with complete understanding.

A few clouds had filled the sky, but the weather was still picture perfect for liftoff. "Now remember to bend your knees when you come in for a landing," the instructor said, and pulled on the straps to double-check the security. Then he stepped back.

Riley held on to the support rope as the big man released the pulley and raised them into the air. With each passing second, they left safety and terra firma farther and farther behind.

His heart raced, much as it did after throwing a successful touchdown pass in the Super Bowl. "Isn't this freaking awesome?"

Sophie laughed, and he heard the sheer terror shaking her voice.

He wrapped his arms around her waist and pulled her tight against him. "Relax and enjoy," he whispered in her ear.

"Easy for you to say."

He stroked the side of her head, caressing the throbbing pulse point in her temple. "I'm proud of you," he told her. Proud of her determination, spirit and courage, even if it was wavering now.

"My parents died in a plane crash."

He took the words like a punch in the gut. Though he knew she'd been orphaned, he hadn't known the details.

Though Spencer had abandoned him, Riley had always possessed the knowledge that his father was alive. For a while he'd lived for the opportunity to make Spencer proud. Even when he'd given up on ever having a relationship with the man, he'd known Spencer was living somewhere in this world. Until now, he would never have believed the thought would bring any sort of comfort. He realized now, it had.

He wanted to be the one to help Sophie work through some of the effects of her tragic loss. "So what's it feel like to let go?"

"Good question." Sophie looked over the vast ocean, the smattering of tiny-looking homes and the Southern landscape, so different from home.

Up in the air, away from the land, her life and her problems seemed very far away. Riley was her only anchor and she leaned into him, giving him her trust as completely as she'd given him her body last night.

She'd never have believed she could throw caution away so easily or enjoy it so much. Now that she had, she allowed herself to embrace the sensation if only for the moment. "I feel free," she called out, suddenly giddy with laughter.

The scary part was that she owed it to this man who, like everyone else in her life, would soon be gone.

CHAPTER EIGHT

WHO'D HAVE THOUGHT parasailing would be almost as intimate as sex? By the time they returned to the house, Sophie was wound up both physically and emotionally. Arousal thrummed through her body, due in large part to the rush of adrenaline from her activity. She recalled reading about the effect of adrenaline on the nervous system. It was no surprise she couldn't wait to wrap her arms around Riley's neck and her legs around his waist.

She followed him into the house, staring hungrily at his tanned legs and powerful muscles flexing beneath his damp, sand-caked T-shirt. She swallowed hard. Then again, that throbbing, pulsing need just might have more to do with the man himself than with her parasailing adventure.

She shut the door to the house behind her and began to methodically take off her clothes so as not to make a huge, sandy mess all over their borrowed home. When she was through, she was clad only in her bikini.

Halfway through the large living room that led to

the master bedroom and its spacious shower, Riley turned to Sophie. Even from a distance, she felt the heat in his stare and the welcoming warmth in his expression. Her heart beat more rapidly in her chest and flutters took up residence in her stomach.

He crooked his finger and no words were necessary to clarify his meaning. She sprinted forward, meeting him halfway.

He grabbed her around the waist, his big hands branding her bare skin with their heated touch at the same time his lips came down hard on hers. This was what she'd been burning for all afternoon and she threaded her fingers through his windblown hair, ready to pull him into an embrace that went deeper than a kiss. He was faster, easing her forward then lifting her onto her tiptoes so their hips meshed at exactly the right point.

On contact, waves stronger than the ocean current raced through her body and she savored the sensation, swaying to the rising current of pleasure he created. Her hips rocked in unison with his. With each roll of his waist, every deliberate thrust of his groin against her body, desire built higher and higher. His mouth worked similar magic, tasting, nipping and exploring.

She moaned aloud, the first sound from either of them.

His body trembled and he moved his hands from her waist to her shoulders, his thumb caressing her flesh in circles, the pressure of his fingers increasing, matching the harder thrust of his lower body. At the same time, he led her across the room.

Her back hit the wall and she finally had the support she needed to hold her up against the sensual onslaught. Through mind-numbing kisses, he nudged her legs apart and shifted until his thigh came in contact with her *there*. She was out of her mind with need, practically panting with unfulfilled desire.

The next thing she knew, he'd shifted her forward. He slipped his hands inside her bottoms so his hands cupped her cheeks and thrust her directly against his hard, muscular thigh. She was full and wet, on the verge of what surely would be the most spectacular climax in the history of climaxes. Whimpering and completely out of control, she ground herself against him over and over, seeking relief that seemed just out of reach.

"Come," he whispered in her ear, pumping his leg up and down, teasing her and yet somehow, increasing the pressure each time.

"Riley—" Her voice broke on a sob.

"Don't hold back, baby." He slipped one hand around her hips and into the front of her bathing suit. His fingers sliding through her damp heat to ease one finger between her folds. "I'll catch you. Come on, Soph. I won't let you go," he said in a roughened voice.

She shut her eyes and let her head loll back, ecstasy overwhelming her. And all the while he continued to rock his thigh, hard and fast beneath her.

She imagined him pumping thick and hot inside

her body. Harder. Faster. Deeper. And she splintered in his arms, the most intense pleasure she'd ever experienced washing over and over and over her.

"Wow." She opened her eyes to find him watching her intently and tried not to squirm in embarrassment.

"You can't hide anything from me."

She merely nodded, then realized how one-sided this had been. "I…let's go to the bedroom so I can take care of you," she said, leaning forward and nipping lightly on his earlobe.

He shuddered with pleasure. "Much as I'd love to do just that, it's unnecessary." A twitch worked at one side of his mouth.

"You mean you already—"

"Uh-huh. Taking you there and watching you come did it for me."

"Oh, wow." She'd never had that kind of effect on a man. Either that or she'd never met a man who would admit that she had, she thought. "I guess I'm pretty potent, huh?"

He grinned. "We could bottle you and make millions."

She laughed. "Shower?"

"You read my mind."

Hand in hand, they were halfway there when the telephone rang.

"I'll get it and meet you in there," she offered. Her body still trembled with aftershocks and she could use a minute before stepping under the hot spray.

She ran for the phone in the bedroom, drew a deep breath and lifted the receiver. "Hello?"

"Who's this?" a young female voice asked.

"Who is *this?*"

"This is Elizabeth Nash. Who are you and where's my dad?"

Riley's daughter, Sophie thought. He must have given her the house number when he'd checked in with her earlier. Obviously the young girl wasn't into polite niceties or preliminaries. "I'm Sophie Jordan and…" Sophie trailed off. Did she tell Lizzie that her father was in the shower, making things sound, oh, about as tawdry as they were, or did she go get Riley?

"Hold on and I'll get your dad." She placed the phone on the counter and knocked on the bathroom door.

"Come on in." She opened the door and peeked inside.

"No need to knock, darlin'. You've already seen it all," he said as he stepped naked beneath the spray. "You gonna join me?"

"Your daughter's on the phone."

He frowned. "Tell her I'm in the shower."

She grabbed the door frame. "I thought about that and it doesn't sound like she'd take that too well. At least not from me."

He picked up the soap and began lathering his gorgeous body. "Then just tell her I'll call her back in a minute."

She nodded. "Will do," she said, and turned to go.

"Sophie?"

She pivoted back around. "Yes?"

"Don't let Lizzie intimidate you. Her bark's worse than her bite."

She smiled. "Don't worry," she said, shutting the door behind her. She walked back to the phone, thinking how Riley adored his daughter and probably made untold allowances for her.

She lifted the phone again. "Elizabeth?"

"Yeah."

"He said he'd call you back."

The young girl let out a prolonged sigh and Sophie gripped the receiver hard, preparing for an argument.

"Okay, just tell him it's *important*. Life-or-death important." But the bored tone sounded anything but distressed.

A pop sounded in Sophie's ear. Bubble gum? she wondered. "I'll give him the message."

"Yeah. Thanks." Click.

Left holding a dead phone in her hand, Sophie merely blinked before hanging up and easing herself down onto the bed. Her body still tingled, a delicious reminder of what they'd just shared. She shivered and rubbed her bare hands up and down her arms. She would have thought their behavior was as juvenile as two teenagers behind the school, except her feelings were far more adult and intense.

Riley strode out of the bathroom, towel-drying his hair as he came up beside her. "What'd Lizzie have to say?"

"I don't think she likes me," Sophie said, recalling the young girl's defensive attitude that had quickly turned bored and dismissive.

He slung the towel around his neck and laughed. "She doesn't know you."

Sophie raised an eyebrow. "Something tells me she wouldn't want to. Let me guess. Daddy's little girl?"

Riley's mouth lifted in a grin that said it all.

Just what Sophie didn't need—a teenager with an attitude and a proprietary air about her father.

Riley winked at Sophie before he picked up the phone to call his daughter.

Lizzie answered on the first ring. "Dad?"

Hearing her voice warmed him. "Hey, Lizzie baby, how are you?"

"Not good! Mom's being so unfair!"

He rolled his eyes at the familiar refrain. "What's going on?"

"My friends are going to the Seaport and *she* won't let me go."

Riley didn't have to see the pout to know it was on his daughter's face. He hated her being unhappy and wanted to fix whatever went wrong. Sometimes Lisa drove him crazy with her rules. In this case he didn't see what was wrong with shopping with friends.

"When's the day?" he asked.

"Next week. We have school vacation, remember?"

He lowered himself onto the bed. "Of course I remember. We're going to Playland sometime next week, right?"

"Yeah. Right. But I really want to go to the Seaport and Mom says I can't go unchaperoned at night."

"Night?" he asked, his ears perking up.

"*Evening,*" she said, clarifying. "Like five o'clock."

Happy hour, he thought. "Who would be there?"

"Dad!"

He chuckled at her outrage. "I have to ask. Now spill. Something has your mother upset enough to say no." Aside from the hour, which would inevitably turn into eight or nine o'clock.

"Miranda and Ashley," she said, naming her two best friends. "And their parents already said yes."

Riley reserved judgment on that bit of news. These kids were notorious for telling each set of parents that the others had already agreed, hoping to sway things their way.

"Who else?" he asked.

"Mmmadjkr," she mumbled.

He couldn't help but grin. "Say it again clearly this time."

"Mike and Joey and Rick and Frank," she said on an indignant huff, clearly annoyed at being forced to reveal all.

"I'd say the boys are your mother's problem. That and the hour."

"But…but…you don't trust me?"

He shook his head. "It's not you we don't trust."

"It's everyone else out there." She parroted the words he and Lisa had used with her before. "Dad, this is so unfair! I just want to hang out with my friends at the Seaport. I don't see what's so bad about that. Everyone's going to go and I'll be left out, and then they'll talk about it at school and I'll be the only one who's not part of things!" Her voice trembled, tugging at his heart.

"I'll talk to your mother."

"She'll never agree. Can't I just sleep at your house so I can go and we won't tell her? Please, Daddy, please."

He groaned, hating the pleading tone in her voice. "We'll talk when I get home tomorrow."

"You're the best!" she squealed into the phone.

"Lizzie, I didn't promise anything," he reminded her.

She laughed. "But I know you and I love you." She blew a kiss into the phone. "Gotta go now! Bye!"

The phone clicked on her end. Lizzie, he realized, had twisted his words into what she wanted to hear. If he didn't agree, she'd blame him even more than she already blamed her mother.

"Teenagers should come with an instruction manual," he muttered.

"Nobody ever said it would be easy."

He turned, startled at the sound of Sophie's voice. Wrapped up in Lizzie's drama, he'd forgotten she sat patiently by his side. "It amazes me how easy it is for someone who's never been a parent to offer platitudes."

She inclined her head. "Good point."

At least she didn't seem insulted.

"I take it she wanted to go somewhere and her mother said no?" Sophie asked.

He nodded. "South Street Seaport during happy hour."

"And you agreed with…" Sophie trailed off.

"Lisa," he said, helping her out with his ex's name. "I didn't agree and you know it. You heard my side of the conversation. I said we'd talk about it when I got home."

Sophie curled a leg beneath her and studied him. "Lisa," she said. "The woman you married because you were young and in love? Or she was young and pregnant?" she asked.

He liked that she didn't pull punches. "Too young to know what love was, too young to have kids, too stupid to know we didn't know any better." He shook his head and laughed. "But we did get Lizzie out of the deal. Lisa's married to a stuffed-shirt accountant now and they tend to follow the rules."

"Aha," Sophie said, nodding. "You, the nonconformist, don't want to follow those rules." A gleam of certainty sparkled in her eyes.

He shifted uncomfortably. "It isn't that simple."

"So explain." She leaned forward, waiting.

He felt certain, once he revealed his motives, she'd come down firmly on his side; after all, she'd already shown she understood him when it came to Spencer. Her insight had provided him with much-needed support this trip.

He'd never shared his feelings about Lizzie with

anyone in his life, but he wasn't surprised he now wanted Sophie to be the first. The notion that he was seeking her understanding, or worse, her approval, was a threat to his style of doing things his own way in his own time.

"There's a reason I don't like to do what others expect." He paused and she remained silent, giving him whatever time he needed to gather his thoughts. "I spent the better part of my life, my youth, trying to get Spencer to notice me."

Unable to sit still, and finding it even more difficult to look into Sophie's solemn eyes, he rose and paced the carpeted room. "By the time I won the Heisman and was represented by Yank, with no word from my father, I decided I was no longer going to please anyone but myself."

Sophie swallowed over the lump in her throat. Imagining Riley as a little boy seeking his father's elusive approval broke her heart. That it was Spencer, a man who'd given *her* love and understanding, hurt even more. Guilt pierced through her, making her feel as if she'd stolen something precious from him. Something he'd never get back.

"When Lizzie was born, I held this little bundle in my arms. She was smaller, and a hell of a lot more delicate, than a football." He grinned, but in his face she saw love and emotion, something so deep it took her breath away.

She started to reach for him then changed her mind. What he felt for his daughter had nothing to do with her and she had no right to intrude on it. "Go on," she said softly.

"Right then, I promised myself—and I promised her—she'd never wonder if her father loved her. She'd never look around and question why her father wasn't a part of her life. And she'd never ever resent me." He set his jaw tight.

Sophie glanced down, knowing she had to phrase this exactly right. "Just be her father."

"It's not that simple. I'm not there when she goes to sleep at night or when she wakes up in the morning."

"So you want to give her what she wants to make up for it."

He shrugged. "That's my job as her father."

"Your job is to make sure she grows up safe and sound and loved. The best way to do that is to set rules—"

"To hell with that," he muttered, rising from the bed. "Control and rules are your thing, not mine. But because of everything you've seen down here, I thought you'd understand my relationship with my daughter. Apparently I was wrong," he said in a suddenly frosty voice.

She blinked, startled by his change in tone. "Of course I understand." But that didn't mean she totally agreed.

Because Sophie and her sisters had been raised by their bachelor uncle, she'd always worried about him getting it right. To his credit—and in no small part thanks to Lola—he had. Partially because they'd known the importance of rules and discipline.

Sophie had taken it upon herself to learn from her uncle's way of parenting. Maybe Riley could do the same. "This isn't about my rules. It's about children and what they need, and what it means to be a parent."

He raised an eyebrow. "And you'd know this because you are one?"

"Whoa." She stood and squared her shoulders. "Where's the hostility coming from?"

He faced her, the arrogant athlete she'd always seen him as in the past. She couldn't be more disappointed. Or more hurt. Her throat swelled painfully as she realized she'd let him into her heart only to have him trample on it at the first sign of their differences.

"It isn't hostility, it's fact," he said, oblivious to her feelings. "You'll never understand where I'm coming from. You're a stickler for rules and I'm not. No way am I going to inflict that kind of control on my daughter."

He was talking about Lizzie but he was condemning Sophie, too, and with each word his emotional walls rose higher. He wanted to block her out and he'd succeeded. She couldn't find the words for a cutting comeback nor did she want to try. Riley had been scarred by his childhood and was so obviously overcompensating with his daughter, it was downright scary.

"I'm in her life and she's going to grow up appreciating that fact, not resenting me or wishing I was gone."

Sophie looked into his cold eyes. "So you'll buy her instead. Well, good for you. Maybe one day you'll grow up and realize she's better off with a real parent rather than an overindulgent one with poor judgment."

He scowled and started for the door. "I'm going to pack," he muttered, and walked out without looking back.

South Street Seaport at night. Sophie shivered and hoped Riley wasn't seriously considering letting his thirteen-year-old daughter go there. Then again, he had one valid point. Now that he'd decided she didn't understand him, it wasn't any of her business.

Unfortunately, there was no telling herself she didn't care. Sophie headed for the shower he'd just vacated and inhaled the scent of soap he'd left behind. Her heart pounded in her chest, disappointment in both Riley and how their relationship had turned out filling her.

She'd been stupid enough to invest more than her body in this short relationship even though she'd known from the beginning how it would end. Too bad she hadn't trusted her instincts and steered clear.

Because although she'd expected a parting of ways when they returned home, she hadn't expected him to turn on her before they even left South Florida.

CINDY REPLAYED the voice mail telling her Sophie would be home later today. Hallelujah. She loved being a publicist, dealing with people and nabbing PR coups, but she hated running the place on her own. Though Spencer had returned, he was too busy handling damage control with his own clients to worry about the mundane things like bill keeping and doling out new assignments to the other publicists. She appreciated Sophie's faith in her, but she was more than ready to return to the role of employee.

Especially since they'd just experienced a major computer crash in the office. The techs didn't know what had caused the problem. They'd mentioned the possibility of a virus attacking the system, but until they'd worked on it some more, they couldn't be sure.

Her cell phone rang and she pulled it out of her purse, answering on the first ring. A pathetic occurrence that happened way too often since she'd shared drinks with Miguel Cambias the other evening.

She looked at the incoming number on the phone. As if on cue, her stomach performed an excited flip. "Hello?"

"Good morning," he said in that sexy tone.

"Hi," she said, feeling like a tongue-tied teenager.

"I've been e-mailing you all morning. Are you avoiding me?" he asked in a confident voice that insinuated she'd never do such a thing.

He was right.

"Not avoiding you. Just unable to reply. Our server is down," she explained, thrilled by the notion that he'd been trying to reach her.

"Aah, that explains things," he said in an understanding tone. "I was hoping I could steal you away for lunch."

She wanted to say yes, but she and Sophie would have to play catch-up for most of the afternoon. "Not today, unfortunately. How about tomorrow?"

"You drive a hard bargain, Cynthia."

She loved the sound of her full name coming from his lips. "I think you'll find me worth the wait," she said, laughing.

"Of that I have no doubt. Lunch tomorrow it is. I'll be in touch." He disconnected the line, leaving a humming feeling dancing through her veins.

She enjoyed his company and not just because the man knew how to treat a lady, from insisting he pick her up at work, to opening doors, to pulling out her chair before she sat. He listened intently to details about her life and asked questions as if he were truly interested in both her family life and her job, unlike many men who only wanted to talk about themselves. Miguel was solicitous and sexy and when he'd walked her to her door, he'd done nothing more than kiss her cheek. His aftershave had lingered in her memory long after he'd gone.

She couldn't recall the last time she'd been wined and dined and romanced like that. In addition, he'd sent her fresh flowers as a thank-you and e-mailed her just to say hello.

How could she not be interested in the man? Yet how could she not feel guilty when her boss didn't know about Cindy's growing relationship with their competitor?

She consoled herself with the fact that Sophie

would be back this afternoon and she'd fill her in then. In the meantime, she'd enjoy the excitement of knowing she was finally on the right track in a relationship and enjoying every minute.

DESPITE THE TYPICAL craziness of Kennedy Airport, Sophie still heard her cell ring. A few seconds later, she was no longer worrying about the chill between herself and Riley because her business was a mess.

She shut her phone, slid it into her purse and turned to her companion, who'd been as silent as she for the duration of the flight. Her only consolation had been that he'd been too preoccupied to flirt with the flight attendants.

Despite the sudden urgency to get to the office, Sophie still couldn't help but drink in what was probably her last look at Riley for a while. Every inch the rebel with the collar of his jean jacket raised and his eyes hidden by sunglasses, she'd never felt more distance between them. It was hard to believe she'd slept with him. Made love with him. Let him begin to get into her heart.

She glanced at the moving carousel, which had begun to circulate luggage from the flight. "As soon as my bag shows up, I'm out of here."

"Work calls?" he asked.

Was that sarcasm she heard in his voice? "The computers crashed. The tech people are trying to get things back online, but right now it's a nightmare." Some sort of computer virus had completely disabled their system. Checks couldn't be printed or signed and neither could contracts. Internet access was nonexistent.

Just then her bag came into view. Recognizing it, he swung it off the conveyor belt for her.

"Thanks."

"No problem."

Silence hung between them. Uncomfortable and not wanting to prolong things, she pulled the handle on her bag so she could wheel it to the taxi line.

"Good luck at the office," he said.

She swallowed hard. "Good luck with your daughter."

"No luck needed," he said flippantly.

Too flippantly, Sophie thought. Could he find this parting as awkward as she did?

She wondered if he'd been at all affected by their time together or if she was just another fling. She'd never know, Sophie thought sadly. She could hazard a guess though, and the answer was as painful as the lump in her throat.

"RILEY NASH, you are a first-class jerk," his ex-wife muttered.

It wasn't anything he hadn't thought about himself since leaving Florida, but Lisa's reasons for calling him the name were way different than his own.

"It's not like I brought her back a huge gift. It was just a stuffed animal from the airport." The gift wasn't behind Lisa's anger—that much Riley knew.

He just wanted to buy himself time before dealing with the real issue between them.

Riley leaned back in his chair in the small restaurant his ex had chosen as a neutral meeting ground. Though he steeled himself for an argument, he remained outwardly relaxed and in control, leaving the hysteria for Lisa.

"You cannot be that stupid," Lisa muttered. "You know that's not what I'm upset about."

"I think we can refrain from name-calling," Ted, the ever rational one said, patting Lisa's hand to calm her down.

Riley had to refrain from gagging at the other man's patronizing, too fatherly manner. "All I did was let my daughter sleep over," he said to her for at least the dozenth time.

"And you let her go to the Seaport with friends *after* I said no!"

He couldn't deny part of her statement, but there had been extenuating circumstances. Like it or not, he'd come to the conclusion that Sophie's words made sense. Lizzie needed a father not a friend. Still he hadn't wanted to deprive her, nor had he wanted her to end up resenting him the way he resented Spencer.

He couldn't stop thinking of Sophie for many reasons, not the least of which was how he'd treated her their last day in Florida. She deserved so much better. But from the moment he'd realized he cared enough about Sophie to want her to understand his motivations regarding his daughter, he'd been scared by the implications. Scared that he'd come to care for Sophie Jordan as much more than a one-night stand. The minute she'd hit on his weak spot—his relationship with his daughter—his defense mechanisms had kicked in and he'd latched on to the first excuse to push her away.

That he regretted his actions was an understatement.

"Riley," Lisa said through clenched teeth. "Let me know if we're boring you."

He refocused at once. "I let Lizzie go to the Seaport, yes, but I was there the entire time. Which I've been trying to tell you, but either you hung up on me or screamed so I couldn't get a word in edgewise."

Yet another reason their marriage had failed. Too much screaming and not enough communication skills. Skills that Sophie certainly didn't lack, Riley thought, surprising himself with his train of thought.

"Well. That changes things," Ted said.

Lisa shot her husband a scathing glare. "It certainly does not." She leaned closer to Riley. "Did she know you were there, watching her?"

He shook his head. "Of course not. She'd have been good and pissed, and—"

"You'd have been the bad guy. Instead, you allowed her to think she was defying me, making you her hero and me the bad parent. Again."

He winced at her description. "I didn't do it deliberately. I didn't think—"

"That's just it! You didn't think. You never do." Lisa clenched her fists and pounded on the table.

"As long as your needs are met, as long as you look good to Lizzie or the press, all's well in Riley's world. To hell with the rest of us." Tears of frustration sparkled in her eyes.

Riley had seen those tears many times before. During their marriage they had argued over many issues, although since the divorce, the only one they ever had to agree on was Lizzie. And until his daughter had hit adolescence, their differing parenting styles hadn't caused real conflict. Riley suffered a pang of remorse that it did so now.

"This can't continue," Lisa said, squaring her shoulders defiantly. "It isn't fair to me and it isn't fair to Lizzie, allowing her to think she can circumvent authority by going to her daddy."

"The reason we wanted to get together today was so we could agree on some ground rules." Ted inserted himself in the middle of their war of words.

Riley forcibly bit back a nasty retort. Knowing that his reaction to the word *rules* had set him on the wrong path with Sophie, he gritted his teeth and merely nodded. He knew one thing for sure. They all had Lizzie's best interest at heart and they had to get along in order to share custody.

"So what did you have in mind?" he asked, wary but willing to listen.

"A simple thing called *joint* parenting. In other words, if I tell Lizzie something, you back me up in front of her." Before he could argue, she held up one hand. "And if *you* tell her something, I'll back you up. In private, we can disagree but we present a united front to her. And if we change our minds, we do it together. No divide and conquer. Not anymore."

"Why do I sense an *or else* coming?"

Lisa sighed. "Or else I'm going to have to sue for full custody."

"The hell you will!" Riley rose quickly, knocking over his chair in the process.

The other customers in the small restaurant stared openmouthed, but he didn't care. "You will not take my daughter from me."

Ted tossed his napkin on the table and stood. "That isn't going to happen. Lisa spoke without thinking. Nobody's going to do anything rash. We…" He gestured to the three of them. "We are going to find a way to co-parent through the rocky adolescent years. And we're going to do it like a family. Elizabeth's family."

Riley met Lisa's gaze and nodded in agreement. For the first time, he actually agreed with the stuffed-shirt accountant. He'd better, if he didn't want to find himself in court fighting for custody of the person he loved most.

CHAPTER NINE

SOPHIE RUBBED her eyes, exhaustion nearly overwhelming her. Although the tech guys had gotten the computer system up and running within twenty-four hours of the crash, the damage had been done. Despite the firewall, a nasty virus had infected the system via e-mail and Athletes Only's form contract, one carefully negotiated and containing a confidentiality clause, had been distributed to everyone in the main computer's database of e-mails. A.O.'s contract was no longer confidential and a week after the story about Spencer's sexual orientation had broken, everyone had something else on their minds.

A knock sounded and she glanced at her office door. "Come in."

Her sister Annabelle strode in and shut the door behind her. "How long were you going to wait before calling in reinforcements?"

"Where's my nephew?" Sophie asked, ignoring work for the most important thing: family.

"He's home with his grandparents. It's way past

time I came back to work. As much as I love him, I'm losing my mind," Annabelle said.

Sophie rose, came around the desk and pulled her sister into a huge hug, then stepped back to check out the changes since she'd seen her last. Her always curvy sibling was even more so post-pregnancy. "Motherhood agrees with you. You look gorgeous. And I am so glad you're here."

"Believe me, I'm thrilled to be here. Now fill me in on the computer crash." Annabelle pulled up a chair and settled in. "I thought our system was secure."

Sophie seated herself on the corner of her desk. "Apparently nothing's foolproof. This was a form of the Klez virus that comes in an e-mail attachment. Once a computer is infected, the virus automatically sends out copies of itself when the machine is connected to the Internet. And it's usually without the user's knowledge."

"Somebody's been researching again," Annabelle said, teasing Sophie.

She shrugged. "How else could I understand what's going on around here?"

"And try to control it?" Annabelle squeezed Sophie's shoulder.

"It's not like anything else around here is falling into place," she muttered.

"We'll fix things. How close is Spencer to signing Cashman?"

Sophie rolled her eyes upward. "Your guess is as good as mine. His father has this good-old-boy

Southern attitude. He expects Spencer to take him at his word that he's a client of Athletes Only. He says he operates on trust and Spencer should, too."

"A little *Jerry Maguire* thing going on?" Annabelle asked.

"That's what has Spence nervous. Add the computer crash, plus Cambias sniffing around courting Cindy—"

Annabelle's eyes opened wide. "He's what?"

Sophie shook her head. "There's no other word for it. He sends her flowers, shows up to take her to lunch, that kind of thing."

"Do you think he's really interested in her?"

"I hope so, because she's falling hard and fast. He'd better not want access to anything business related," Sophie muttered.

Without warning, Frannie came storming through the door. "You have to see this. Come to the conference room quick."

Sophie shot Annabelle a worried glance and together they followed Frannie out the door, down the long hall and into the conference room, where they had a fifty-inch LCD screen. To her surprise, there was a clip of Tom Arnold, special correspondent for Fox's irreverent *Best Damn Sports Show Period,* talking to Uncle Yank at an airport.

"Where is that?" Annabelle asked.

"Kennedy," Frannie said.

"I didn't know he was coming back early from his cruise." Sophie eased herself into an oversize chair, knowing that whatever happened next, she wouldn't like it.

"Nobody knew." Frannie clicked a few buttons and soon they were watching the beginning of the interview.

"Good flight, big guy?" Tom Arnold asked.

"The best," Uncle Yank said in a voice as loud as his Hawaiian shirt and baggy Bermuda shorts.

"So what's so important that we came out here to meet you instead of waiting until you could come on the show? Because I know Chris and John were looking forward to talking to you next week."

"They were?" Sophie and Annabelle asked in unison.

Yank chuckled and slung an arm over Tom Arnold's shoulder as if they were old buddies. Which they were, but that wasn't the point. Uncle Yank had a gleam in his eye and Sophie leaned forward in her chair.

"A man can't wait to brag about his honeymoon, Tom."

"Yeah, I've had a few of those myself." Tom grinned.

Sophie figured Lola was standing in the background, waiting to throttle her husband.

"So you return to pure chaos at home."

"Nothing we can't handle. The draft is all ours next week."

As far as Sophie knew, nobody had been in contact with Uncle Yank, but obviously she was wrong. "Who's spoken to him?"

"It must have been Spencer," Frannie whispered. "Unfortunately, you haven't seen anything yet."

Tom raised an eyebrow. "Your firm's signed Cashman? Because Miguel Cambias has also mentioned some serious talks with the first-round draft pick."

"Anybody with half a brain knows there's no contest between Cambias and Athletes Only. It's like choosing between a prostate exam and a blow job. What's an intelligent man gonna pick?"

"Oh God," Annabelle muttered, covering her face with her hands.

"Why doesn't he just wave a red flag in Cambias's face?" Sophie asked.

Once he stopped laughing, Tom leaned in closer to Yank. "Now I have to ask the question everyone's wondering about. You lose any clients after Spencer got pushed out of the closet?"

"Spencer Atkins is the *best damn sports agent, period.* Besides me, of course. No fool's going to leave A.O. because the man prefers receiving to passing."

"Fair enough. Are you ready to return to work?"

"Damn straight. Get it? *Straight.*" He belted Tom on the back. "With the draft in a few weeks, I've got a boatload of work ahead of me. Not to mention my personal mission."

"Could that personal mission have something to do with your gorgeous nieces?" Tom asked, as if he'd planned to make this transition.

Goose bumps like warning signals prickled along Sophie's skin.

"It just so happens it does. You know I'm just

coming home from my honeymoon. I waited too long to get hitched, but now that I have, I'm a spokesperson for commitment."

"Oh, brother." Annabelle, who'd taken a chair beside Sophie, reached over and grabbed her sister's hand.

"Two of my nieces, Annabelle and Micki, have also gotten themselves shackled."

"And that leaves Sophie," Tom said, nodding slowly as if just catching on.

Sophie's stomach cramped and she closed her eyes for a brief moment. Of all the harebrained, half-cocked, stupid ideas…

Yank abruptly turned and began waving his arms. "Hey, honey, come on over here and hand me my bag."

The camera panned to Lola, who looked fit to be tied, as she crossed her arms over her chest and glared at her husband. "I will not be a party to this spectacle, Yank Morgan. And it's not too late for you to leave now before more damage is done."

"Poor Lola," Sophie said.

Annabelle turned to her, her expression incredulous. "Poor Lola? Poor *you!*"

Sophie rolled her eyes. "I'll survive. I can't do anything now anyway. What's done is done. Besides, the man raised all three of us. We're used to his humiliating comments."

And it was inadvertent. Everything Uncle Yank did, he did out of love. Unfortunately, he didn't think before he spoke, which often landed him in the doghouse with those he cared about most.

They turned back to the screen. The camera had panned away from Lola while Yank pawed through his duffel bag, then to Sophie's complete mortification, he pulled out a photo. Of her.

"She's sexy, smart and single," Uncle Yank was saying.

"He's making me sound desperate!" Sophie's cheeks burned with humiliation. "And I'm going to kill him."

"I thought you said, what's done is done," Annabelle reminding her, trying to suppress a laugh.

"*He's* done. And if he's smart, he won't show his face around here anytime soon." Sophie rose and headed for the door, passing a silently sympathetic Frannie as she departed in search of a brown paper bag to put over her head.

In fact, maybe she'd wear it for the rest of her life.

AFTER HER HUMILIATION on TV, Sophie had taken a mental step back and decided to cool down before confronting her uncle. The difficult thing about getting angry at Uncle Yank was that he always had good intentions. His way of going about things was much more questionable.

She'd decided to stop at the gym for the early-evening yoga class in order to relieve stress, before heading to his apartment for a long talk. Now as she stepped off the elevator onto Yank's floor she heard Noodle's high-pitched bark. Apparently her uncle and Lola had already picked up the pooch from Cindy, who'd taken over doggie duty.

She rang the doorbell and immediately smacked her hands over her ears in time to block out the worst of his extraloud chimes. Uncle Yank had installed them before he'd married Lola. He hadn't wanted to miss a visitor. After almost going deaf the first time she'd visited and heard the noise, Sophie had learned her lesson and protected her hearing.

She turned and shot a covert glance at the door across the hall, expecting his neighbor to stick her head out and complain about the racket as she always did.

"She's off visiting her daughter," Uncle Yank said from behind her, tapping her on the shoulder at the same time.

Sophie swirled around. She hadn't heard him open his apartment door. "You drove her away, huh?"

He shook his head. "Don't go giving your uncle a hard time. Give me a big hug instead."

Despite her anger and frustration with him, Sophie loved the man and wrapped her arms around him tight. "I missed you, you old coot." She stepped back. "But I'm still going to kill you," she told him.

"Hey, it's my job to see you're taken care of."

She raised an eyebrow. "And you think prostituting me to every man with a TV set is taking care of me?"

"If you'd just settle down like your sisters, I wouldn't have to worry about what'll happen to you when I'm gone."

Sophie grabbed her uncle's weathered hand, a

knifelike pain settling in her heart. "Nothing's going to happen to you. Unless you trip over Noodle or fall off another chair," she said, making light of the serious fact that he was getting up there in years, though still only in his late sixties.

He chuckled. "It's something I can't help thinkin' about. I want to know if I kick off, I won't have to worry about you."

"There's not going to be any kicking going on unless it's me kicking some sense into your thick skull." Lola stepped into the hall. "Apologize to Sophie right now."

Sophie pulled the woman who'd raised her along with Uncle Yank into a hug. "You always were his conscience," Sophie said, laughing.

"I may be blind but I'm not deaf, and I can hear you just fine. I don't need a conscience. There's nothing wrong with taking care of my own," her uncle insisted.

Sophie sighed. "There's no getting through to him."

"Amen." Lola shook her head. "Why don't we take this inside?"

As they settled into seats in the living room, Uncle Yank said, "So Spencer tells me you've been spending time with Riley Nash."

At the mention of Riley's name, Sophie's heart did a little leap inside her chest. She knew better than to share the truth about her relationship, or whatever it had been, with her uncle. He'd rip Riley's head off, and Sophie still cared about him too much to subject him to Uncle Yank's wrath.

She swallowed hard. "Riley came to Florida with me when I was looking for Spencer." So much more had happened between them and she hoped her fair skin didn't show a blush.

"So he finally decided to go looking for his old man." Her uncle nodded approvingly.

Apparently Uncle Yank was focused on Riley and Spencer's relationship, not Sophie and Riley's. Knowing she'd escaped, she jumped on the topic at hand and leaned forward in her seat. "You knew Spencer was Riley's father?"

Uncle Yank shook his head. "Until last month, all I knew was that in Riley's senior year Spencer called me and said he wouldn't be taking on Riley Nash as a client. He asked me to represent him before some other shark could step in."

"Didn't you wonder why Spencer would give up a prime athlete?" Sophie asked, confused.

"A man doesn't always have to explain himself. That's the way it was between Spencer and me."

Lola let out a sigh. "We found out Spencer's motives last month after the big revelation. He just wanted to protect Riley from the pain of having a gay father, so he called Yank and asked him to represent Riley. To take care of him the way Spencer couldn't."

Sophie rubbed her aching temples. Suddenly she had a better understanding of Spencer. She no longer considered him the man she didn't understand, or the dear friend who'd let her down. Instead she saw a ter-rified human being who'd done what he thought was necessary for his child, no matter how misguided his actions had turned out to be.

"Riley doesn't know this," she murmured, her heart with the man who thought himself unworthy of his biological father's love.

"I wouldn't think that he did," Uncle Yank said. "Spencer told me that there was an ugly confrontation in Florida and Riley wants nothing to do with him."

"It's confusing, but that's about the gist of it."

Lola rose from her seat, smoothing the creases in her slacks. "Sophie, honey, would you stay for dinner?"

Sophie nodded. She didn't have any other plans and she'd missed her uncle and Lola.

As she helped Lola chop a salad and put dinner together, Sophie's mind whirled with what she'd learned. She couldn't stop wondering how Riley would feel when he found out that Spencer had looked after him from behind the scenes, taking care of his career through Uncle Yank.

Knowing Riley's defiance when it came to Spencer, she doubted the truth would change much, especially the betrayal Riley still felt to this day. Spencer's deliberate absence had affected Riley's life in a profound way, from how he raised his daughter to how he maintained his distance from anyone who lived by rules and order.

No matter how much Sophie understood what made Riley tick, he'd never get past *her* need for stability and routine. Inevitably they'd clash over every decision he made that was spontaneous or unexpected, and he'd hate the way she made him feel boxed in. For her part, there was no possible way she could change the habits of a lifetime, ones that gave her comfort and security.

In fact, the more she thought about their short affair, the more she realized that he'd done her a favor by distancing himself in Florida before things between them got even more complicated or serious. A little heartache now was nothing compared to the damage he could have done to her if he'd gotten an even tighter hold on her heart.

RUNNING ON THE TREADMILL was a damn good way to release stress, and since returning from Florida just a few short days ago, Riley had had plenty of aggravation. First the scene with Lisa and Ted, and then the fact that his daughter was upset with the new regime, as she called it, and didn't like that all three parents had read her the riot act. She'd decided to take her anger out on Riley by not making herself available to see him. His daughter turning on him was the one thing he'd wanted to avoid and he didn't know how to make things better.

Then there was the issue of his burning desire to see Sophie again in someplace other than his dreams. And definitely someplace other than on the television screen being promoted as *sexy, smart and single* by her crazy uncle. Riley pounded on the rubber at a steep incline. Willing himself not to focus on his problems, he turned up the volume on the headset and set the channel to one of the sports channels before running harder.

But as usual, he couldn't stop thinking about Sophie. He missed her like crazy. Yank Morgan's close-up photo of Sophie had been like a kick in the head, reminding him she was even more beautiful than he remembered. Not to mention more vulnerable than she liked to let on and more sexy than any woman had a right to be.

Her uncle had held her out like a piece of meat in the marketplace. Unfortunately Yank's description was dead-on accurate and every red-blooded male in this country probably now knew it, too.

Riley came to a skidding halt and grabbed the towel he'd slung over the handlebar.

"She's hot." Mike, his best friend, running back and occasional weight spotter, gestured to the television where they were rerunning clips from Yank's interview, including the headshot of Sophie. "That is the chick from Florida, right?" Mike asked.

Riley had unloaded on his friend last night while at a bar, but only because Mike wouldn't spread the information around the locker room. "That's her."

Mike knew that he'd hooked up with Sophie in Florida and that she'd gotten under Riley's skin, but not even Mike knew about his relationship to Atkins. Growing up in a politician's house had taught Riley the value of keeping a secret.

"I can see why you can't forget about her. So why

not have some fun and let the thing run its course?" Mike suggested.

Riley had asked himself the same question many times during sleepless nights when he'd tossed and turned, images of Sophie's body under—and over—his keeping him aroused and awake.

Riley tipped his head to one side and really pondered the notion. If he couldn't get Sophie out of his head by staying away from her, maybe he should stop fighting it. Maybe he should try and pick up where they had left off and allow the relationship to lose steam on its own. It would. They always did.

Riley glanced at Mike. "Every once in a while, you come up with a not-so-stupid idea." He gave his buddy a friendly punch on the shoulder and started for the shower.

"Where are you going?" Mike asked.

"To act instead of sitting on my ass."

"Mind if I tag along?" Mike asked. "I have some things to follow up on."

Riley shrugged. "Be my guest."

Spencer Atkins had been Mike's agent for years. Riley ignored the stab in his chest brought on by the reminder that other people were good enough for Atkins's representation. Just not Riley.

AFTER A QUICK SHOWER at the gym, Riley headed over to Athletes Only. He knew he must be desperate to see Sophie if he was willing to risk running into his old man to do it. He had his doubts she'd have anything to say to him, but he had to try. His sanity depended on it.

An hour later, after a frustrating trip through heavy city traffic, they arrived at the offices of Athletes Only and The Hot Zone. His heart pounded hard in his chest, along with a suffocating feeling he hadn't experienced…ever.

He stepped off the elevator and into what looked like a flower shop. Vases lined the reception desk filled with bouquets of carnations, roses and other assorted varieties he couldn't possibly name.

"Are we in the right place?" Mike asked jokingly.

"Damned if I know." Riley walked to the desk and peered between the floral displays. "Is Sophie Jordan in?"

The woman he'd met last time glanced up at him, then sneezed. "If you have flowers, put them in the corner," she said, then returned to the work in front of her, ignoring him.

Riley cleared his throat. "I'd like to see Sophie. I'm a client."

Behind him, Mike snickered. "Client, my ass."

"That's what they all say," the receptionist said, all but echoing Mike. "See these?" She gestured to the flowers surrounding them. "They each belong to someone who claims to be a client or wants to be a client of Ms. Jordan's."

Riley's stomach rolled at the revelation. In his wildest dreams, he'd never have thought Yank's pronouncement would result in any real attention showered on Sophie. He'd been dead wrong and now not only did he have competition, but that competition hadn't slept with, then insulted and jilted her all in the same breath.

The receptionist scowled at Riley. "Frankly, Ms. Jordan can do better than all of you. How pathetic to show up here just because her uncle broadcast her photo and single status on national TV."

Ouch.

Riley leaned across the desk, being careful not to knock over the flowers and upset the secretary even more. "I agree. We met last time I was here. You'd just started here temporarily, if I recall."

She narrowed her gaze. "You do look sort of familiar."

"Then here's a friendly suggestion for you. You're doing a great job screening people for your boss, but get to know the real clients. I'm Riley Nash, a long-time client of Yank's and more recently of Sophie's. So how 'bout you cut one of the good guys some slack and tell Sophie she has a visitor?" he asked, emphasizing his accent, since most women found it charming.

She pursed her lips and scanned what he hoped was a client list. Finally her eyes opened wide and she jumped up from her seat. "Good gosh, I am so sorry! You're Riley Nash." She ran around the desk and reached out to grab his hand, pumping it hard.

"That's what I said." He couldn't help but grin. "And this is Michael Putnam, one of Spencer's clients." He turned to Mike, only to find his friend gawking at the young brunette.

She wasn't Riley's type, but since Sophie, he wasn't sure he had a type.

"You go on in and I'll just let Sophie know she has company. And please don't tell Ms. Jordan I almost didn't let you through. I've already messed up once and I am really hoping for a permanent position here."

Mike strode up to her and placed an arm around her shoulder. "I'll put in a good word for you. As a matter of fact, why don't we talk while Riley goes in to see Sophie?"

Riley said a silent thank-you that Mike would remain behind. Riley didn't need Mike by his side when he faced Sophie for the first time since he'd messed up.

As Riley walked down the hall, all he could think about were the flowers. He wondered who'd sent them, and noted how much satisfaction he'd take in breaking each and every bloom, stem by stem.

"You're sick," Riley muttered to himself. *Lovesick?* a little voice in his head asked.

Sophie's light laughter captured his attention. "No dinner, no date, no, thank you," she said, then hung up the phone as Riley stepped into the doorway and drank in the sight of her.

She was every inch the woman he couldn't get out of his mind, and more. From the top of her perfectly styled hair to the tailored suit that molded to curves he'd held in his hands, to the tips of her high-heeled pumps, she was *his* hot item and he'd be damned if another man or his flowers would get anywhere near her ever again.

CHAPTER TEN

SINCE UNCLE YANK'S television interview three days ago, Sophie had been inundated with phone calls from persistent men asking her on dates. She'd been pointed to on the street and inundated with flowers. All because *Dateline NBC* had picked up on the interview and included it in a special broadcast entitled "Matchmaking Relatives: Are they a meddling nuisance or a prime way to hook up in an uncertain world?" Sophie, herself, had been avoiding calls from the producer to do a follow-up interview. Talk about unwanted publicity. She really couldn't take much more harassment.

Sophie hung up on her most persistent caller of the day, her sister Micki's best friend, John Roper. He was looking for a replacement confidante while her sister was away, and he'd turned to Sophie. If she were to date a ballplayer, she had to admit Roper had potential. He was more refined than most, a metrosexual type who enjoyed the finer things in life. Though trouble followed Roper like a magnet, he was definitely fun to be around.

Fun or not, Roper was still a ballplayer with a thick head and a stubborn personality. Oh wait. That was Riley, she thought, laughing at her own joke.

"Hey, babe."

Speak of the devil. Sophie glanced up, startled at the sound of Riley's voice. It was as if she'd conjured him. Her attention flitted over him and she hated to admit he was still a feast for the senses. His faded jeans molded to his strong thighs and his unshaven face and light tan looked sexy paired with a pale blue collared tee.

"Well, well, well. What brings you to this side of the world?" Forcing herself to remain behind her desk—the only protection she could find at the moment—she aimed for a casual and unaffected air.

He walked inside as if Florida had never happened and settled himself on the corner of her desk. "I wanted to see how you were handling your fifteen minutes of fame."

He treated her to a grin that had once melted her defenses, but now she knew better. She'd let them down once before and lived to regret it.

Riley glanced at the flowers surrounding her, a definite frown marring his handsome face. "Your allergies must be bothering you with these things taking up so much air space," he said, his tone sarcastic.

"Not a bit," she said, and tried not to smile. If she didn't know better she'd think he was jealous of her newfound attention. She checked her watch, eager to have him gone before she did something she'd regret.

Like throw herself into his arms just one more time. "I'm busy so…"

"Want to get a bite to eat?" he blurted out.

She raised her eyes. A nervous muscle actually twitched in his jaw. She immediately rejected the thought. No way was Riley anxious about seeing her again. Nothing about women rattled Riley.

As for his question, she would not go out with him. Been there done that, she thought, quelling temptation. "Thanks anyway but I have plans."

"With one of your suitors?" he asked with definite distaste. "You can't be serious."

She tried not to laugh, but with his use of the antiquated term, now she was certain. Riley was squirming. And she was female enough to enjoy his discomfort.

"I didn't realize our relationship dictated I had to explain or answer to you." She focused on her freshly done nails. "Oh, that's right. We don't have a relationship."

He rose and rounded the desk. Looming over her, he gripped the sides of her chair and leaned close. She inhaled, taking in his fresh scent and trying to ignore the sexual desire galloping through her. Apparently her body didn't understand what her mind and heart already did.

"I thought when two people slept together, they had *something*," he said, his eyes flashing with equal parts desire and determination.

She didn't know where this change of heart had

come from, and emotionally, she couldn't afford to find out. Around Riley, self-protection would be a smart tactic.

"And I thought when the last words exchanged after sex were 'I'm going to pack,' that *something* equaled *nothing.*"

"I don't call what's happening between us right now nothing." His lips hovered over hers, teasing. Tantalizing.

She fisted her hands, digging her nails into her skin to avoid acting on that *something* and kissing him senseless.

"Riley?" she said on a husky purr, one she couldn't control.

"Hmm?"

"We had fun and all, but I am not going there again." She couldn't get a handle on his varying mood swings. She didn't know how to deal with a man like him, nor did she have the inclination to try.

He'd already proved how easily he could turn on her. Since she couldn't control Riley—or her feelings for him—she had to send him away now. Before she let herself care even more. It was the only means of preservation she could think of, because he was a man sure to leave again. At some point, it would be for good.

"Would it help if I said I was wrong?" he asked.

She shut her eyes, steeling herself against his gentle voice and implied apology. "We're different, Riley."

"Opposites attract."

"We're like oil and water. We don't mix."

"I prefer to think of us as a more combustible combination." He turned his head and his lips settled on her cheek in a soft kiss. "Want to see the sparks?"

She lifted her hands to his shoulders and pushed him away. "It was fun but it's over. No more quickies for us." She spun her chair back around and stood, gesturing toward the door. "Now if you'll excuse me, I have business to attend to."

"You must be extra busy. I heard about the computer virus and how the contracts were distributed without permission," he said, understanding and sympathy in his voice.

"You don't have anything to worry about. None of our clients do. Our lawyers are on top of the situation. Everything's fine."

He grinned. "Glad to hear it. Then you can come for dinner. You have to take a break to eat anyway."

"I told you I have plans," she lied.

He shrugged, seemingly undeterred and unfazed. "Break them."

"No."

"You can't possibly want to go out with one of these bozos," he said, waving at the flowers.

"You mean after having experienced the great Riley Nash?" she asked, forcing a laugh. "You know what? It's time for you to leave. You have no right to show up here and make demands. You have even less right to act like a jealous idiot. You made your choice, now I'm making mine." She turned her back and waited for whatever comeback he had.

Seconds that felt like minutes passed in silence. Suddenly she heard footsteps walking away.

She exhaled hard, grateful that she could now deal with the lump in her throat and lead weight in her chest. Slowly she retreated to her desk and lowered herself into her chair, closing her eyes.

When she opened them, Riley still stood in the doorway. "I'm glad to see you're more affected than you wanted me to realize."

"You're a weasel," she muttered.

"No, babe, I just don't do the things you expect, and you know what? You *like* that about me. You don't know how to deal with me, but you do enjoy me."

She lifted the first thing she could find, a block of sticky notes, and leveled it across the room, but the lightweight object dropped uselessly to the floor.

"When you decide to come around, we could work on your throwing arm." He grinned.

She grabbed for another object.

He laughed and ducked out the door before she could hurl the paperweight at him.

Alone, she slammed her hand on the intercom button and told her secretary to hold all her calls and turn away any visitors.

The urge to run after him was strong, but Sophie knew better and she was not going to give herself a chance to second-guess her decision to turn him away. No, she was going to move on. She was going to go out and have fun, to heck with the man who wanted to turn her life upside down.

   She headed to Cindy's office and they agreed to go to Quarters, the new *it* sports bar in town, for drinks after work. Anything to keep her mind off of Riley, she thought. And when Roper called once more, she invited him to join them.

RILEY LEFT Sophie and met up with Mike by the elevators. They headed for Houston's for some decent ribs and a good amount of beer. Riley knew he was feeling sorry for himself for not getting through to Sophie, but he couldn't help it. He was a man who usually got his way with a charming smile or good-old-boy wink. Sophie made him work for what he wanted and he knew damn well that was part of her allure. Not that he desired her only because he couldn't have her, but he did admire her resolve.

   Like a good, solid football game, the one who hung in there the longest was bound to win. If Riley understood nothing else, it was determination.

   He was preoccupied with his thoughts and, thank God, Mike was smart enough to shut up and eat. His friend didn't push for conversation, nor did he give Riley a hard time about obviously striking out with Sophie. For that, Riley paid the dinner bill and when Mike suggested they hit Quarters Sports Bar next, a place co-owned by one of their ex-teammates, Riley agreed. Some more liquor felt like a good idea about now.

   No sooner had he entered the bar than his cell phone rang. He glanced down, saw his mother's Mississippi number and stepped outside to take the call in private.

"Mom?" he asked, as he snapped the phone open.

"No, son, it's your father," Harlan said.

Riley leaned against the glass front beneath a large awning. "How are you?" he asked. He'd been meaning to call home, but dreaded the inevitable conversation with his mother about Spencer.

For a long time, he'd thought he wanted more information, but since actually meeting the man, he'd done everything he could to avoid learning the truth. Had they been in love? Or had Riley been Spencer's misguided way of trying to get over being gay? He wasn't sure he wanted to know, so he'd sidestepped the very people who probably had the answers.

"Life's good. Your mother said you've been impossible to reach lately and I promised her I'd get in touch."

Riley heard the unspoken reproach. "I'm not in a place where I can talk. I should've called but I've been busy. Tell Mother I'll call first thing in the morning."

His stepfather cleared his throat. "What happened in Florida?" the senator asked without warning.

Riley stiffened. "How did you know I was in Florida?" He hadn't told his mother he'd gone to seek out Spencer.

"Knowledge is my business, son."

Riley studied the dirty underside of the awning. He didn't appreciate his stepfather keeping tabs on him. "I like to think my life is my own."

"It is, but you have to realize my right hand and I

need to stay on top of this tawdry gossip story about your…er…about Spencer Atkins," Harlan said, lowering his voice.

Ridiculous, Riley thought. It wasn't as if anybody was listening. "So far nobody's found out about my relationship to the man. I don't see that changing."

"It's in all of our best interests that it doesn't."

"I realize that." And he'd intended to ask Sophie to keep an ear out at the office for any sign of trouble, but he'd never gotten that far.

The fact was, the woman had him so tied up in knots, he couldn't think straight.

"Riley? I asked how your off-season workouts are going."

"Just fine. Listen, I have to run but give Mom my love and don't worry about anything. Things here are under control," he said to reassure the older man.

"I know that they are," Harlan said in his typically self-assured way. "I'm certain Spencer Atkins has his hands full with his own crises, and reporters are too busy digging into his current problems to worry about his past."

Riley nodded. "I take it you also heard that his agency had a major computer meltdown and his form contracts were sent out over the Internet? Hundreds of contacts and business associates who had no business knowing what was in those documents now do."

Harlan actually chuckled. "I did hear something to that effect."

Riley shook his head, as always in awe of the

man and his ability to unearth private information. "You *are* good."

"Yes, well, as a politician, I must keep myself informed of everything and anything that might affect my position or my family."

"I understand." He'd grown up with Harlan's philosophy imprinted on his brain.

Position first, family a close second, both intertwined, Riley thought. Harlan would do almost anything to make sure his senate seat and run for the White House was protected. "I'll talk to you soon," Riley promised.

"You bet."

Riley disconnected and headed back for the bar and a nice strong drink. A hard drink, one a step up from beer. Before he had the chance to order, he heard a familiar laugh and his gut clenched with unmistakable awareness.

Following the tantalizing sound, he turned his head and caught Sophie's startled wide eyes. She lifted her glass to him, in silent acknowledgment, before returning her attention to—another man.

SOPHIE HAD BEEN at the bar for half an hour before Riley suddenly showed up. No big surprise, since this was the newest sports bar in town, but she'd come out for a break from the phone calls and flowers. She'd also wanted time to not think about Riley. Obviously that wasn't going to happen.

She took one look at him and her breath caught

and her throat grew tight, longing filling her. "Why can't I catch a break?"

Cindy shot her a look of silent understanding, one only another woman could achieve, and continued to talk about the fixed computer files in order to distract her.

Nothing could take Sophie's mind off the man at the bar, not even the white-wine spritzer in front of her, but she appreciated her friend's attempt. As for the office computer system, they'd gotten back on track finally. The tech guys insisted it wasn't a real derivative of the Klez virus, but more like someone had tampered with the system. They'd backtracked and tried to figure it out, but the trace led nowhere and they'd chalked it up to a freak occurrence.

"Good evening, ladies." Miguel Cambias approached the table. "I'm so glad you called," he said to Cindy, then leaned down and kissed her on the cheek.

Cindy flushed pink. "And I'm glad you could join us." She patted the empty seat they'd saved for him.

Another chair for Roper remained open next to Sophie and she wished her sister's friend would hurry up and join them.

She looked up and smiled at their new guest. "Hello, Miguel," Sophie said in her most gracious voice.

She still didn't like the man, but she trusted Cindy's instincts. Until she had a reason to think otherwise, Miguel was a presence she'd put up with when she had to. No reason to make her friend uncomfortable.

"We were just talking about the sudden change in

weather," Cindy said to her date. "From warm to roasting hot in mid-March. It's so unusual."

To Cindy's credit, she smoothly changed the subject from the problems at work, keeping Miguel in the dark—where he belonged. Sophie relaxed, her shoulders lowering as her tension eased a notch.

"If you think this is hot for March, you should come to my country. The Dominican Republic is always hot. You would love it there." As he spoke, he slid his arm behind Cindy's chair in a gesture that seemed natural, not forced.

According to Cindy, they'd begun seeing each other exclusively. She was happy for her friend, who deserved someone to treat her well. She rarely spoke about her life in California, but Sophie sensed it hadn't always been an easy one.

"I'm sorry I'm late," John Roper said, joining them.

Miguel signaled for the waitress and ordered a Chivas Regal, while Roper requested a green-apple martini.

Sophie suppressed a grin as she watched Miguel's shocked look at Roper's choice in drinks. Obviously he'd never experienced the man in all his metrosexual glory.

An Enrique Iglesias song replaced the latest pop tune and Miguel gestured to the small dance floor. "Would you like to dance?" he asked Cindy.

She met Sophie's gaze, silently asking if she was comfortable enough for her to walk away.

Sophie glanced over her shoulder only to find

Riley no longer watching Sophie's table. Instead he was engaged in conversation with his friend Mike, whom she recognized as a client of their agency, and two well-endowed, obviously interested women.

She swallowed hard, reminding herself she'd turned him away tonight. "Go. Dance," she said to Cindy. She didn't need her friend for backup when there was little chance Riley would join them. Besides, she was an adult, and she could handle his disinterest as easily as she'd handled the interest he'd shown earlier today.

They left hand in hand, leaving Sophie with Roper, who enjoyed nothing more than good conversation. About himself.

Though distracted by jealousy, Sophie plastered a smile onto her face and tried hard to pay attention to the story of Roper's latest escapade. Her sister, Micki, had her hands full keeping her best friend out of trouble, and with Micki away, John Roper had dug himself a nice-sized hole.

He lifted his glass, took a large sip, swallowed and said, "It would have been nice if the lady I met at the gym had told me she was married before I slept with her."

Sophie blinked but before she could reply, John continued. "Can you believe she lied to me?" he asked, painting himself and not the husband as the wounded party.

She figured John had a point though, since the woman's husband had tracked him down and threatened to smash his face in if he went near his wife again.

"It also would have been nice if she'd mentioned that he was an amateur boxer." Roper downed the rest of his fruity alcoholic drink. "Glad I ordered another," he said.

"It's amazing the media hasn't picked up on this one."

Roper laughed. "It's early in the season. Give them time."

Sophie sipped her drink. "Perhaps you ought to know a little more about a person before jumping into bed with them?" she suggested, trying to think about what her sister would tell her friend. Thank goodness Micki would be back in two days. Then *she* could handle Roper's latest crisis.

"And take the mystery out of it?" Roper asked, laughing. "No, you're right. And contrary to popular belief, I don't pick up strange women often."

"Well, now you've been reminded about the reason why."

The waitress suddenly appeared and placed an unopened bottle of wine on the table.

"There must be some mistake. We didn't order this," Sophie said.

The other woman turned and pointed across the room. "Compliments of the man at the bar."

Both Sophie and Roper glanced over. A blond stranger smiled at her.

Sophie also noted that Riley had disappeared in the few minutes since she'd last seen him. She tried not to care, but her hands sweated and nausea overtook her at the thought of him leaving the bar with another woman.

Roper examined the bottle. "Nice vintage, Soph."

She didn't care about the cost. "I can't go anywhere without being harassed," she said on a frustrated groan.

"I'd hardly call a ninety-dollar bottle of wine harassment," Roper said.

"It is if you aren't interested." She looked up at the waiting cocktail waitress. "Please tell the gentleman that I appreciate the offer, but no thank you."

The other woman inclined her head. "Whatever you say."

"Hey wait!" Roper complained, as she left with the bottle.

Sophie couldn't help but laugh. "Don't you think that instead of wishing you could take the free drink, you ought to be insulted that strange men are sending expensive bottles of wine to me despite the fact that I'm sitting here with you?" she asked.

He leaned back in his seat. "Nah. We're obviously platonic friends. Not like those two." He tipped his head in the direction of the dance floor, where Cindy and Miguel were locked tightly together.

A real pang of envy flooded Sophie, for what she'd had with Riley and what they'd never have again. She turned away from the sight of Cindy and her new love.

The waitress returned, this time with a bottle of Dom Pérignon champagne. "He's stubborn. He said to ask how you liked the flowers."

"I've received so many I lost count," she muttered.

The other woman laughed. "Apparently he knew you'd say that, because he said to tell you that his name is Steve Harris and his were the two dozen red ones along with chocolates from your favorite store."

Sophie shivered, recalling asking Nicki, their temp, how the man knew where to buy her chocolates. Nicki had assumed Sophie wouldn't mind and had questioned Sophie's secretary, then divulged the information to the stranger. Sophie had nearly fired her on the spot. Only her begging and promise not to mess up again had saved her job.

Roper laughed. "Do you like persistent men?" he asked Sophie.

She rubbed her forehead with her hand. "I have a splitting headache and this man's pushiness is border-line scary." She waved away the second bottle. "Please tell him no thank you and I'm not going to change my mind." Sophie had had enough and rose from her seat. "No offense, but I really need to go home."

John immediately stood, too. "Are you taking a cab?"

She nodded.

"I'll walk you out and help you hail one." Reaching into his pocket, he withdrew some bills and left them on the table.

She placed a hand on his forearm. "You stay," she urged. "Why should you lose a perfectly good table just because I'm a spoilsport?"

He raised an eyebrow. "You sure?"

She nodded. "Tell Cindy I'll see her at work in the morning, okay?"

"No problem. You take care." He gave her a friendly hug.

Sophie smiled. "Thanks, John."

A few minutes later, she'd wound her way through the crowded bar and ended up on the street. The sun had set while they were inside and a warm breeze, too warm for the time of year, settled on her shoulders.

She brushed her heavy bangs off her forehead and searched uptown for a taxi with a light indicating it was vacant, but typical of New York City at night, she had a long wait.

Suddenly she felt a tap on her shoulder. She whirled around and found herself face-to-face with Steve Harris, the man who'd sent her the flowers, chocolate and both bottles from the bar. Bottles she'd turned down. And he didn't appear too pleased with her.

CHAPTER ELEVEN

RILEY WAS PISSED OFF. Sophie had deliberately ignored him, and Mike, hoping to work the jealousy angle in Riley's favor, had hooked them up with two gorgeous women at the bar. Mike had taken off with one of them in a cab, assuming Riley would do the same, but Riley's interest wasn't there. Not one iota.

There'd been no point in going home with her when he wouldn't have been able to get it up. He didn't want to be with any woman other than Sophie and to pretend otherwise just to soothe his ego had been a damn stupid move.

They'd had to walk a long way to find an empty taxi, but eventually he'd hailed her a cab and sent her on her way alone. Then he headed back to the sports bar. No sooner had he turned the corner where Quarters was located than he heard the sound of Sophie's voice.

"What part of *no* don't you understand?" she asked, her voice rising.

A guy Riley didn't recognize stood too close,

invading her personal space. Riley hadn't liked it when he'd seen her with Roper, a baseball player he knew by sight not acquaintance, and he liked this even less. He stepped closer so he could hear the conversation.

"Come on. I saw the interview on TV. You're single and available. How many guys bother to find out where you buy your favorite chocolates? Quit playing hard-to-get." The jerk placed a hand on her arm, which Sophie promptly shrugged off.

Riley stiffened.

"Back off," she warned the guy in an angry tone, one tinged with fear.

"Are you trying to tell me you like it rough?" the guy asked.

"She doesn't, but apparently you do." Riley had had enough and he lunged forward, shoving the guy away from Sophie with enough force to make him stumble backward on the sidewalk.

"Hey! Mind your own business," the guy said, pulling himself together.

"She *is* my business."

The other man shot him a disbelieving look. "That's not what her uncle said on television and it's not what it looked like in the bar."

"But it is what I'm telling you and unless you want me to smash your face into that building over there, I suggest you take my word for it." Riley took another menacing step forward, knowing his adrenaline was pumping and his body primed for a fight.

"Riley, no!" Sophie grabbed his arm and held on tight.

Only her panicked voice kept him from taking a swing.

"Okay, okay." Sophie's attacker backed off first. "She's probably not worth much in the sack anyway," he said, stepping away.

Riley waited until the man had disappeared around the corner before facing Sophie. "You okay?"

Her cheeks were flushed pink, her blue eyes flashing with a mixture of emotion. "I am too worth something in bed," she muttered.

Riley burst out laughing, then reached to run his hands up and down her arms. "Are you sure you're okay?"

She nodded. "I'm fine." But she swayed slightly, making her words a lie.

"You're dizzy."

"Light-headed. There's a difference. Dizziness is usually vertiginous. You know, vertigo, the sensation of spinning like a top. I'm just light-headed and unsteady on my feet—" She suddenly paused, her eyes narrowing, focused on his face. "What's with the smile?" she asked.

"You're just so predictable. If a situation makes you uncomfortable, you reach for the safety of an explanation. That's all."

"First I'm not worth much in bed and then I'm predictable?" Her voice rose, trembling with what he guessed was a release of the fear she'd experienced.

He snaked his arm around her waist and pulled her against him. "The first is untrue. I can vouch for how good you are firsthand."

He inhaled and his body hardened at the familiar, intoxicating scent. He reminded himself she needed reassurance, not another come-on, but he almost lost it when a purr of contentment escaped from her throat.

"Let me get you home," he said in a voice rough with desire.

Sophie stepped back. "This is where I should tell you I can get home all by myself." But she was too tired to play games and too scared to actually let him leave. And she wasn't ashamed to admit it.

She ran her hand through her hair. "My uncle means well, but someday he's going to be the death of me. Things were awkward after he did the initial interview, but since *Dateline* picked up on the idea, lunatics have been coming out of the woodwork."

Riley frowned. "You didn't say anything about that today."

She shrugged. "I didn't think it would get so out of hand. Besides you're not responsible for me." Even if she liked it when he took charge.

Sometimes she grew tired of being the one who oversaw everything in order to prevent problems or tragedy. As if she could control such an outcome anyway.

He strode into the street and held his hand in the air, flagging a cab. "Since you're not planning on telling me to take a hike, let's get out of here."

As soon as the cab screeched to a halt, Riley opened the door and waited for her to climb in before sliding in beside her. Sophie gave her address to the driver and settled in for the short ride. Riley didn't crowd her in the back seat and, as much as she appreciated the sentiment, she craved his arms around her and the security he offered more.

Before she could act on her feelings, they pulled up to her building. "We're here." The driver stopped the meter.

Riley pulled cash out of his pocket and slipped it through the Plexiglas divider. "Keep the change."

A few minutes later, she let Riley into her apartment for the first time. He stalked the place, a man unashamed to study the unfamiliar environment and take it all in.

Her cheeks flamed as he studied her wall of photographs. Each had been meticulously chosen and framed by Sophie herself. They were spaced one inch apart on the wall directly across from her bedroom, so she could make out the outline of each picture at night. Even if she couldn't see the individual photos, Sophie knew which picture held which place, and why.

She swallowed hard. "Can I get you something to drink?"

He straightened from where he'd focused on a photograph of Sophie, Annabelle and Micki, taken the day they'd come to live with Uncle Yank. Each sister wore a matching frilly dress in order to make a good impression. What the picture didn't show was the bow on each of their behinds, she remembered, and laughed aloud.

He shot her a curious look at her abrupt outburst. "I'd love a Coke. I'm thirsty."

"Coke it is," she said, grateful for something to keep her busy.

"What was so funny?"

She pulled a can from the cabinet and filled two glasses with ice, dividing the soda between them. "I was just wondering what Uncle Yank must have thought when he saw the three of us for the first time." She handed him his glass.

"He probably calculated the distance to the nearest exit." Riley grinned.

She smiled. "No kidding. I don't know how he did it," she murmured. "I was always so afraid he'd go away and leave us alone the way Mom and Dad had." They walked to the sofa and she settled in, curling her legs beneath her.

Riley sat beside her, his knee touching hers. He remained silent, obviously giving her time to think and relax. She was grateful for the security he brought her and, for now, their earlier disagreements and all they didn't have in common faded away.

"You'd think that after all these years, those issues and insecurities would disappear." She placed her glass on a coaster on her cocktail table.

He shrugged. "I don't know about that. I mean, if childhood crap didn't stay with us, shrinks would be out of business."

She laughed, but knew that deep down he was also referring to his own issues. It helped to know she wasn't alone.

Sophie yawned suddenly, the events of the night taking their toll, especially now with the danger gone and the rush of adrenaline dissipating fast.

"Come on. Off to bed." He held out his hand.

In his eyes, she saw warmth and caring. She'd be lying if she said she didn't view the flicker of desire in their brown depths, a desire that had stirred to life inside her, too.

He must have sensed her hesitation, because he lowered his hand to his lap and curled it into a fist. "I'm not going to attack you in your bedroom, Soph. I just want to make sure you're okay."

A huge lump formed in her throat. Not because she'd insulted him, but because she couldn't remember the last time anyone had taken care of her, without her pulling the strings behind the scenes. Before she knew it, an actual tear fell down her cheek. She wiped the moisture away with the back of her hand.

"I didn't think for one second that you'd take advantage of me," she whispered.

"Then why the hesitation? And why the tears now?"

She smiled. "I was just surprised, that's all. I'm usually the one in charge of taking care of everyone else."

He extended his hand again, this time grasping her hand in his. "Well, it's time you let yourself go. If you're exhausted, feel it. If you're going through a release of tension, then collapse. I'm here to catch you," he said in a gruff voice and pulled her to her feet.

She stood, but to her surprise, her knees buckled, another rush of light-headedness assaulting her.

He was there in an instant, wrapping his arm around her waist and leading her to the bedroom. "When was the last time you ate?"

"Um…lunch, I think?"

"And you drank on an empty stomach? For a smart woman, that was pretty stupid." He flicked the light switch and her night-table lamp flickered to life.

"I had some peanuts," she said, her words not much of a defense.

"If you think you'll be all right alone in here, why don't you change into something comfortable and I'll see what I can scrounge up in your kitchen?"

"I'll be fine." But she chuckled at his other comment. "I take it your own kitchen is pretty bare?"

He cocked his head to one side. "I'm a bachelor. What do you think?"

She opened her dresser drawers, pulling out a change of clothes. "I think you'll be pleasantly surprised by what you find in mine. The question is what you're able to do with it."

He shook his head and laughed. "Oh ye of little faith. My mother loves to cook as a way to release the stresses of living with a man constantly on the run and scheduling events. If I was home, I'd sit and watch her. Sometimes I even helped. I can get by." He winked at her and headed for the kitchen.

Her knees turned weak, but this time not because she was hungry. At least not for anything except this sexy man who seemed to want nothing more than to tend to her every need.

At least for now. A little voice in her head warned her to tread lightly and carefully, to accept what he offered now but not to read anything into it for the future. Which was fine with her. She knew herself. Knew what would happen if she and Riley even attempted to make this…this…*thing* between them work long term.

She already knew what would happen. To keep the fear of losing him at bay, she'd compensate with her need to control and end up trying to control him. Like she had with Uncle Yank's vision problems and then with his broken hip. Like she had with her sisters until they'd argued back. Like she had with prior men in her life who hadn't meant nearly as much to her as Riley already did.

She'd already stepped into his hang-ups in Florida. Without a doubt, she'd blow it with him again. It was only a matter of time before an independent, free-spirited man like Riley would run again, this time for good.

Better to remember to protect herself first. That settled, she quickly changed into silky drawstring pants and a matching T-shirt, then washed up for the night.

She devoured Riley's delicious and impressive fluffy omelet loaded with freshly chopped vegetables and cheese, along with toast and a large glass of orange juice before heading off to bed. With Riley by her side.

RILEY WATCHED Sophie sleep. No sooner had she crawled beneath the covers than she passed out cold. Of course there had been the few seconds when she'd moved and wrangled beneath the light yellow bedding. While his imagination had been running wild with thoughts of what she could be doing under there, suddenly her pajama bottoms had come flying out from beneath the covers.

"I can't sleep with pants on," she'd explained through a yawn, oblivious to how those words had turned him on.

Then she'd fluffed her pillow, laid her head down and promptly fallen asleep, leaving him worked up on top of the comforter—where he planned to stay, for her sake as well as his own.

She needed her sleep. He needed her. There was no point in denying the obvious. It was a fight within himself that he was destined to lose. He had no choice but to go with the flow. See where this thing took him. That she'd let him bring her home was a sign she was softening toward him.

With his ex-wife, everything had been a rush. He blamed it on the foolishness of youth. They had to have each other, had to get married right away, had to have unprotected sex and of course Lisa had ended up pregnant—even though three or four nights a week, Riley would come home later and later to avoid the inevitable argument. Why couldn't he work out at home? Why did he have to hang out with the guys after a game? They were all wrong for each other, he and Lisa. But they had done one thing right and that was his daughter.

He needed to make peace with Lizzie. She needed to accept that he was her parent as well as her friend. And he knew just how to make it happen and who could help him accomplish his goal. He rolled over and propped his head on his hand and continued to watch Sophie sleep.

Her hands were beneath her cheek as she breathed in and out evenly. Without makeup and with her hair tousled around her face, she looked softer and more vulnerable. The kind of woman who was capable of reaching out to Lizzie without earning her disdain and snotty attitude. Oh, she'd start off trying to control the situation but his badass daughter would quickly learn that Sophie Jordan couldn't be manipulated.

He grinned, satisfied with his decision and looking forward to the fireworks. He'd never let Lizzie meet any woman he'd been involved with before. Never even considered it. But as he'd thought many times before, Sophie wasn't just any woman.

Unable to fight the urge, he reached out and stroked her hair near her temple. She shifted slightly, sighed and settled back into deep slumber. Meanwhile he had a hard-on to match the Empire State Building, he thought, resigning himself to a long, sleepless night.

SOPHIE AWOKE at seven o'clock as always without the help of an alarm clock. She'd never had to use one, because she was always prompt—anal, as Uncle Yank liked to tease her. She immediately remembered that Riley hadn't left her alone last night and she rolled over, already sensing he'd gone.

On the pillow where he'd slept was a handwritten note. "Went home to shower for an early-morning meeting. Car service will be downstairs at eight-thirty. Don't make plans this weekend. You're mine. R."

Last night, she'd been so shaken up by the guy who'd harassed her, she hadn't thought about anything beyond Riley and the security he represented. Now she realized she just might have given him the wrong message. Apparently he was back in her life.

How long would he stay this time? she wondered, and shivered.

She rose, showered and had a quick cup of coffee. She was grateful for the car waiting downstairs, which meant she didn't have to stand in the street alone and hail a cab. She owed Riley a huge thanks for that and, she realized, so much more. He'd remained by her side all night, a complete gentleman in every way. She realized now what a great father he probably was. What a lucky girl Lizzie was to have him as her dad.

She was so preoccupied with her thoughts, she

barely registered arriving at the office and stepping off the elevator. But as she did so, she stopped short. Uniformed police officers were swarming the hallway.

Her stomach clenched with fear. "What's going on?" she asked.

"Are you Annabelle Jordan?" one of the men asked.

She shook her head. "I'm Sophie Jordan."

He tipped his head. "Nice to meet you, ma'am. The alarm company already called Annabelle seeing as how she was first on their list. And of course they called us."

In the back of her mind, Sophie noted that they'd never taken Annie off the top of the alarm company's emergency list after she'd moved out of Manhattan. It would take her sister a while to drive into the city in an emergency.

"What happened?" she asked, barely able to take in the men measuring the break in the untempered glass.

One of the officers rose from a kneeling position and walked over. "We're not one-hundred-percent certain, but it looks like someone broke in." He gestured to what she hadn't seen before. The hole in the glass was bigger than she'd realized.

"Could someone fit inside?" Sophie asked.

"Someone could, but not without great care and expertise or else they'd probably cut themselves. We're dusting for prints and checking for bloodstains."

Sophie gagged, a reflex she'd had since childhood. One that only showed up in situations that included bloodshed.

"Why don't you have a seat?" The officer gestured to the window ledge. "We'll let you know once you can go—"

"What in the dang hell is going on here?" Uncle Yank walked off the elevator, Spencer and Lola by his side, and Noodle in his arms. Not in front of him on a leash, the way a normal guide dog ought to be.

"We've had a break-in," Sophie said, repeating the obvious.

Uncle Yank frowned. "I can see that." He paused. "Well, I can't exactly *see* everything but I can make out enough to know we got ourselves a problem."

Noodle barked and wiggled to go free, probably sensing her owner's distress.

Lola patted Noodle's head in an effort to calm the pooch. Sophie thought she ought to be patting Uncle Yank's head instead.

"Officer, what happened, exactly?" Spencer asked, stepping up to take charge. "I'm Spencer Atkins."

The officer with the notepad nodded. "Your reputation in the sports world precedes you, Mr. Atkins. My nephew's a fine baseball player. He's hoping you'll get him a contract like A-Rod or Jeter one day. He'd take you, too, Mr. Morgan."

Sophie swallowed a laugh, relieved her uncle merely muttered beneath his breath instead of giving the man a hard time about how much better an agent he was than his partner.

Spencer grinned, his mind off the robbery at least for the moment. "How old is the boy?"

"Ten," the cop said, laughing.

"You tell him if he practices, anything is possible." Spencer turned, taking in the mess once more. "I can't believe this happened. And it's all my fault."

The police officer tapped his pen against his pad. "Why do you say that?"

"Because he's one of those guilty types, that's why." Uncle Yank patted his friend on the shoulder. "He's got no good reason to say a thing like that."

Spencer cleared his throat, his eyes steady on the officer's. "If you already know who I am, then you must know about the recent scandal."

The other man nodded.

"I don't see what that has to do with anything," Sophie said, jumping in before the cop could answer.

There was no reason for Spencer to discuss his private life with a stranger, even if that stranger was a law-enforcement officer. Spencer's homosexuality was irrelevant and would only embarrass him here and now.

"They're just trying to protect me," Spencer insisted.

The young cop scratched his head. "From what? You folks are confusing me."

Spencer groaned. "I think it's possible that someone targeted our offices because it was recently revealed that I'm gay. Maybe one of our clients is angry or feels betrayed. I'm fully aware there are homophobic people out there, especially in the sports world. Nobody wants their own masculinity questioned because they're associated with someone whose sexual preferences don't match their own."

Sophie ran a hand over her burning eyes. She hated that he'd take something as random as a robbery and place the blame on himself. He had enough problems right now. She stood and placed her hand on his arm. "Spencer, we haven't lost any clients. No matter how you're feeling, this idea of yours doesn't make any sense."

In her heart, she believed her own words. She wasn't a Pollyanna but she refused to think anyone she or Athletes Only associated with would do something like this.

"I agree with Sophie," Lola said. "The motive could be something as simple as robbery. Was anything taken?"

"We'll know more once the guys tell me what they've found inside," the first cop who'd spoken with Sophie said. "While they're doing their job, I need to ask you folks a couple of questions."

Her uncle narrowed his gaze. "Oh, here we go. Focus on the good guys while the bad guys go free." He raised his hand to poke the officer in the chest.

Good old Uncle Yank, doing his bit to divert attention from his best friend's problems and creating more in the process, Sophie thought. Before she could dive between the older man and the cop, Lola stepped in.

She grabbed Yank's offending finger. "Keep it up and I'll break the other hip," she said. Then she turned to the officers and offered them her most sincere smile. "You'll have to excuse Yank. Between the break-in and the recent stress, he's a little cranky."

The younger man eased back, away from Yank and harm's way. "I understand, ma'am. Nobody ever knows how to react to a violation like this one."

"What do you need to know?" Sophie asked.

"Who would do something like this, for starters?" This question came from another man she hadn't seen before. He had stepped over to join them. "I just came from inside. Nothing obvious looks taken. No major equipment is gone. Nothing ransacked. Well, except for the flowers in the office around the corner. Those were all trashed."

Sophie stiffened. "*My* flowers were trashed? The ones in *my* office?"

The man scratched his head. "Is there another office loaded with more flowers than a cemetery?"

She merely shook her head.

"Then I guess that makes it your office. And it certainly rules out the gay-bashing theory. So any other ideas?" he asked, his focus directly on Sophie.

"I don't know." All she did know was that her life was completely out of control. First she'd been harassed last night and now this. She began to shake, trembling, unable to stop.

Her uncle wrapped his strong arm around her shoulders. "It'll be okay. We can talk about everything once you've calmed down."

"Well, actually, it would help if we discussed possibilities now," the cop said, "while everything's still fresh. Has anything like this happened before?" He addressed Sophie.

"Hell, no!" Uncle Yank shouted. "If it had, I'd be the first to know."

"Well actually, yes. Something unnerving happened last night," Sophie said.

"What?" Uncle Yank asked.

"Where?" Lola demanded, her fear and concern etched in that one word.

"Why didn't you call one of us?" Spencer asked.

Sophie ran a hand through her hair, pulling it out of its binding and not caring a bit. She turned to her well-meaning uncle, knowing how hard he'd take what she was about to say next.

"I don't know where to begin. But even before last night, everything's been wrong. All the flowers," she said, her voice rising and the tension mounting as she thought of all she'd been through over the past few days. "That's not normal. I mean, I don't even know who sent over ninety-five percent of them. And the phone calls, the visits from total strangers. Men accosting me in the street. Does that sound okay?"

"Hell no, it isn't okay. Nobody bothers my niece." Uncle Yank straightened his shoulders, but he must have stiffened and squeezed the dog too tight, because she barked and Lola grabbed her out of his arms.

"Well, it's your fault!" Sophie shouted, unable to control her frustration. "You did that damn interview. You plastered my picture on the news, advertising me as single and desperate."

"Now, Sophie, Yank never said you were desperate." Lola's voice trailed off. "Never mind." She waved her hand, dismissing her words. She obviously realized the futility in defending her incorrigible husband.

"Your uncle only wants what's best for you, even if he does have a unique way of expressing himself," Spencer said.

Uncle Yank bowed his head. "I'm sorry, Sophie. I love you. Spencer's right. I only wanted what was best for you."

"That's why you look familiar," the first officer said to Sophie, snapping his fingers as things became clear. "I saw you on *Dateline*."

"Lucky me. One of the major networks picked up on the story and all the desperate men of the world decided I was their patsy." She pinched the bridge of her nose.

She already had a headache and now she added fear to her problems. She was truly afraid of what this nutcase would do next, not that she'd tell her uncle as much and worry him more.

She reached out a hand and grabbed his forearm. "Look, I love you. I just want you to let me live my life in peace, the way I prefer it."

He nodded. Sophie knew he understood and agreed—until this crisis passed and he picked up on his next bright idea.

"We're going to need a list of everyone who sent you flowers. If you have the cards, we'll take those.

If not, just what you remember, including names and florists. We can run leads from there."

"Okay. I can give you the cards as soon as you let me inside." She'd make sure she handed over one man's in particular, Sophie thought, recalling Steve Harris's behavior last night. But she didn't want to discuss that in front of her uncle. "The cards are in my desk," she explained to the officer.

"She's anal," her uncle said proudly.

Sophie sighed.

"When you're ready you can come down to the precinct and give a full statement. For now is there anything else you can think of? Anyone in the office you fired, anyone who might be suspect?"

Suspect? "None of our employees would do something like this."

"She's right," her uncle said.

Nobody mentioned their competition in the industry, but Sophie couldn't help wondering if Cambias had anything to do with the break-in. She still questioned his motives for dating Cindy, and immediately felt guilty for her thoughts.

Sophie couldn't bring herself to mention her friend's boyfriend to the police without talking to Cindy first. After all, what did she have to go on other than instinct and dislike?

"We did have that computer glitch," Lola said. "And we never did track down the source of the so-called virus. Our tech guys are suspicious, but whoever hacked in was so good, they can't prove a thing."

The cop continued to take notes.

Lola's words took Sophie by surprise. She hadn't even considered that the computer issue could be related to this break-in.

"Miss Jordan, you never did tell me what happened last night," the policeman said, reminding her.

Needing a minute to compose herself, she shut her eyes. Riley's face appeared in front of her, full-blown, providing comfort, reminding her he'd cared for her after she'd been accosted outside the bar.

Envisioning Riley gave her the strength to tell her story. "I went to Quarters with some friends last night," she began.

"You went where?" Uncle Yank yelled. "What was my niece doing in that pickup joint?"

Lola groaned. "He's leaving," she promised Sophie and the police. "We'll wait over here." She prodded him over to the window ledge where Sophie had sat earlier.

Sophie just wanted the inquisition over. She folded her arms over her chest. "A guy sent over a bottle of wine. I turned him down and then he sent a bottle of champagne. I realized then that he'd also sent flowers and chocolates from my favorite store." She drew a deep breath before continuing. "I sent the champagne back, too. But when I left to hail a cab, he was waiting for me outside." She shivered at the memory.

What would have happened if Riley hadn't shown up to scare him away? Sophie had no doubt she could handle herself, but whether or not she could best a determined man much taller and heavier than her, well…

"I asked if you caught his name," the officer said.

She nodded. "Steve Harris."

"Good." He nodded approvingly. "We'll check into him. Maybe he's a regular. If we're lucky, a bartender or waitress knows him."

He jotted down the information and shoved his pad into his shirt pocket. "I'll follow it up and get back to you. In the meantime, the forensics guys will run the information they collected. I'd appreciate it if you came by at your earliest convenience, okay?"

"She'll be there," Uncle Yank called from down the hall.

The cop shot her a sympathetic look.

"I'll come by," she promised.

"Thank you." The officer gestured to the rest of his team, who'd almost finished packing up. "We'll be in touch, folks. And Ms. Jordan?"

She inclined her head. "Yes?"

"Try not to go out alone."

CHAPTER TWELVE

SOPHIE COULDN'T BEAR to remain in her office. The crews worked on fixing her door, which had also been broken, and cleaning up the broken glass. She headed for the small kitchenette, poured herself a cup of coffee and sat down at the little table and chairs in the room.

"May an old man join you?" Spencer stepped inside and pulled out a chair.

She gestured for him to sit. "Since when do you go around calling yourself old?" she asked the handsome man.

"Since I started feeling that way."

She wrapped her hands around the hot mug. "And would that have anything to do with the news hitting the papers?"

"Actually, it started when my son told me he wanted nothing to do with me." He bowed his head in dismay.

Sophie sighed. "Are you upset because he wants you to keep your distance or because you finally realize what you put him through all those years?" she asked softly.

A smile lifted his lips. "You're too smart for my own good," he said, laughing.

"What can I say? It's easier to figure out other people's problems than my own." She stared into the muddy coffee. Somebody had to teach Nicki how to measure coffee grounds before they overdosed on caffeine. "Spencer?"

"What's on your mind?" His hazel eyes, so much like Riley's, stared into hers.

"I owe you an apology." She said what had been on her mind since she'd seen him at the police station in Florida. "I had no right to judge you or the decisions you made. I couldn't begin to guess what you were feeling back then."

He reached out and squeezed her hand. "No need to apologize. I was an ass then and now, to quote one of your uncle's favorite phrases."

"Still, I am sorry." When Spencer had stepped up and taken responsibility with the police, assuming the break-in had been related to him and his issues, Sophie had seen how seriously he took his role as a protector of the people he cared about.

She'd seen him make decisions for his clients that were in their best interests, not his own. She should have trusted in Spencer and his motives regarding his son. It wasn't for her to criticize him. She wondered if it was too much to hope that one day Riley would come to feel the same way.

"So this is where you two are hiding." Yank stood

in the doorway. "Sophie, they want you in your office."

She stood and paused to hug Spencer before heading to deal with the mayhem once more.

SPENCER WATCHED Sophie leave the room and his best friend take her seat. He was grateful to these people who'd given him unconditional love and acceptance, even after he'd kept a huge secret from them—a secret that could destroy their business, their livelihood, their worlds.

Okay, so that was an exaggeration, but lately everything that had happened felt huge. Larger than life, almost. Devastatingly awful in some ways, and in others, too good to be true. Like his best friend and partner not holding his omission against him. In fact, Yank hadn't once demanded to know why Spencer hadn't shared the truth. Instead Yank had given Spencer a pat on the back along with his unwavering support. Humbling, for certain, Spencer thought.

Yank settled himself into the chair. He seemed more agile now than immediately after he'd broken his hip, but he was still more fragile than he had been before. Not that he'd admit it and not that Spencer would mention the fact. Yank was too damn proud for his own good.

"Are you feeling okay?" Spencer asked.

Yank slowly straightened in his seat. "I'm just fine."

"Good. So we're still on schedule for this weekend?" Spencer and Yank had planned on keeping

John Cashman too busy to think about Miguel Cambias on this weekend before the draft. They'd wine him, dine him, arrange interviews for him and they'd be by his side all the way, giving him no time to fall under their opponent's spell.

"We're on, all right, but with everything that's happened around here, I'm worried 'bout leaving Sophie alone."

Spencer nodded in understanding. He'd thought about the same thing. "Send her to Annabelle's for the weekend."

"Annie's going with Vaughn to speak at a college in Massachusetts."

"Can Lola watch over her?"

Yank snickered. "Like Sophie would accept a baby-sitter? Besides I already suggested it, and Lola wants to do it, but her aunt's in the hospital and she's going to oversee her care until she moves to a rehab center."

Spencer rubbed his palms against his eyes. "When did getting one damn guy through the draft become so difficult?"

"Since dirtbags like Cambias began sneaking around."

"Well, we'll show Cashman our proposal this weekend. I've got a draft of a five-year plan that includes salary and savings. He also needs to hire a financial advisor, because if he lets his father run his income the way he's been running his life, chances are it'll all go on moonshine before his first season's out," Spencer said, reciting what he'd been thinking since his last meeting with Cashman.

"That's what happens when a kid's mama dies too young. He ends up relying on the adult influence in his life and copying their habits, for better or for worse." Yank's eyes glazed over as he obviously withdrew into himself.

"You're talking about you and the girls, aren't you?" Spencer had been Yank's closest friend since before he'd become their guardian. He'd seen what a solid job Yank had done with the "little women" as he'd called them. Spencer had also seen his friend struggle within himself to come to terms with the commitment. Yank couldn't turn the girls out, but being responsible for them had scared him to death. So he'd pushed Lola away instead.

Heaven only knows why Lola had remained by his side all these years, but she had. Until she'd finally given him an ultimatum and even then Yank Morgan hadn't come around and admitted he both needed and loved her. At least not right away. Yank wasn't known as a stubborn bastard for no good reason, Spencer thought.

He met his friend's gaze.

Yank scrubbed his hand over his unshaven face. "You're lookin' at me like you have me all figured out."

Spencer grinned. "You think I don't?"

"That still don't change the fact that I'm worried about Sophie and not just because she needs someone to watch out for her."

"Yank," Spencer said, a clear warning in his tone. The other man had already caused Sophie enough trouble.

"I owe it to her to see she finds the right match."

His tone was insistent and Spencer knew better than to think he'd talk him out of it. Still, he gave it one last shot. "I suppose it would be too much to hope that you've learned your lesson after your last attempt at matchmaking?"

"I haven't decided yet," Yank muttered.

Spencer figured it was only a matter of time before Yank came up with another crazy plan and he steeled himself for what lay ahead. He silently promised he'd guide Yank so he caused the least amount of damage to the niece he loved. Well, Spencer thought, at least he now had a focus beyond self-pity.

Yank frowned. "Don't tell me you didn't do the same thing when you hooked me up with Riley all those years ago. You looked out for your kid same as I want to look out for mine."

Well, there he had it. The means to guide Yank and help Sophie. He'd be no better than Yank if he acted on the idea spinning around in his mind, but he couldn't stop the words from flowing. Even if he knew he'd regret the admission to Yank.

"Riley's a good match for Sophie," Spencer said. "I saw them together in Florida and they definitely clicked." And Spencer would love to see Riley with a woman as loving as Sophie.

Yank bolted upright from his chair, faster than he'd

moved in ages. He pulled Spencer's head against his chest and kissed him square on the crown. "You are the best friend a guy could have. Lola!" he bellowed.

Spencer rolled his eyes toward the ceiling, then smoothed his hair with his hand.

"What's wrong? Who's sick? Do you need an ambulance?" Lola practically skidded to a halt as she ran into the room.

"Spencer said Riley's a perfect match for Sophie. How do you like that?" Yank asked proudly.

Lola reached for a newspaper left lying on the table, rolled it and smacked Yank on the top of his head. "You screamed so loud I thought someone had a heart attack!"

"Someone nearly did. When I heard the news, I knew we had the answer to all of our problems."

"Oh good Lord. Remind me why I married you again?"

Spencer snickered.

Yank ignored him. "Lola, baby, you eloped with me and when you did, I promised you a big old party when we returned, remember?"

She visibly inhaled, searching for a way to calm down. "And what does that have to do with Sophie and Riley? Because I know you, Yank Morgan, and you have an agenda. You always do," she said, calmer and obviously resigned.

After years with Yank, she'd perfected dealing with him, Spencer thought. He envied them the easy give and take of their relationship. Sometimes he even wondered now that he wasn't hiding anything, if he'd find a companion of his own.

"Once your aunt's settled, I want you to plan our party. We can even renew our vows in front of friends and family like we talked about on the ship. Spare no expense and throw a huge bash," he said, waving his arms in enthusiasm.

"And?" Lola prodded. "Get to the real point."

"It's obvious. Get Sophie involved in the planning. Give her a wedding and some romance to focus on instead of all the bad stuff happening around here. Just make Sophie itch for happily ever after. That's not so hard, is it?"

"No, Yank. It's not hard at all. But I don't think Sophie's going to appreciate being manipulated." Lola propped her hands on her hips.

Spencer had watched the byplay without saying a word. Until now. "She's got a point. And the girl's smart, Yank. She's going to know something's up."

"Only if Lola let's on. Which she won't because she doesn't want Sophie upset. So, Lola, you have your instructions. Spencer and I will handle the rest."

"Oh, swell. The two great minds of the Western World teaming up to matchmake. We already had a floral shop in this office and a break-in. I wonder what can happen next?"

Spencer narrowed his eyes. "Oh please don't group me in with his shenanigans."

Yank waved them away with a dismissive hand. "I meant *I'll* handle the rest." He reached for the phone and dialed. "Riley? It's your agent. I need to talk to you so get your ass down to my office immediately." He hung up before Riley could reply.

Spencer rose, his muscles suddenly stiff, his heart suddenly hurting. "I think this is where I make my exit," he said, trying to sound light when he felt weighted down.

"Spencer, wait," Lola said, her hand on his shoulder, stopping him from walking out. "Why can't you make peace with Riley? Start over?"

He inhaled deeply. "Because he asked me to stay the hell away. And since I've never done anything he wanted during his childhood, it's the least I can do for him now."

Staying away from Riley had never been as easy or as simple as his son obviously believed. But doing so now that they'd had their first face-to-face confrontation, now that Spencer had seen the man Riley had become, was damn near impossible.

And he lived with regret every single day of his life.

SOPHIE CANCELED a photo shoot for a sick client. She returned some phone calls and in between she arranged a *Sports Illustrated* interview for Roper, who was looking for some positive publicity to counteract the negative and the magazine was doing a piece on athletes in touch with their feminine side—though they promised a masculine title and approach. She did everything and anything to avoid thinking about the fact that the office had been broken into and she might be the target.

But she couldn't ignore the truth. And it only reminded her that she had no control over anything in her life. She headed to her private bathroom, hoping if she splashed cold water on her face she'd feel better.

After running the water for a while, she let the icy stream hit her wrists. Her body temperature cooled and she immediately felt better. She patted her face with a water-dampened towel, then rolled her neck from side to side, stretching her stiff muscles.

She wished she could visit with Annabelle to escape this nightmare, but her sister was going away for the weekend. Though she could stay at Annabelle's house upstate anyway, she hated to run away.

Besides, Riley's note had asked her not to make plans and she wanted to see what he had in mind for them. She still promised herself she'd keep her walls high, but she knew better than to think he'd leave her alone while she was being targeted. And, she admitted, she didn't have the strength to turn him away just now.

She reached her arms above her head, laced her fingers together and stretched the way she'd learned in yoga class. Come to think of it, maybe going to another yoga class would calm her nerves.

She tipped her head upward and opened her eyes. What looked like the lens of a video camera stared back at her from the lighting in the ceiling.

She screamed.

RILEY HAD BEEN at the gym near Athletes Only when Yank called and left a message on his voice mail demanding Riley meet him at the office ASAP. Riley had been in Yank Morgan's office long before he heard Sophie's shriek. He turned and ran, reaching her office half a step before everyone else at A.O. He didn't see her immediately and spun to find her standing inside the small bathroom.

"Who died?" Yank came to a halt behind Riley, stopping himself by grabbing onto the younger man's shoulders.

Sophie blushed, her soft skin turning a flattering shade of pink. "Everything's okay. I'm okay. I'm sorry I scared everyone."

"You heard her. She's fine. Everyone get back to work." Yank waved his hands, shooing everyone away.

Riley waited until everyone except Yank had taken off. "What's wrong?" he asked Sophie.

"That is wrong." She pointed to the ceiling.

He looked up. A camera lens had been not so subtly hidden in between the overhead lighting.

"What is it? What's up there?" Yank squinted at the ceiling.

"It looks like a camera lens. Like the ones they put in department stores," Riley explained. "Get me a chair, will you, Sophie?"

She nodded and walked out, then returned from the other room, rolling her desk chair in front of her. "Here you go."

She held the wheeled chair steady while he climbed up on it.

"You know that's how I broke my hip," Yank said.

"Leave him alone," Sophie chided.

Riley tried not to laugh.

"All I meant was that he should be careful or else he'll end up ass down like I did."

Riley grinned. "Thanks for the warning." He carefully pulled the tiny round lens, which protruded from between the light grating, expecting it to be connected by wiring. Instead the lens pulled right out in his hand.

"It's not connected to anything." He jumped down to the floor.

Sophie stepped closer.

Her luscious scent assaulted his senses immediately. It had been just one day since he'd seen her last, but he'd gone to sleep imagining he smelled her fragrance beside him and he'd woken up reaching for her. Now she was here, inches away.

"I don't understand," she murmured.

He held the tiny piece up to the light. "It's a dud."

"As in a practical joke?" Yank asked. "I'm going to kill the bastard who tried to scare my niece that way."

Sophie exhaled hard.

Beside him, Riley felt her tremble.

"It's no joke, Uncle Yank," she said. "It must have been part of the break-in. Someone probably planted this here when they broke all the flower vases."

Riley didn't know what was going on. He'd rushed in here so fast he hadn't noticed the flower shop was no longer in her office. And as for a break-in, he'd seen men fixing the broken glass outside but he'd never considered that it'd been more than an accident. He was unprepared for the feeling of protectiveness that swept over him at the thought of anyone wanting to scare, let alone hurt, this woman.

"I'm going to let the police know 'bout this." Yank started for the door.

"That's a good idea," Sophie said softly. "Uncle Yank? Can you also call your friend Curly who does security? Ask him to come down and see what he thinks of this thing before the police take it away."

"That's my girl. Always thinkin'," Yank said, and left.

She lowered herself to the closed toilet seat. "I just don't understand who'd want to do this to me."

Riley placed his hand on her shoulder. He noticed the damp towel in the sink and shut off the still-running water. "How about we talk it through. Sometimes that helps to figure things out."

She nodded. "Okay."

"If it wasn't the break-in, if someone else did this, who could it be? Who has access?"

"But…"

"Humor me. Just to cover all bases."

She glanced down at her hands. "There's the cleaning crew that comes in at night, the security people who patrol in the evening, and everyone in the office who passes by when I'm not here."

"Have you fired anyone recently?" he asked.

She shook her head. "We're a small office and all get along."

"Okay then, let's talk about the times you aren't here. You and I were just in Florida. Could anyone have let themselves in here then?"

"No!" Sophie jumped up from her seat. "No way is it anyone who works for us. We're like a family here. I'm not stupid or naive, but I refuse to believe someone within this office would do this to me."

He followed her out of the bathroom back into her office, watching as she paced the room, silently mouthing the expected number of steps across the carpet. He couldn't control his grin as she reverted to the comfort of counting, the same thing she'd been doing the day he'd come looking for his old man.

At the thought of Spencer, Riley realized that not once since he'd been here had he worried about running into him. Instead his thoughts had been occupied by Sophie.

"There is one person who might be behind all this," she said, stopping in her tracks.

Her words caught him off guard. "Who?"

"I don't like suggesting this. It hurts me because he's dating one of my closest friends, but…"

Riley tipped his head to one side and studied her. "Nobody's going to do anything without proof, but if your gut's telling you something, I suggest you listen. At this point we can't afford to overlook anything, no matter how remote it seems."

Sophie swallowed hard. "Miguel Cambias."

"No!" Cindy had entered without Sophie realizing it and stood with her mouth opened in horror.

"How could you say such a thing? How could you even think it?"

Sophie's heart skipped a beat, then began pounding harder. "I'm sorry, it's just that—"

"What? You think he'd use me to get to you? That he doesn't care about me? He just wants to sign your uncle's draft pick? You're wrong. I know him." She pointed to her heart. "I know him in here."

Sophie closed her eyes for a brief second. This was exactly what she'd wanted to avoid. "I'm not saying it is Miguel. I'm just saying it's possible."

"And how do you think breaking in here and planting a camera would get him any closer to John Cashman?" Cindy folded her arms across her chest.

"I don't know." Sophie looked out the window over Manhattan. "It's a stretch," she admitted.

"What about the idea of deflecting Yank's and Spencer's focus? If they're busy worrying about you, looking out for you, then that would leave Cashman open and vulnerable to another agent." Riley stepped between the two women. "To *any* agent. Not necessarily Cambias."

"That's what I thought." She shot Riley a look filled with gratitude for attempting to salvage her friendship with Cindy.

"Everyone's shaken up from the break-in. Sophie's rattled about finding the camera. I suggest nobody holds anything said in the heat of the moment against the other."

Cindy, with her pale face and defensive posture,

appeared unsure, shaken and still very upset. "I have to go."

"Don't say anything to him," Sophie called out to her friend.

Cindy turned back. "Why not? So the police can handle it instead? I don't think so." With that, she was gone.

Sophie stepped forward to stop her.

"Let her go," Riley said.

"But…"

He grabbed her by the shoulders. "Wouldn't you warn the person you cared about if you thought someone was out to get them?" The intensity in his eyes was enough to make his question seem infinitely more personal.

Wouldn't you warn me? he seemed to ask.

Don't you care that much about me?

She shivered, unable to process the implications and feelings when everything around her was falling apart.

"Listen, I know you need to go down to the police station this afternoon. But once that is done, I think you could use a break from all this." He swept his hand around the office. "I want to bring Lizzie home to see her grandparents and I'd like you to come with us."

She knew he'd had something in mind for them this weekend but traveling with his daughter to meet his parents? It was too much for her to take in right now.

"I don't think it's such a good idea."

"You'd rather stick around the city this weekend

alone? Worry about stalkers, nut jobs, admirers, cameras in your bathroom and break-ins at your office."

"I'm not alone," she said, shivering.

"I overheard your uncle's secretary making plans this weekend for him to keep Cashman busy. Do you really want to divert his focus the weekend before the draft by having him worry about you?"

"You're not playing fair."

"Neither are you, pushing me away. What happened to the brave Sophie who went parasailing with me? Who planned to go to Florida alone to find Spencer without a clue where to start?" He propped one hip against the desk and crossed his arms over his chest, pinning her with a knowing stare.

He was taunting her. Calling her on her fears. Daring her to say yes. She'd grown up with siblings and a dare was something she couldn't possibly refuse. Apparently, she couldn't refuse him, either.

Sophie never considered whether she was a brave person or not, but she certainly didn't want to be known as a coward. "Mississippi?" she asked.

"Brandon, Mississippi."

She swallowed hard. "I hear it's nice there this time of year."

A slow, sexy smile spread over his face. "It sure is."

"And how's the mood this time of year with thirteen-year-old girls?"

"Unstable," he said, laughing.

He was taking her home with him. And *that* had her more frightened than when she'd found the camera in her ceiling.

YANK WOULD HAVE DANCED if his bum hip allowed it. Before he could get caught eavesdropping, he headed for his office. He couldn't stop at Spencer's office to share the news, because his friend had decided to work from home for the rest of the day.

"Work from home, my ass," Yank muttered. Spencer was just afraid of runnin' into his son.

After all the years of being aggressive, going after what he wanted and doing things his way, Spencer Atkins was running scared because some pansy politician didn't want to acknowledge a fruit in his family tree.

Well, screw him, Yank thought. Spencer deserved as much happiness as Yank had in his life, and he was going to do everything he could to make sure his friend got it. And he'd succeed. Things had been going his way of late, after all. First Riley was taking care of Sophie without even having to be told to do it. Why should he stop there?

Lola was going to whip him but good, Yank thought, laughing. But he could handle her. He knew how to keep her happy now, he thought and grinned.

Yep, Yank was going to reunite father and son. Just as soon as he figured out how to bring the two men together without Riley blowing the whole thing by turning and walking away.

CHAPTER THIRTEEN

CINDY RAN from Athletes Only. She took an elevator to the street, then did something she never did, hailing a cab instead of taking the cheaper subway. She paid for the fare all the way to the Bronx, straight to Miguel's office, not stopping to check in with the outer receptionist and practically flying past his personal secretary.

All the while, her heart pounded like a sledgehammer in her chest as she silently repeated the mantra, *Please don't let Sophie be right. Please don't let him be using me.*

She entered his inner sanctum without knocking. Sleeping with the man gave her *some* privileges, she thought. And if she'd been misreading him, if he did have an agenda, well, better she find out now by gauging his reaction to her barging in on whatever he was doing inside.

She entered and came to a stop, breathing heavily. She could only imagine the wild look in her eyes, but she refused to second-guess the impulse that had brought her here. She'd dated the man, despite

Sophie's warnings, and she'd fallen in love with him, despite her own. If he'd betrayed her—

"Cynthia!" Miguel rose from behind his desk, bracing his hands on the edge of the dark wood. "What's wrong?"

She never took her eyes from his face, watching every nuance she could capture. So far, all she viewed was surprise and concern that she'd shown up unexpectedly. Still, the man was a master at masking his emotions.

He knew how to wine and dine her. His ability to treat a woman well and make her feel like the rarest diamond was unmatched in Cindy's experience. But as much as he did and said all the right things when they were together, and as often as he called when they were apart, he'd been hurt badly by his first love. A woman who'd remained in his home country after promising she'd join him in the United States. Instead she'd stayed and married his best friend, who owned a small fleet of boats on the island, betraying Miguel in a way that had broken his heart and caused him to put up walls.

He claimed she was the first woman he'd let in ever since. He said that the other women in his life had been ways to pass time, but she was his *único y verdadero amor,* which meant his "one true love." She prayed he was telling the truth.

"Cindy?" That he used her nickname told her he was worried.

Well, she was worried, too, but now that she stood

in front of him, fear overwhelmed her and the words didn't come as easily as she thought they would.

"Nicholas, let's call it a day. I have an emergency," he said to a man Cindy hadn't even realized was there.

"Not a problem," the other man said. He rose, gathered his suit jacket, nodded at Cindy and left the room.

Miguel wrapped his hand around her waist and led her to the leather sofa. "Sit and tell me what brings you by."

She couldn't relax enough to sit. "How badly do you want to sign John Cashman?" she asked.

He shook his head. "I do not understand."

"It's a simple question," she said, stepping out of his warm, comforting grasp. She couldn't think when he touched her like that. "How badly do you want to sign John Cashman?" she asked again.

"As much as I want to sign any young athlete with years of potential ahead of them. What are you really asking me?"

She tried to swallow, but the inside of her mouth was too dry. "We all know Cashman's father is pulling strings, manipulating his son. He wants the best deal and he's unsure of who can get it for him."

Miguel inclined his head. "Your point?"

"You're doing your best to convince him that you can do a better job for him than Spencer Atkins or Yank Morgan."

He nodded, not denying the obvious truth. "And

they are doing their best to convince him they can negotiate a better deal than I can. That is the nature of the business. You knew we were business rivals before we started seeing one another. I do not understand why you have a problem now." His voice held a frustrated edge.

She understood but she didn't yet have the answers she sought or the settled feeling she needed. "Did you sabotage the computers at Athletes Only? Did one of your e-mails to me contain the virus that disabled the system?"

He stared at her in shock, not replying immediately.

At his silence, she continued to ask the questions pounding at her brain. "Did you hire someone to break in? Put a hidden camera lens in Sophie Jordan's bathroom?" Tears filled her eyes as she questioned him and she wiped away the moisture that prevented her from seeing him clearly.

This time *he* stepped away. "I am insulted you would even ask if I did such terrible things."

"I can't help it. There've been a lot of unsettling incidents. Scary things are going on over there. I need to know you aren't behind them."

He ran a hand through his neatly combed hair. "I love you, Cynthia. I've trusted you not only with what has hurt me in the past, but with my heart now. I have never given that to another woman. Not since Lisette. If you cannot trust as I have, there is nothing I can say that will convince you." He turned and started back for his desk, not facing her again until he was behind the large piece of furniture. Far away from her, physically and emotionally.

She trembled, but inside she heard Sophie's voice, questioning Miguel's motives and actions. And she felt swamped by guilt over the possibility that she'd willingly accepted his love without question. She hadn't thought about her employers, only about herself.

"You've swiped talent from other agents before," she whispered.

He stiffened. "I have never resorted to illegal behavior. Your boss and your coworkers can have their suspicions, but either you believe in me or you do not. I refuse to dignify these accusations with more answers." He straightened papers on his desk, waiting while she thought things through.

If she believed in him and he'd betrayed her, she in turn would have betrayed her employers and friends in favor of a man. If she didn't have faith in him, she could lose him forever. All she had to go on was experience—she and her father had trusted someone with the keys to their restaurant and in the end it had cost her father his life.

Cindy wanted to trust Miguel, but how could she really know he was telling the truth?

"Cynthia?" he asked, his dark eyes meeting hers.

She was shaking as she replied. "I...I need time to think," she said at last.

"That is too bad, because if the situation were

reversed, I would believe in you. In us." A muscle pulled at the side of his mouth, a sign he was holding back emotion.

"Miguel, please understand—"

"I understand you don't know me as well as I thought you did. If you think I am capable of doing these things, hurting your friends…" He shook his head. "If you'll excuse me, I have business to take care of. Legitimate business." His voice had turned frosty, lacking the sensual warmth he normally reserved for her.

Confusion and pain overwhelmed her as she stepped back. Turning, she reached for the doorknob and let herself out. Not just out of his office, but likely out of his life.

IMMEDIATELY AFTER landing in Mississippi, Sophie checked her voice mail and discovered that she must have crossed paths with her sister, Micki, midair. Her sibling had landed in New York, home from her long honeymoon. With all the chaos at the office, Sophie had forgotten about her sibling's return. She would call Micki later. She had other things to deal with now.

As much as Sophie appreciated Riley's attempt to take her away from her problems, his daughter's sullen greeting, which had been followed by a persistent scowl, told Sophie she was hardly in for an easy time this weekend. She also knew she was merely postponing dealing with whomever was tormenting her. But if it meant her uncle and Spencer could focus on the draft, she'd just have to get through this trip.

While she was here, she planned to make notes and work through who could possibly want to scare or even hurt her. As afraid as she was, Sophie was also angry that someone would try to rule her life by fear. She refused to be cowed by her so-called stalker. Like everything else, she'd deal with this by analyzing all possibilities.

Riley's stepfather had sent a limousine to pick them up at the airport, and Sophie stared out the window, watching the passing scenery. And despite their moody teenage chaperone, Sophie couldn't control her awareness to being so close to Riley. Every time she inhaled, his cologne teased her senses. She imagined she could feel the heat emanating from his body. But most unsettling was the indulgent, even tender way he looked at and spoke to his daughter. Sophie's heart melted watching him play the role of father.

All of which cemented her fears of allowing herself to get too close to Riley. She'd have preferred to stay in a hotel, but Riley wouldn't hear of it. He'd insisted that his parents had enough room for a small army and she wouldn't be imposing.

Sophie glanced at Lizzie, who hadn't taken her iPod headphones out of her ears since Sophie had met up with father and daughter at the airport. Sophie could hear the music blasting from across the car but doubted the teenager would appreciate a lecture on hearing loss, so she remained silent.

From the side, Lizzie looked like her father, possessing the same profile except with smaller, feminine features. She had long brown hair she'd flat-ironed straight and wore a hot-pink Juicy Couture sweat outfit, which sat low on her hips and hugged her still-developing curves.

Riley tiptoed around her mood, deferring to her rude behavior without comment. To his credit though, he didn't try to excuse her attitude, for which Sophie was grateful. And from his unusual silence, she decided he wasn't all that thrilled with the awkwardness hanging over them.

She hoped he'd think about doing something to deal with his daughter's behavior. But hope was all she could do since she knew better than to criticize his parenting or step in the middle of his relationship with Lizzie. She silently promised and hoped she could keep her vow.

The car drove up to large black wrought-iron gates. The driver checked in and the massive doors slid open wide so they could drive through.

"Okay, ladies, we're here," Riley said as the car came to a stop.

Without waiting for the driver to hold the door, Sophie exited, stepping out into the Mississippi humidity, glad she'd opted for curls rather than any kind of sleek hairstyle that wouldn't hold up in this weather.

Lizzie slid out from behind her and ran up the huge front lawn where a slender woman in navy slacks and a silk blouse waited on the front steps, then pulled her into a warm hug.

"Ready to meet the parents?" Riley winked at Sophie.

The gesture did little to ease the growing nerves in the pit of her stomach. "I really don't belong here."

He frowned. "You do, too. You're my guest and they're expecting you. There's nothing to worry about."

"Except the little fact that your daughter hates me," she muttered as they started walking up the driveway.

He wrapped an arm around her shoulder, comforting her. "She doesn't hate you. She hates sharing me."

Sophie let out a laugh. "Pardon me for thinking there's little difference."

"Riley!" The woman walked down the steps and drew her son into her arms. "It's been too long. I've missed you," she said, sounding just like Sophie always imagined a mother should sound.

An unexpected swell of emotion rose in Sophie's throat, emotion she should have been way beyond feeling. She was used to seeing little children and their mothers all over Manhattan and she'd passed the point where the sight would arouse feelings of loss and longing. She'd never watched two adults embrace and been hit with all she was still missing out on in her life. Until now.

Which said something about her connection to Riley, Sophie thought and shivered despite the sticky heat.

"You must be Sophia." The elegant woman held out her hand and welcomed Sophie with a warm smile.

"My friends call me Sophie."

"I'm Anne."

Sophie inclined her head. "Thank you for having me for the weekend."

"It's not like you gave anyone a choice." Lizzie stood behind her grandmother, leaning against the wooden front door, glaring at Sophie.

Sophie stiffened. She waited for someone, Riley's mother or Riley himself, to react.

"Lizzie, go inside and let Marabel give you some milk and cookies." Once the girl had turned and stomped inside, the older woman turned back to Sophie. "Maybe she's tired from the trip."

"Maybe she just has a smart mouth and I've had enough." Riley walked around Sophie and up the steps to the front door. "It's high time I had a talk with her."

Sophie exhaled in relief.

"Riley, wait. Just give her some time to calm down. You can talk to her later," Anne pleaded with her son.

Sophie had little doubt he'd give in, leaving her odd woman out around this family. A place she ought to remain, if she was smart.

Riley gritted his teeth at his mother's unreasonable request. Until today, he hadn't seen how badly behaved his daughter could actually be. Or maybe he hadn't wanted to see. Until Lizzie had turned her anger on Sophie, Riley had been content to let her mouth off, telling himself he deserved her frustration because he no longer lived with her mother. And of course, because he was afraid of having no relationship with her, as he didn't with Spencer Atkins.

He finally understood Sophie's frustration with him in Florida and Lisa's constant angst over his handling of their child. However, his mother saw Lizzie infrequently, and keeping the peace for a little while longer was a small price to pay for her happiness. Especially now, with the Spencer situation hanging over her.

He nodded, indulging his mother, but only for now. "I'll show Sophie to her room. While she's getting settled in, you and I can talk."

Although he'd made peace with not finding out information about Spencer from the man himself, Riley had a lot of questions for his mother. Questions he'd waited to ask in person, so he could see her face and judge her reactions for himself.

"Anne, why don't you show our guest to her room?" Senator Harlan Nash joined them on the front porch. "Riley and I can retire to the study and catch up."

The senator posed his words as a suggestion, but Riley knew that tone and it indicated pure expectation. The man, in his navy power suit, white shirt and conservative red tie, was the epitome of a Washington power broker. Without a doubt, Senator Nash was on his way up in politics. Heaven help anyone who stood in his way, Riley thought.

"Still issuing commands, I see." Riley laughed as he shook the man's hand, then pulled him into a brief hug. "Some things never change."

"Any reason they should?" the senator asked easily.

Riley grinned. "Not a one." He glanced over, wondering how Sophie was handling all this family at once.

In her expression, he saw interest and understanding. He was glad. She was seeing the Nash family as they really were, and clearly she approved.

If only she felt the same about his daughter—and vice versa, he thought, frustrated. He'd just have to find the right time to bring the two women in his life together somehow.

"Aren't you going to introduce me to this lovely lady?" the senator asked.

Now there was a pleasurable task. "Senator Harlan Nash, meet Sophie Jordan." Riley turned to Sophie. "Sophie, this is my father."

The two shook hands and the next thing Riley knew, the senator had directed his mother and Sophie upstairs, while he closed Riley in the study with him. Unfortunately, Harlan received a phone call that took up an entire hour.

By the time Riley had finished reading the paper and decided his father being off the phone "in a minute" wasn't happening, his mother had left the house with Sophie for a tour of the city. No sooner had Harlan exited his office than Lizzie had pleaded to be taken for ice cream, and Harlan had immediately agreed.

Riley begged off. Left alone, he hit the home gym in the basement. So much for conversation with his mother or Lizzie. So much for reconciliation between

Sophie and Lizzie. If Riley didn't know better, he'd think the senator had orchestrated the entire thing, isolating Riley and precluding a conversation of any kind.

SOPHIE CLIMBED on top of the bed in the comfortable guest room. One of about four guest rooms, if she'd counted correctly. The stately mansion befitted the senator and his family, gorgeous yet homey at the same time. She yawned and stretched, snuggling into the huge bed. Her exhaustion came more from travel than anything else she'd done today.

Along with Riley's mother, she'd taken a tour of the town, and then Anne had shown her the capitol, half an hour away. Sophie had enjoyed her time with Riley's mother. The other woman had chatted about everything and anything, including stories about Riley as an incorrigible youth. The bond between mother and son was obviously strong, yet Anne hadn't made Sophie feel like an intruder at all. In fact, his mother had commented on the fact that Riley had never brought a woman from New York back home with him before.

Still feeling warm and fuzzy from that comment, as well as from the Lizzie-less dinner, as the teen had gone for pizza with local friends, Sophie knew she wouldn't unwind fully unless she mapped out the possibilities of who was stalking her back home. She pulled a pen and pad from her travel bag and began to take notes. Steve Harris and Miguel Cambias topped her list. They both had motive. Miguel had already proved himself adept at gaining what he wanted, be it Cindy or an athlete he wanted to represent, while Steve Harris had shown his ability to dig into her life.

But only Cambias had opportunity because of his access to Sophie and Athletes Only via Cindy. Sophie had no doubt her friend was an unwitting accomplice if it was Miguel who was looking to divert her uncle's and Spencer's attention from the draft. Yet she wasn't convinced the man would go that far and she didn't want to think he'd use Cindy as a means to an end. She sighed, no further along in her thoughts than she had been after talking with the police following the break-in at the office.

Somehow the knock on the door a few minutes later didn't surprise her and it provided a welcome distraction. "Come in." She laid the book on her lap and waited for Riley to let himself inside.

He walked in, dressed in faded jeans and a light blue T-shirt. Still sexy with the shadow of a day's growth of beard. Still so appealing and desirable.

"Hey, gorgeous."

She blushed and grinned. "Hey, yourself."

He lowered himself onto the mattress, his thigh touching hers. "Working?" He picked up the notebook, took in the scrawled names and frowned. "I'd rather you *were* working than dwelling on this."

She shrugged. "I have to figure out who's doing this."

He shook his head. "That's a job for the cops. I brought you down here to get away from it all and that's what we're going to do."

She raised an eyebrow, definitely interested. "What did you have in mind?"

"Would you believe my father still has a vintage Corvette convertible? I thought we'd drive around, I'd show you the sights at night and we could end up at the local *parking* spot."

She couldn't help the smile pulling at her lips. "Aren't you afraid of getting caught?" she asked, teasing him.

"Lizzie's been asleep for hours and I can't think of anyone else who'd care. What do you say?" He leaned forward, his lips inches from hers. "When was the last time you experienced some good old-fashioned necking?"

She couldn't resist him on a good day, let alone on one when her defenses were down and she was on his turf. She was still in self-protection mode, but she wasn't about to turn down what was probably her last opportunity to be with him.

"I need to change first."

He glanced down, his attention settling on the cleavage revealed by her favorite lemon-colored satin camisole, then traveling down the length of her matching drawstring pants. He trailed a finger over one bare shoulder, his roughened skin caressing her flesh. She shivered, feeling her nipples pucker into tight peaks and knowing for certain he noticed them, as well.

"We could stay here," he said, tempting her even more.

She swallowed hard. "And definitely risk getting caught." Suddenly taking that convertible ride sounded even more appealing.

She scooted around him and poked through the drawers for a bra and shirt, then grabbed jeans from the closet. "Be out in a sec," she promised, closing herself in the bathroom.

Ten minutes later, they drove through the gates and into the muggy night air. A cool breeze didn't lessen the high humidity but Sophie didn't mind.

She was in a vintage convertible, Riley by her side and her problems back home in New York. How could she complain about that?

He drove down a dark stretch of road, made a sharp right and suddenly a school came into view.

"Is this your high school?" Sophie asked, glancing at his profile.

He nodded. "Brandon High," he said, laughing. "And that field over there?" He gestured with a wave of his hand to the football field, complete with electronic scoreboard. "Riley Nash Field."

She squinted, unable to read the writing on the sign. "You lie."

He laughed. "Yeah. But they should name that place after me. I scored enough goals to earn it," he said with a grin.

"Your lack of modesty is unbelievable." But it was one of the things she admired about him.

His faith in himself was probably one of the traits that made him such a solid, dependable team player. He hadn't let Spencer's rejection hold him back. If anything, his birth father's absence drove Riley to push himself harder.

She remembered how easily he called the senator *Dad*. The word rolled naturally off his tongue. Riley clearly had a solid support system here at home, one filled with love and affection. Her heart squeezed tight for Spencer, yet she couldn't stop the feeling of gratitude she felt toward Harlan for raising Riley without prejudice over the lack of common blood between them.

He drove past the school and soon they entered the small center of town. "I thought we'd grab some DQ before we went parking."

"DQ," she repeated. "Dairy Queen?"

He nodded. "You pampered city girls don't know the first thing about good ice cream." He pulled alongside a drive-through window. "What would you like?"

Sophie leaned back against the car seat. "Since you claim to be the ice-cream connoisseur, why don't you go ahead and order for both of us?"

"Two vanilla cones dipped in chocolate," he said. Then he turned back to her. "I'm going to go with the classic, so you can get a real feel."

He paid and took the cones, handing them to her while he drove the quick few minutes back to the school. He pulled into the dark parking lot and shut off the engine.

She handed him his cone. "So what's with the hard topping?"

"Is there another way to have hot fudge or caramel on a cone?" he asked, a teasing note to his voice.

Sophie laughed. "Guess not." She bit into the cone, knowing the pieces could fall all over her and were likely to stain. "Delicious," she said through a mouthful.

They ate in comfortable silence. Sophie didn't want to break the mood by asking too many questions, so she remained quiet, enjoying Riley's company.

"How are your mother and the senator handling the news about Spencer?" she asked when she couldn't hold back anymore.

He shrugged, licking the last of the ice cream off his bottom lip. She tried not to stare, but he looked so darn sexy sitting in the convertible, eating his treat and staring as if he wanted to devour *her* the same way he'd consumed his ice cream.

"I wouldn't know," he said at last. "I haven't had five minutes alone with either one of them since I arrived. Either Harlan's sending my mother off to take care of Lizzie or she's out giving you a tour of the town. And he's not making time for idle chitchat either. All he talks about is politics when we're alone. I think they're both trying to avoid the subject."

"Does that bother you?" She rolled her used napkin into a ball and tucked it into the car's ashtray.

"It makes me think they knew about Spencer all along and don't want to have to answer my questions.

Why else avoid conversation?" As he spoke, he stretched one arm over her seat.

Unable to stop herself, she reached out so her fingertips touched his. "Makes sense. I'm sorry you have to go through all of this."

He let out a groan. "It's an odd thing. Sometimes everything about Spencer and the situation feels like it's happening to someone else and I shouldn't be affected at all."

"But you are affected. He's your biological parent and you have questions you want answered. And you have the right to those answers," she said, defending his feelings.

"Thank you for saying that." He tipped his head toward her.

Sophie leaned in closer, meeting him halfway across the console of the car, until their lips touched and lingered. Her mouth had been frozen from the ice cream, but as soon as their tongues met, warmth replaced the cold and heat surged through her body. Suddenly the light caress wasn't enough. She wanted to crawl into his lap and wrap herself around him until she didn't know where she ended and he began.

The need he inspired was unlike any she'd felt before. She doubted she'd ever feel anything like it again. Reaching out, she wrapped her hand around the back of his neck and pulled him closer, angling his head so she could taste him even more.

Desire pummeled at Riley. He loved kissing

Sophie, making love to her with his mouth, mimicking exactly what he wanted to do to her with his body. From the erotic purrs escaping the back of her throat, Sophie wanted the exact same things.

He wrapped one hand around her waist, but short of physically climbing over the center divider, there was no way he could get as close to Sophie as he needed to be.

Frustration filled him. He leaned back against the car seat and groaned.

She rolled her head to the side. "I thought you said parking was fun." Her eyes glinted with a teasing light.

He managed a laugh. "Are you telling me that wasn't fun?"

"It was fun." Her smile gave his heart rate another boost. "You just never mentioned how much torture parking would be."

"That's because I didn't remember it being quite so bad." Then again, he'd never had *this* woman sitting in the passenger seat beside him, ready and willing.

Suddenly he remembered his parents using this car for family picnics. They'd always used an old blanket his father kept in the trunk.

"Wait here." He climbed out of the car and walked back to the trunk. He held his breath as he looked inside and exhaled a huge sigh of relief.

Sophie slammed the passenger door shut and joined him as he pulled out the old blanket. "What's going on?" she asked.

He propped a hip against the car. "Just how frustrated are you?" he asked, his tone rougher than he'd intended.

"Well, I don't know. You've already managed to get me to go parasailing, to come to Mississippi, to leave my comfortable bed and go *parking*. What else did you have in mind?" Her blue eyes twinkled with curiosity and more.

He reached out and stroked her cheek. "I want to make love to you right here, right now."

She gnawed on her lower lip. "Where?"

"Over there." On the field that held so many other memories for him. "Well?"

Her eagerness was almost tangible as she shifted from foot to foot. Just like in Florida, the uptight Sophie who needed control as badly as she needed to breathe was nowhere in sight. But something was definitely wrong. Though her flushed cheeks told him she wanted to be with him, too, she still hesitated.

He waited, giving her the moment she obviously needed.

"I just want to make sure we both understand the ground rules," she said at last.

He bit the inside of his cheek. "Now that sounds like the Sophie I know—" He'd been about to add, *and love.*

Here, on an open field beneath the stars, Riley admitted to himself that he'd fallen hard for Sophie Jordan. Forget good old-fashioned necking, he was talking about good old-fashioned *love*.

He shivered despite the heat unfurling inside him. Not because he was actually in love for the first time in his adult life, but because of the possibility that she wouldn't let herself return the feelings. He didn't doubt that she loved him. Hell, he'd bet she'd known it back in Florida, but he'd pushed her away because of his own insecurities. He'd yet to win her back and he was afraid, based on her own issues, he never would.

"Riley? Ground rules," Sophie reminded him.

He nodded. "On the field I'm a rules man myself," he said, keeping things light. No sense losing her before they even began. "Name your terms."

She inhaled deeply. "This one night with no expectations afterward."

Oh, this was rich, Riley thought. She was handing him the stuff of male fantasies. "The words any man would want to hear." Just not the words he wanted from Sophie, he thought and forced a smile.

Until now, Riley had defined his life by going after what he wanted and making it happen. The only glaring failure was his relationship with his biological father, a situation too complicated for him to accept all the blame. Failure wasn't in Riley's vocabulary and that included how things would end up with Sophie.

Between her fear of being abandoned and her need to control, she had walls higher than any Riley had ever constructed. Which meant that for the first time, he was going to have to play by someone else's rules in order to win the endgame. He just wished the outcome of this one was guaranteed.

CHAPTER FOURTEEN

RILEY SPREAD the blanket over the ground, using the time to gather his thoughts and his resolve. He had played many big games before and never suffered performance anxiety. He didn't intend to do so now, even though this was the one time he had the most to prove.

He needed Sophie to see that what they shared was more than one night. That they were more than a brief fling. He almost laughed at the irony. He'd never planned to think beyond the moment. Even when he'd been with Sophie in Florida, there'd been an inherent understanding that they were giving in to temptation. Nothing more.

He'd cemented that impression by turning on her when she'd tried to point out his mistakes with his daughter. Any positive feelings Sophie had begun to develop for him had evaporated fast. He'd given Sophie no reason then or now to think she was special to him. After all, she'd seen him flirt with every woman in a skirt.

But he knew now that she was the only woman he truly wanted. If he thought it would make a difference, he'd hand over his heart as quickly as she'd captured his. Yet he knew that baring his feelings would send her running far and fast, because in Sophie he'd found someone who'd mastered the art of self-protection far better than he had. And he'd caused her to raise her barriers high. She couldn't allow herself to trust him and he promised himself he'd gauge her reactions and pace himself accordingly. The endgame mattered more than the short-term goals.

He sat down on the blanket and patted the space beside him. "Join me?"

She curled up close, the cool air from the ride in the convertible giving her incentive to want body heat. He just plain wanted her.

"This is a nice place to grow up," she murmured.

He smiled. "Glad I could share it with you."

She leaned back on her elbows and glanced up at the stars, which were barely visible through the haze and clouds. "Did you ever wish upon a star?" she asked.

"Can't say that I have. I'm more of a practical, make-my-own-luck kind of guy."

She shook her head in mock pity. "You really missed out on one of childhood's great moments."

"Star light, star bright?" he asked lightly.

"First star I see tonight. I wish I may, I wish I might, have the wish I wish tonight."

As he studied the delicate features he'd come to adore, he suddenly found a reason to indulge in whims and fantasy. He stared upward and found the brightest star in the night sky, the one that called to him in a way that the others did not. The same as Sophie did, Riley thought.

He shut his eyes and wished for what he desired more than anything else. "Sophie—"

"Shh."

She placed her finger over his mouth to silence him and his lips tingled beneath her touch.

"Don't tell me your wish or it won't come true," she said.

"That means you can't tell me your wish, either," he said, unable to contain his disappointment. He'd wanted her to let him inside her heart.

"But I can tell you that it's the same wish I've been making for as long as I can remember." A wistful smile passed over her lips, vanishing as fast as it came.

He pushed her long curls off the back of her neck. "It hasn't come true yet?"

"Nope." She tipped her head, obviously enjoying the brush of his fingertips against her skin, so he kept up the soft contact.

"But I keep hoping it will." Her lashes fluttered closed.

He swallowed hard. He wanted to be the one to make her dreams come true, but first she had to believe in him.

Goal in mind, he leaned over and nuzzled his face into the sweet spot between her neck and shoulders. She smelled delicious and when he licked her soft skin, he discovered she tasted even better. A seductive purr escaped the back of her throat and she trembled against him.

God, he loved just being with her, Riley thought, and he refused to contemplate what he'd do if she pulled away after tonight.

A quick sweep of his hand over the front of her shirt and he felt her hardened nipples, proof that in Sophie, when it came to passion, he had a willing partner. Riley decided it was a damn good start.

He wrapped one arm around her waist and drew her down, protecting her from the hard ground by rolling her on top of him. Her full breasts pressed hard against his chest as her lower half settled into the vee of his legs.

He groaned aloud, unable to control his reaction to having her exactly where he wanted her.

She grinned and wiggled her hips enticingly, causing his erection to swell.

"Tease." He laughed.

"You love it," she whispered, planting kisses over his face until her lips settled over his.

He loved *her*. Thinking it at the same time he held her in his arms caused a rush of warmth and a sense of rightness to flood through him. His heart pounded hard and heavy in his chest with the desire to make himself one with her overwhelming.

His tongue tangled with hers. Heat flared to life in his belly, the friction of their twisting, grinding bodies bringing him too close too fast. He didn't want to come without being inside her, deep inside her, so she'd *feel* how right they were together. How wrong they were apart.

He slipped his hands up the back of her shirt so he could embrace her bare skin. He also managed to still the rhythmic motion of her hips that had him teetering on the edge.

She eased a bit, allowing her breath, hot against his neck, to slow, giving him time to take over. After a couple of tries, he managed to unhook her bra, then watched in fascination as she maneuvered enough to pull the female contraption out of one sleeve and then toss it onto the blanket beside them. Her shirt came next.

He took a moment to relish the sight of her naked in the moonlight. Then he reached out and cupped her breasts in his hands, feeling them heavy and aroused.

She arched her back, pressing her taut nipples into his palms. Seeking to enhance her arousal, he responded by rolling each bud between his thumb and forefinger. He wouldn't last long once they began and he needed her tightly wound and ready to explode. Because he sure as hell was ready to blow.

Sophie's entire body shook and trembled, on the edge of something so much bigger than she'd anticipated or experienced before, even with Riley. He knew just where to touch her to make her burn, exactly how hard to squeeze in order to push her past reason and sanity.

Unable to wait, she reached down with shaking hands and unbuttoned Riley's jeans. She hooked her thumbs into the waist and quickly helped him shove them down his legs and past his ankles, until they joined the growing pile on the ground.

She was crazed with wanting, practically panting with desire, yet she was still partially dressed. Riley's eyes were glazed and dark with need, but he didn't reach to help her. Instead he clasped his hands behind his head as if he were relaxed and composed, with all the time in the world.

But his penis thrust upward, demanding attention, making a mockery of his so-called composure.

"Undress for me," he said in a gruff voice.

At the request, a liquid trickle of desire pooled in her panties. A desperate throbbing pulsed low in her belly and she vibrated with unfilled longing. She rose to her knees and slowly, deliberately, wiggled her jeans down her thighs, stopping when they reached her ankles.

Sophie was braver than she'd given herself credit for but she couldn't muster the courage to strip completely in the great outdoors. She glanced at Riley and saw only understanding in his eyes. He wasn't going to push her further than she could handle.

His understanding was enough to bring her to tears. The little things—like the way he read her mind, and the way he understood her and accepted her anyway—chipped at the walls around her heart. But all his sweetness and decency couldn't change the differences between them that would drive them apart in the end.

Sophie feared loss more than she feared anything else, but she couldn't lose what wasn't hers. Her wish upon a star had been for someone to love her and cherish her forever. That might be in the cards one day, but not with Riley. Not with a man who'd tried and failed at marriage, and who'd decided he wasn't someone to be closed in by rules. But that didn't mean she couldn't have him now.

And once again, being with Riley made her want to push beyond her security level, beyond her normal comfort zone. For Riley, she wanted to be braver than she'd ever been before. And she couldn't wait a minute more.

She rose over him, his thick head poised between her legs. Then his erection disappeared as she slid down, fusing their bodies and filling the emptiness inside herself with everything that was Riley. She enclosed him completely, feeling him all the way through to her soul.

"Sophie." He called out her name on a rough gasp, his pleasure evident in his tone.

Sophie shut her eyes and let herself feel. She rose upward, squeezing her inner muscles around him, and released as she slid back down. The friction between them was sweet and intense, taking her by surprise. Her throat filled with emotion with every slick glide up and down, with each thrust of her mound against him.

His breath quickened without warning and she realized he was near his peak. She wasn't far behind and when he grabbed onto her hips and pumped his body up into hers, slick, hot and harder each time, he took her closer still. He found the rhythm she needed, and she soared up and over, wave after wave of the most intense climax washing over her, pummeling her relentlessly, until finally, she peaked and saw stars brighter than those she'd wished upon all these years.

Just when she thought she was sated, he thrust upward once more and she squeezed him tight, causing one last wave of ultimate sensation to sweep through her body.

She thought she'd heard herself scream but was too embarrassed to ask. All she knew for sure was that, once again, Riley had engaged not just her body but her heart and soul.

Heaven help her when he walked away after this.

SOPHIE AWOKE, her body aching in sinfully delicious ways. When Riley had said good-night outside her bedroom door, the kiss had been achingly slow and beautiful. She'd felt so cherished and loved, even without the actual words having been said. Thank God. Because her fears were knocking loudly and she was having one hell of a time ignoring them.

She showered and dressed for breakfast, choosing a casual peasant skirt, T-shirt and loosely draped belt before heading downstairs. She didn't know who she'd find in the dining room where staff set the long table each morning. She was hoping to run into Riley's mother, Anne, whom she'd truly enjoyed spending time with. She prayed she'd miss Lizzie, who, as was the tendency of teenagers, may have slept in.

Instead she discovered Senator Nash sitting at the head of the table, drinking coffee and reading the morning newspaper. Food had been set up buffet style on the credenza, and Sophie chose to indulge for a change, picking scrambled eggs and hash browns along with a large glass of orange juice before joining Riley's father at the table.

She eased into a seat beside him and set her plate in front of her.

"Good morning," he said, folding the paper and placing it aside.

Sophie smiled. "Good morning to you, too."

"Looks like we're the early birds."

She nodded. "Force of habit, I guess."

"I never set an alarm clock. I'm up at five forty-two every morning."

Seeing a kindred spirit, she couldn't help but laugh. "It's six forty-six for me."

In the comfortable silence that followed, she ate her breakfast while he rose and served himself. Seconds, he informed her, hoping his wife didn't catch him overindulging.

He appeared warm and friendly and Sophie couldn't help but be drawn to the man, since she could relate to him on many levels, including his need to control the world around him, she thought wryly.

"So tell me about your PR agency," he said when they'd moved on to just sipping their coffee.

She enjoyed talking about her job, which inevitably entailed discussing her family, and she dove into the subject. "My uncle started a sports agency called The Hot Zone years ago, way before my sisters and I came to live with him."

"I'm sorry about your parents," he said somberly. "Riley's told me your history."

"Thank you," she murmured.

She was used to the comment. It was the revelation that Riley had informed the senator about her family that surprised Sophie. Had Riley passed on the information in preparation for her visit here—or for other, more personal reasons? Did he want his stepfather to know about Sophie as a person Riley cared for? she wondered.

She shivered and paused for a large sip of her hot coffee.

Senator Nash nodded, encouraging her to continue when she was ready.

"Anyway, after Annabelle—the oldest sister— graduated from business school, she suggested the idea of starting up a PR firm as a subsidiary of the sports agency. Uncle Yank loved the notion. He saw it as a way of continuing to care for his athletes once their playing days came to an end."

"In what way?" he asked.

Sophie sensed true interest, not forced conversation, so she indulged in a longer explanation. "If a client signs with both Uncle Yank as his agent and The Hot Zone PR firm, we can negotiate not only big-money endorsements while an athlete is in their prime, but also lay the groundwork in preparation for the future. Whether they're injured a year into a big-money contract and need a source of income, or whether they play out a successful career, we can help them plan for both."

"Very interesting," he said, nodding.

Sophie blushed. "I'm sorry. I tend to get carried away when I start talking about something I'm interested in."

"No need to apologize. Riley has said he finds your knowledge on all subjects fascinating and I tend to agree."

She glanced into her now-empty cup. No way would she explain the need that drove her to overlearn about everything. Her control issues were too personal.

"So do you have anything to do with the agency side of the business or are you exclusively involved in PR?" he asked.

"I do PR for the most part, but we have a weekly meeting of partners only, so everyone's up to speed on the key clients and issues. That way nobody's ever left high and dry in an emergency," she said, proud of the system they'd made work over the years.

He leaned back in his chair and nodded approvingly. "Although I'm in politics, I do consider myself business savvy and I think that's a smart way to run things. So you're close with Spencer Atkins?"

Sophie suspected Riley's stepfather had been gradually leading to this moment. By questioning her about her business, he'd been able to work his way around to Spencer without being obvious. Well, without being too obvious. She was definitely onto him.

She glanced down, uncomfortable with the subject of Riley's real father, while buying herself time to think.

"Riley told me he's trusted you with the information," the senator said. Reaching out, he patted Sophie's hand. "If my son trusts you, so do I. I'm sure you realize how sensitive this is. Mississippi isn't known as part of the Bible Belt for no reason."

Now Sophie really was uncomfortable. "Senator—"

"Please call me Harlan."

Either he was as honest and good as Riley believed or he was the ultimate politician. She wanted to believe the former and operated under the assumption that she could trust his word. "Harlan, Spencer's been like a part of my family for as long as I can remember."

"So you knew about his…" He loosened his tie and cleared his throat.

"Sexual orientation?" She shook her head. "No, I didn't. No one in my family knew. But he's entitled to his privacy," she said defensively.

"No one agrees more than I do. It's a shame the way someone chose to repeat what they'd discovered. Whoever it was probably made a huge amount of cash by revealing the truth."

Sophie frowned. "As much as I know that's the way of the world, it makes me sick."

"I know. Now my biggest concern is keeping the news quiet."

She toyed with the napkin in her lap. Finally she glanced up, deciding to jump into the conversation all the way. "I understand how sensitive a subject gay rights is, but why would your constituents hold Spencer's affiliation against you? You aren't even related by blood!" Sophie hated how bigoted individuals could affect so many innocent people's lives.

The senator rose and paced the floor. "I married the man's wife when she was pregnant with his child. I raised the man's son. The implication will be that I condone his lifestyle."

"That's ridiculous. Doing something noble doesn't mean you condoned anything, or even knew the truth about Spencer." She stilled, recalling Riley's suspicion about that very thing. "Or did you know the truth?" she asked softly.

He shook his head. "Neither did Anne. All she knew was that her husband no longer wanted to be married. We met soon after and I fell hard. She was wise enough to trust that we could make a lasting union—Anne, her unborn son and myself."

Sophie exhaled long and hard. She knew how much Riley feared his parents had been lying to him all along. Though she was saddened at how alone Spencer must have been, she was definitely relieved that Riley's family hadn't been hiding the truth.

"The fact remains, Mississippi has had a law banning gay marriage since 1997, and in 2004 the voters passed a Constitutional Amendment declaring marriage as being between one man and one woman. It passed by eight-six percent," he said solemnly. "In my mind that leaves no room for close family ties that make my future decisions suspect." He shook his head. "Doesn't matter what I think or feel, that's the way of things."

Sophie had no intention of delving into the senator's true views on gay marriage, even assuming he'd tell her the truth. Nor did she plan on asking him if he'd ever taken into consideration Riley's right to get to know his birth father.

She suspected the senator wouldn't like her opinion and opted to remain silent. "I can promise you the truth won't leak from me. I'm loyal to those I care about." That much she could say with ease.

Besides, Spencer wanted things hidden, as well. Like it or not, Sophie would stand by everyone's choices.

Harlan stopped his pacing. "You can't imagine how glad I am to hear that."

She wondered what he would have said or done if she'd planned to spill that carefully hidden secret. She glanced into his steely-gray eyes and decided she was darn glad she wouldn't have to find out.

"I trust Spencer feels the same way?" he asked, unapologetically probing her.

She pursed her lips. "Despite the way things

looked over the years, Spencer has always had Riley's best interest at heart and Riley has asked him to keep silent. I'm certain that's the end of things as far as Spencer is concerned." She hated discussing this and wanted the subject dropped.

Harlan gripped the back of a chair in a tight clench. "With all the unfortunate events at your place of business, he's probably too busy to focus much on himself anyway."

She leveled him with a curious glance. "How did you know?"

"Riley's filled me in on the break-in, the camera and those men who just won't leave you alone," the senator explained. "I'm sure your uncle and Spencer are distraught with worry."

Sophie narrowed her gaze. "But I thought—"

"Good morning, everyone," Anne Nash strode into the room, her mood as bright and cheerful as her patterned silk blouse.

Sophie had been about to ask just when Riley had found time with his stepfather to provide him with all that information since, as far as she knew, he hadn't had a moment alone with the man.

"Harlan, are you torturing Sophie with stories about Riley as a baby?" Anne asked.

Her husband chuckled and pulled out a chair for his wife to sit. "Actually, I leave those memories for you to divulge. You're a much better storyteller than I." He smiled indulgently at his wife.

Sophie resisted the urge to scratch her head. The

senator was an enigma. A man with an agenda, but one who obviously loved his family so much it eclipsed anything else in Sophie's mind.

Footsteps running down the stairs echoed through the house and seconds later, Lizzie joined them for breakfast, scowling when she saw Sophie. She didn't bother to hide her dislike from her grandparents, who obviously indulged her tantrums and spoiled behavior even more than her father did.

Sophie rose and poured herself more coffee, deciding maybe the caffeine would help her deal with the demon child. Lizzie was Riley's daughter, and Sophie was determined to win over the young girl.

The teenager chose a chair far away from Sophie, near the other end of the rectangular table. There was some chatter among her grandparents, but Lizzie remained quiet.

"Lizzie?" Sophie asked.

"Hmm." The young girl didn't look up from her cereal as she ate.

"Have you seen any good movies? My sisters and I get together for a girls' night and we're trying to pick something light and fun. Do you have any suggestions?" Sophie tried to engage the teen in conversation.

"Like you care. You're just trying to be nice to me to suck up to my dad."

Sophie gritted her teeth and glanced around the table. The senator had taken a phone call in the other room, which left only Riley's mother as a buffer.

Anne gave Sophie a sympathetic glance but said nothing in the way of real support.

Sophie was on her own. As much as she wanted to tell Lizzie off and be done with her attitude, Sophie felt sorry for the child who feared losing her dad to some strange woman.

Sophie clasped her hands in her lap and leaned forward. "Lizzie, you don't know me at all, but I'm going to tell you a little something about myself."

"I'm not interested."

To Sophie's surprise, Anne sucked in a shocked breath. "You may not be interested, young lady, but you will listen to what Sophie has to say. You're in my home and we treat guests politely here. Do you understand me?"

"Yes, ma'am," Lizzie muttered.

Sophie smiled, grateful for Anne's interjection. "My parents weren't divorced like yours, but they died when I was younger than you are now."

She watched the teen carefully for signs of reaction and was grateful when Lizzie cast her eyes down to her lap. At least Sophie knew she was listening and decided to continue.

"I was raised by my uncle who happens to be your father's agent. So I know something about not wanting to be left out and I know even more about being afraid of losing someone you love."

Although Lizzie remained silent, her cheeks had turned pink, making Sophie wonder if she was embarrassed by her earlier outburst.

Sophie paused and thought about what to say next. "I'm here as a guest and I'm a friend of your father's, but I have no intention of taking him away from you and I don't want to compete with you in any way. You come first for him. You always will."

Lizzie didn't respond. If Sophie had reached her, she had no way of knowing it and the silence around the table grew, until Anne tossed her linen napkin down and rose from her seat.

"Elizabeth Nash, I know your parents have taught you better manners than what you're displaying now," the older woman said in obvious frustration. "Sophie was nice enough to reassure you despite your behavior. Now I suggest we go on from here. She asked you a question about the movies and I think you should answer it. *Nicely*," Anne added, emphasizing her point.

Sophie hadn't expected the verbal support and she mouthed a thank-you to Anne. The other woman smiled in return and eased herself back into her chair.

"She's not my mother and I don't see why I have to have anything to do with her." Lizzie's stubbornness rivaled her father's.

"Because your father said that you do."

At the sound of Riley's voice, Sophie jerked around in her seat.

He stood in the doorway of the dining room, his broad shoulders filling the space. Even though she'd just seen him last night, Sophie couldn't take her eyes from him now.

He wore a tan-colored shirt and had rolled up the sleeves halfway, exposing his muscular forearms, which he'd folded across his chest as he eyed his daughter with a determined stare.

"But…"

"No buts." Riley strode into the room. Pausing by Sophie, he leaned down and kissed her cheek, making a statement to everyone in the room.

Especially to Sophie. At the unexpected and blatant gesture, her heart skipped a beat and her breath caught somewhere between her chest and her throat.

As if he'd done nothing out of the ordinary, Riley headed for the credenza, poured himself some coffee and joined the rest of the stunned people at the table.

"Elizabeth?" Riley prodded his daughter. "Either you answer Sophie's question as your grandmother suggested or you apologize for being rude. Either one works for me."

Lizzie glanced up, tears filling her big eyes. "You never used to be so mean to me. You used to take my side. Now all of a sudden, you're ganging up on me and I know why. It's because you want me to spend more time with Mom so you'll have more time alone with her." She jerked a finger toward Sophie. "Mom said you have someone special in your life and I should respect it," she said, a mixture of disgust and jealousy icing her tone.

"Then why don't you?" Riley asked his daughter softly.

"Because I don't want to lose you." Big teardrops fell from Lizzie's eyes and Riley held out his arms so his daughter could come for the hug she so desperately wanted.

Sophie watched the emotional scene play out and slowly eased her chair back so she could slip out of the room. Her own emotions were raw and at the surface, tears threatening to swamp her, too. She knew what it was like to lose a parent in some way and she couldn't help but empathize with the young girl. At thirteen, Lizzie was reacting to her emotions. Thinking about other people's feelings wasn't within her frame of reference right now and Sophie couldn't blame her.

Sophie made her way back to her room, grateful nobody had followed her. She needed time alone with her thoughts, which were already hammering at her hard.

Sophie had been a few years younger than Lizzie when she'd lost her parents, but Sophie finally understood the panic and fear in the teenager's eyes and comprehended the source of her defiant attitude. Sophie was only sorry she hadn't equated the two things on such an elemental level earlier, but now that she had, there was no way she would be the cause of that kind of pain for Riley's daughter. There was no way she'd let Riley lose the most precious person in his life.

Sophie pulled her suitcase from the closet and began to pack for home. No need to wait for their flight later today when she was certain she could leave now.

CHAPTER FIFTEEN

RILEY PATTED Lizzie's back, and she stepped away and headed back to her seat. "You okay?" he asked her.

She nodded.

He turned to Sophie, intending to make peace between the two ladies in his life, but saw an empty chair instead. His stomach plummeted and a wave of emptiness swept through him. "Where—"

"She slipped out," his mother said.

"I'm sorry." Lizzie glanced at him through wide, too-innocent eyes.

He doubted her sincerity, but now wasn't the time to get into it. As much as he wanted to go after Sophie, he intended to settle some things within his immediate family first. His father had rejoined them, and if the whispering was any indication, his mother had filled him in on what had just happened.

Based on recent experience, he'd never have them all together in one room again. "I have something I want to discuss. It's something that affects us all, and Lizzie needs to be part of the conversation."

"What's up?" Lizzie asked.

Riley drew a deep breath. He hadn't slept last night and, as much as he'd like to blame his insomnia on thoughts of making love to Sophie, he'd had other things on his mind as well. Like winning Sophie back.

And cleaning house, he thought. There was no way he could try to bring Sophie into his life until he proved to himself and to her that he was a man capable of dealing with some serious issues in his life. He knew she thought of him as a guy with a girl in every city, and for a while, that hadn't been far from the truth. The fact that he wasn't like that anymore didn't matter without proof that he wanted to set his life in order.

He'd caused much of his daughter's attitude and problems by spoiling her. He'd acted with the best of intentions, but he'd screwed up and it was time he admitted it.

"You were right when you said that I never called you on your actions before Sophie came into the picture."

"You see? I knew she was the problem!" Lizzie said triumphantly.

He shook his head. "Not the problem, but the solution."

"I don't get it," Lizzie said warily.

"I don't either, son." Harlan held his wife's hand and spoke for them both.

He smiled grimly. "You will once I explain. I let Lizzie get away with having an attitude, with acting like a spoiled brat—"

"Hey!" She interrupted, jumping from her seat.

"Sit down and let me talk," he said in his sternest voice.

She sat.

"I didn't want to be the bad guy because I was afraid of losing you, of having no relationship with you the way—"

"The way we did for a while, right?" Harlan asked quickly.

Too quickly. He had interrupted Riley in order to keep him from mentioning Spencer's name. Riley glanced at the man who'd raised him. "It has to be said."

His mother raised a trembling hand to cover her mouth, but she said nothing.

"What has to be said? What's going on?" Lizzie asked.

"Nothing," Harlan said.

"Everything," Riley countered. "Mom, Dad? You raised me well and I love you both. But you raised me to value honesty above everything else and I can't move forward with my life if I don't come clean with Lizzie now."

Harlan clenched his jaw. "She's thirteen. I think you're asking a lot of a thirteen-year-old to keep this kind of secret."

Riley's attention settled on his daughter. Her face was contorted in confusion. "I trust her," he said, hoping to convey his love for her, as well.

Harlan rose. "Well, pardon me if I don't sit here

and watch you bury this family and my career," he muttered and walked from the room.

"I'll calm him down." Anne turned to Riley. "I understand why you need to do this," she said, granting him the one thing he needed most right now: her understanding.

"Thanks. Just one question before you go. When did you find out about Spencer? Did you know all along?"

"I found out through the papers like everyone else," she said, and from the sad tone in her voice, Riley believed her.

"We'll talk later," he promised.

She nodded and followed the path her husband had taken. Riley trusted in his parents' marriage as much as he trusted in…in Sophie, he realized. And he knew that he was sitting here now, about to divulge his entire past to his daughter, so that he could have a future with Sophie.

The woman he loved.

He'd thought it last night and had only grown more certain after making love to her on the field. In the time since Spencer's disappearance, his life had undergone a bigger transformation than he'd ever thought possible. Finding out his real father was gay had forced Riley to come to terms with so much in his life, he almost owed the old man a thank you.

But first…he faced his daughter.

Almost an hour later, Lizzie knew everything, from Harlan not being his real father to Spencer

Atkins being his biological one. She'd been sincere when she'd promised to keep the news to herself, but she'd laughed a lot, too. Nothing less than he'd expected from a thirteen-year-old girl.

They talked about their relationship and the changes that they'd both have to make going forward, hugging and crying as they tried to negotiate and agree. One of the deals they made was Lizzie's promise to apologize to Sophie.

Riley actually felt good, as if he were making progress. When he'd revealed that he intended to do everything he could to make Sophie part of their family, Lizzie had turned back to his obnoxious, rebellious thirteen-year-old once more.

And all was right with Riley's world.

ALL AROUND RILEY, everything was wrong. From the moment he and his female companions had stepped onto the plane, earlier than planned because he refused to let Sophie fly home by herself, to the minute they'd walked out of the gate at JFK, chaos had reigned.

Lizzie was angry they were cutting their trip short, and though she'd apologized to Sophie as he'd demanded, her *I'm sorry* had lacked any sincerity whatsoever and she'd refused to speak the entire flight home.

Sophie had withdrawn, as well. When he'd discovered her packing in her room, all she would say was that the father-daughter bond was sacred and she refused to come between them and cause a rift. After all, she'd reminded him, his biggest fear had been ending up estranged from Lizzie, as he'd been from Spencer. She was doing him a favor, she'd said, and she felt certain he'd come to see it and even thank her one day.

Like hell.

Riley planned for Lisa to pick Lizzie up from the airport, leaving him time alone to deal with Sophie. Because his ex missed their daughter, she'd agreed. Lisa had shown up as planned and whisked the sullen child away, winking at Riley and shooting him a thumbs-up signal behind Sophie's back.

His ex-wife approved of his choice in women. Whoopee, Riley thought. Still, he appreciated her help in giving him a chance to win Sophie over.

Until he heard someone call Sophie's name. He turned and saw her sister Micki and her husband, retired baseball player Damian Fuller.

"I'm sure I told you I'd take you home," Riley said before Micki reached them.

Sophie didn't look at him. "I didn't want to put you out so I called my sister."

"So I see." And he didn't miss the irony.

When Sophie had insisted he act like Lizzie's parent instead of her friend, Riley had used her words as an excuse to pull away. Now, when he took her advice and laid down the law with his daughter, acting like the parent Sophie had wanted him to be, *she* pulled away from him.

And Riley saw it as the excuse he knew it to be. Unfortunately he had no time to call Sophie on it, because Micki ran to the luggage carousel and threw her arms around Sophie, hugging her hard.

"It's been so long!" Micki exclaimed.

Sophie hugged her sister back, laughing and grinning in a way Riley hadn't seen—ever. This was the Sophie he'd always imagined, the warm, loving woman who had everything she wanted and needed in her life. Except, her sisters were married and Sophie was alone.

Riley was right. She needed him, too. She just didn't know it yet.

"Two weeks and you and Damian deserved every last minute. But I am so glad you're home." Sophie pulled her sister tight once more.

"Women." Damian Fuller gestured to the two blondes making a spectacle of themselves.

Riley nodded. "I'm—"

"Riley Nash, NY Giants. I think I've heard of you." Damian laughed.

Riley nodded. "Same here, Fuller. Good to meet you in person." He shook the other man's hand.

Damian studied Riley for a moment, not hard to do when the sisters were preoccupied with each other. "Mind if I give you a piece of advice?"

Riley shrugged. "Can't hurt."

"The first thing is, don't bother trying to step in between the sisters. Not now. Not ever."

Riley raised an eyebrow. "In other words, grab my bag and call it a night?"

Damian nodded. "Sophie's tough because she's had to be. Middle-sister syndrome along with the same fear they all share of losing someone they fall in love with." The other man slapped Riley on the back.

"Hey, it's not like she's professed her love to me," Riley clarified.

Damian shrugged. "You're obviously in deep with her and the only way to deal is to give her enough space to realize what she's missing. Otherwise she'll keep pushing you away and never be forced to look at herself in the mirror."

Riley hefted his bag off the conveyor. "Did you become a shrink since retiring?"

"Nah. I just became part of the Jordan family. A guy learns about all the sisters real quick that way. And speaking of being part of the family—" Damian led Riley a short distance away from where Sophie and Micki were chatting, completely oblivious to the men.

"Yeah?" he asked, anxious to get home.

"Sophie's my sister-in-law and that makes her family. So if you aren't serious, get the hell out and don't come back. Because if I see you again, I'm going to assume you mean business."

Riley rolled his stiff shoulders back, stretching his tight muscles. "In other words, hurt her and I answer to you?"

"Something like that."

Considering the shape he was currently in, Riley wasn't worried. Not to mention the fact that he and Damian were in complete agreement where Sophie was concerned. "I only want her happiness," he felt compelled to tell Sophie's brother-in-law.

"Good. Then I won't have to kick your ass," Damian said, laughing.

Riley grinned. "No, but if you wouldn't mind knocking some sense into your sister-in-law, I'd be mighty obliged," he said in a thick Mississippi drawl.

Then, without saying goodbye to Sophie or Micki, he tossed his duffel over his shoulder and left the airport. Leaving Sophie on her own as she obviously desired.

Besides, if Damian was wrong and his absence didn't make Sophie's heart grow fonder, Riley would just turn around and kick the other man's ass.

A FEW DAYS AFTER Sophie's return, the partners gathered in the boardroom. Uncle Yank glanced around, and obviously satisfied, began to call their meeting to order. "The weekly meeting of The Hot Zone—"

Spencer cleared his throat loudly.

Uncle Yank frowned but got the message and started over. "The weekly meeting of Athletes Only and The Hot Zone will now come to order." Uncle Yank rapped his gavel, given to him by Judge Judy, on the table with such glee that Sophie jumped in her seat.

He lived for this gig, Sophie thought.

"The secretary should note that all partners are present and accounted for." His gaze settled on Lola, who sat next to him, doodling but not taking notes.

"I *said*, the secretary should note that all partners

are present and accounted for." He nudged his wife with his elbow. "Lola, honey, you're the secretary. That means you take the notes."

"That's what I'm doing. Or don't you hear my pen moving on the paper? I thought you told me that when the sight goes, the other senses get heightened?" Lola asked too sweetly.

Uh-oh. Sophie and her sisters shared amused glances. Obviously husband and wife were arguing again, which, considering the parties involved were Yank and Lola, wasn't a great surprise, nor was it a cause for worry. It was status quo.

"You're scribblin' circles, honey," he said through gritted teeth.

Lola glanced up from her paper. "I wouldn't have thought you could see the difference, *dear.*"

"Oh Lord. Are we going to witness a family squabble?" Spencer asked.

Sophie chuckled. "As if you didn't know what it was like to be a part of this clan."

"What in the world is going on now?" Annabelle asked.

Lola placed her pen down on her pad. "I came home early yesterday and found your uncle making himself a tuna-fish sandwich."

Everyone waited for the punch line.

"The tuna was in a Tupperware container in the fridge. I don't need my full peepers to do that." Yank defended himself, but the color high on his cheekbones said there was more.

"You were cutting a tomato with a serrated knife," Lola said, her voice rising.

Yank exhaled a frustrated groan. "I'm not a child who needs his food cut up for him."

"And I don't intend to be married to a nine-fingered mutant pain in the ass. You push things too far, Yank Morgan. I know you. You'd cut off one finger at a time if it meant keeping your independence." Lola gripped her pen tighter in her hand.

"I'm fine. It was just a little nick." He held up the injured digit. His middle finger stuck straight up in the air, flipping the bird to everyone at the table.

Everyone, with the exception of Lola, snickered at the sight. The sad truth was that Lola had every right to be concerned, but as usual, Uncle Yank managed to turn the situation into a circus.

"I need the afternoon off," Lola announced.

Spencer cleared his throat. "I don't see a problem."

"What for?" Yank demanded to know.

She met his gaze, a smug smile on her lips.

Sophie braced herself for whatever the other woman had in mind.

"I plan to go on over to Toys 'R' Us. I'm going to purchase those babyproof locks so I can secure the drawers and cabinets," she said to her husband.

"Oh no," Micki muttered.

"Here we go," Sophie agreed.

Uncle Yank rose from his chair. "The hell you will. You can't lock me out of my own kitchen."

Lola gathered her papers and stood, too. "Just

watch me, you old coot. Someone has to protect you from yourself." She straightened her shoulders and strode out of the room.

Yank followed right after her, arguing all the way.

The remaining partners glanced around the room.

Sophie grabbed the forgotten gavel and smacked it against the table. "I move we continue without them."

"I second," Annabelle said.

"Third." Spencer nodded.

Sophie hit the table once more. "Motion passed." She grinned. She could get used to this little bit of power, she thought, turning the gavel around in her hand.

"Okay, Little Miss Dictator," Micki said, laughing. "What's the first order of business?"

Although Sophie normally made notes on what they should cover in their weekly meeting, today Sophie's pad was empty. Sort of like her life, she thought.

Since coming home from Mississippi, life had been as conspicuously quiet as it had been crazy busy before the trip. Although only three days had passed, she recognized the distinct change. No more break-ins, no sabotage, no problems. Eerie but true, Sophie thought. Meanwhile the police had come up blank on any leads. A niggling fear remained, but Sophie refused to live petrified until the next incident. For all she knew, whoever had started things had decided he had better things to do than harass her.

"We should discuss the draft," Spencer said into the silence. "On the first day, Yank and I signed

Cashman five minutes before the announcements began. Not only is he our client, but he's signed with the team with the worst record, the San Francisco 49ers." The team with the worst record always received the first pick in the draft.

Everyone around the table applauded. Although the Heisman winner always went to the most needy team in the league, they'd still accomplished much for their newly signed client.

"Did you have any problems with Miguel Cambias?" Sophie asked.

Spencer shook his head. "As a matter of fact, less than none. Go figure. He was present and active, but he didn't go near Cashman."

Sophie bit down on her lower lip. Had she targeted the man unfairly? She'd have to talk to Cindy, but her friend had taken the past few days off, and Sophie hadn't had a chance to apologize again or see what her talk with Miguel had accomplished.

"Anything else on the agenda?" Micki asked.

They discussed the various open client files and agreed to wrap things up until next week. Then the partners headed back to their own offices.

Sophie didn't stop to talk to Spencer alone because she was certain he had no desire to discuss Riley with her any more than she wanted to talk about Riley with him.

RILEY OPENED the pizza box so he and Lizzie could dig in. They each pulled out a slice of pepperoni pizza, took their cans of Coke and headed for his den with the big-screen TV. One of the perks of coming to Dad's was that he let Lizzie eat dinner in front of the television. It was their guilty secret and, even with his new determination to be a real father and lay down rules, he wasn't about to deny her this treat.

"So how's school?" Riley asked.

She shrugged. "Mr. Gordon hates me."

"Science, right?"

She nodded.

"How could anyone hate you?" he asked, looking proudly at his smart, gorgeous daughter and trying to suppress a grin.

She stuffed her mouth full with pizza, then said, "I studied all night and he gave me a seventy-four! Can you believe that?"

Riley raised an eyebrow. "Define all night. Was that all night in between your shower, blow-drying your hair, straightening your hair, talking on the phone and IMing your friends?"

A guilty flush stained her cheeks.

He didn't envy his ex-wife her full-time job of keeping their child in line. "Sounds to me like you earned that seventy-four and Mr. Gordon doesn't hate you as much as he's giving you what you deserve."

She frowned, then picked up the television remote and began channel surfing in reply.

Riley noted that in the few hours they'd been together, she hadn't mentioned Sophie at all. Knowing Lizzie, it wasn't so much out of sight out of mind as it was her wanting to pretend Sophie didn't exist.

Riley wished he could do the same, but the golden-haired beauty was ever present in his mind. Typically he was a man of action, yet all he could do was hope that she missed him enough to get past her insecurities and hang-ups and give them a chance at a future.

Damian Fuller had had a point and Riley knew three days hadn't been nearly enough time for her to come to any realizations. He'd just have to sit tight and wait. However, patience wasn't his strong suit.

"Hey, Dad, look!" Lizzie gestured at the big screen. "Isn't that your agent?"

Lizzie had met Yank quite a few times over the years. But she wasn't a fan of sports TV, and when he glanced up, he realized she was watching the local cable entertainment channel. Yank Morgan was being interviewed by the sports-gossip reporter, inset on the screen were photographs of Riley and Sophie, labeled with their names.

"What's *she* doing up there?" Lizzie asked in her snottiest voice.

Riley closed his eyes and groaned. He didn't have an answer but whatever it was, it couldn't be good. "Make it louder."

Lizzie raised the volume.

"Mr. Morgan, just to remind our viewers, you're considered the sports agent to the stars. You requested this interview, so let's talk about what's on your mind." The brunette leaned forward, her eyes eager and interested.

"As everyone knows, I went on TV a few weeks ago and splashed my niece's picture all over the news, tellin' people she's single and in need of a good man."

"I remember that," the woman said, laughing.

A damn good picture of Sophie, if Riley did say so himself. A little formal for his taste, since she wore her hair pinned back and a prissy, yellow sleeveless dress with a conservative houndstooth design. He preferred her naked and disheveled on his bed.

Shifting uncomfortably in his seat, he glanced at his daughter, then looked back at the television.

"I'm here to issue a refraction of that story. I was wrong."

The reporter smiled. "You mean a retraction."

"That's what I said. My Sophie is not in need of a man, so you guys out there can stop sending her flowers and plants and chocolates and things to the office." He slashed his hand through the air.

Riley agreed with that particular sentiment. The only man Sophie needed was *him* and if Yank saw fit to call off the rest of the testosterone-filled population, Riley was all for it.

"To what do we owe your change of heart?" the interviewer asked.

Yank grinned—a smile that Riley had seen before when Yank was ready to use his trump card and close a big deal.

Lizzie remained silent, watching intently.

"Well, it turns out my niece was holdin' out on me. While I was worried about her future, she was in good hands the whole time."

The woman smoothed her skirt. "You mean she's involved with a man?"

"If you call two recent trips outta town together involved, then, yeah, she's involved," Yank said, laughing. "First Florida, then Mississippi. Yep, she's *involved*."

Riley's stomach clenched and he could swear he felt Lizzie stiffen beside him.

"Who's the lucky man?"

"Football star Riley Nash, of course. Who else would she go to Mississippi with?" Yank asked, as if the question were a no-brainer.

"Dad!" Lizzie yelled, and jumped up from her seat, a horrified expression on her face.

He drew in a deep breath. Riley was used to being a media focus, mostly for football, occasionally for off-season entanglements, but until now his celebritylike status had never affected his daughter in such a direct way.

Riley pressed the mute button of the remote control and turned to her. "Lizzie, I've always told you that you can't let what you see on television affect how you think about people or even life. Reporters and interviewers want to get ratings or sell papers. They'll invade a person's private life to do it. It isn't right, but it happens," he said, opting to stay rational in light of her hysteria.

"But that's your agent and he's on TV saying you're involved with that woman. And it's true, right? I mean she was at Grandma's with us, right?"

"That part is true," he agreed.

"Have you seen her since?" Lizzie asked.

"No." At least he could answer that honestly.

Lizzie met his gaze, her panic and distress palpable. "But you want to, right?"

Riley sighed. He might as well lay it on the line right now, even if it meant dealing with more of his daughter's drama. "Sit, okay?"

Reluctantly, she lowered herself into a chair.

Riley leaned forward, choosing his words carefully. "Your mother married Ted, right?"

His daughter nodded.

"Does that mean she loves you any less? That you're any less important to her?"

She shook her head, her eyes round and huge. "Are you saying you're gonna *marry* Sophie?"

Though he'd set himself up, the question still caught him off guard. As he sometimes did in a big game, Riley decided to wing it. He'd talk to Lizzie as the words came to him and hope for the best.

"When your mom and I divorced, I never thought I'd get married again. We loved each other, but we couldn't get along well enough to make it work. I didn't want to go through it again." She was too young to understand lust not real love, and she deserved to believe he'd loved her mother. He had, in a young sort of way.

Lizzie sniffed. "That's not an answer."

"Eventually, if Sophie agrees, yes, I'd want to marry her," he said slowly, realizing he was speaking from the heart. "But you will always be my number-one girl and anybody I marry would know that. Sophie already knows that, honey. You just need to give her a chance."

Lizzie glanced at him, her lashes damp, her eyes shimmering with tears, and his gut cramped painfully. This was the little girl who always looked at him with love and adoration in her eyes. He'd promised himself he'd never disappoint her, yet here he was, doing just that. He'd never felt lower and yet he'd never been more sure that he was doing the right thing for them both.

"She'll never be my mom." Defiance tinged Lizzie's tone.

Riley gave her a grim smile. "She'll never try to be. Assuming things work out the way I'd want them to, she'd be just like Ted is for you—someone you can trust with anything you need." That was how much faith he had in Sophie.

"This sucks," Lizzie said, and crossed her arms over her chest in that obstinate way of hers.

Riley chuckled. "All things considered, I'll let you get away with that."

His nerves were on edge, his emotions frazzled from dealing with Lizzie and from realizing how he really felt about marrying Sophie. Despite how often he thought about her, he'd never followed the notion to its logical conclusion.

Now that he had, he was overwhelmed with a sense of rightness. "Sometimes," he said to his still-upset daughter, "a person realizes he needs more to be happy. And to be a good father to you, I need to be happy." And Sophie, with her big smile and bigger heart, her neuroses and need for order, made him happy.

Who would have thought it?

Lizzie swallowed hard. "I still don't like it."

"You'll learn to like it," he said, laughing.

Whether or not Sophie came around to his way of thinking was another story. But thanks to Yank's ridiculous impulses, Riley had a chance to get his daughter to understand what Riley needed.

He was willing to give his daughter time to get used to the idea, but he wasn't willing to give up Sophie while Lizzie mulled it over.

CHAPTER SIXTEEN

SOPHIE MET UP with Cindy at Cake 'n' Bake, a little hole-in-the-wall bakery in SoHo. Together they were going to buy the pièce de résistance of Lola and Yank's party, a cake to end all cakes and a surprise for Uncle Yank and Lola. The only catch for Sophie was that she hadn't seen Cindy since their confrontation over Miguel Cambias. Still, Sophie took Cindy's willingness to meet her today as a good sign. Otherwise she'd have to wait until Monday of next week, when her friend returned to work, to see if Cindy had forgiven Sophie.

She waited for Cindy on the sidewalk. A beautiful April day, the wind blew with a definite hint of spring. Sophie wanted to enjoy the beginning of the season, but she was preoccupied with too many things, like the possibility of losing a friendship and a top-notch publicist. Then there was her unresolved situation with Riley.

"Sophie? I'm sorry I'm late. I just had to stop at the dry cleaners on the way over." Cindy ran up to her and screeched to a halt.

"I'm sorry," Sophie said, wanting to get the heart-felt apology out immediately. "I'm sorry you over-heard what I said about Miguel and I'm sorry I said it. But things were in complete chaos and somebody had to be responsible and—"

"It's okay." Cindy met her gaze, only compassion evident in her eyes. "I understand why you'd think he had something to do with the crazy things happen-ing around the office. I thought so myself. That's why I took my anger out on you."

"You thought Miguel was guilty?" Sophie asked, surprised.

Cindy swallowed hard. "It crossed my mind. I thought about the sudden attention, the constant e-mails. I wondered. But when I asked him about it…"

"What'd he say?" Sophie asked.

"Basically that either I trusted him or I didn't." She bit down on her trembling lower lip.

Sophie stepped closer to her friend. "And?"

"And I walked out on him." Cindy exhaled long and hard. "I took the elevator down to the ground floor and I walked the streets of Harlem. Then I realized either I was sleeping with a man I believe in or I wasn't."

Sophie listened, her heart in her throat. She felt as if she were sitting on the edge of her seat, rooting for Cindy and Miguel. "So what did you do?"

"I turned and ran all the way back to his building, up the stairs and back to his office." A blush stained

Cindy's cheeks, evidence of her overwhelming emotions for this man. "I told him I had faith." She shrugged. "It's not like the tech guys were able to track anything back to him."

"That's true," Sophie said.

"And we've been together ever since—every night as a matter of fact," Cindy said, smiling.

Sophie pulled Cindy into a tight hug, glad Cindy had found happiness, and relieved that she and her friend had put their differences behind them. "I'm so happy for you." She stepped back and smiled.

But what lingered in Sophie's mind was that she envied her friend's ability to throw caution away and have complete faith in someone she cared for. Just because their tech people couldn't pin the computer virus on Cambias's e-mails didn't mean they'd exonerated him. Yet Cindy was able to give Miguel the benefit of the doubt.

Sophie hadn't even begun to trust in Riley. But she and Riley had a lot of strikes against them. Sophie had lost her parents and learned the benefits of controlling the things and people around her, while Riley was his own person and did his own thing. That was strike one. He'd turned on her once before in defense of his relationship with Lizzie. Strike two. And as attentive as he could be at times, she couldn't forget how much he loved to flirt with all women; she couldn't guarantee he'd be around beyond the next date. Strike three.

Three strikes and they were out. Game over.

"Sophie?"

"Hmm." Sophie shook her head hard. "Sorry, we can go inside."

Cindy stopped her with a hand on Sophie's arm. "In a minute. I have a question." She stepped closer. "Did I ever tell you that my father was killed before I moved to New York?"

Sophie's throat swelled with emotion. "I had no idea." But she could only imagine the pain her friend had suffered. Was still suffering. "What happened?"

Cindy drew a deep breath. "An employee he trusted broke in after hours and stole money from the register. He set fire to the place to cover his tracks. My father tried to put it out before the firefighters arrived…" She waved her hand, obviously unable to continue.

Sophie grabbed her friend's hand, squeezing it tight. "I wish I'd known before now. Friends should share these things with each other."

Cindy nodded in agreement. "It's not so easy to talk about. But now you know. Just like I know about your parents, and that they're the reason you can't bring yourself to trust that Riley isn't going anywhere. You'd rather push him away before he leaves you like your parents did."

The words, uncomfortably accurate, stung Sophie's already raw emotions. "That's ridiculous. Riley's not going to die on me. God willing," she felt compelled to add.

"But you're afraid he's going to get bored, or fall out of love or just plain leave you," Cindy said pointedly.

"Nobody said anything about *love*." There was a lot in Cindy's conclusion to address, but Sophie chose the most obvious, and the scariest, part of her friend's speech.

Cindy sighed, then linked her arm through Sophie's. "I've given you enough to think about for now. Let's go cake shopping," she said, and led Sophie into the shop.

Grateful for the distraction, Sophie lost herself in the gorgeous confections. Cakes in all shapes, from cupcakes to designer purses, caught her eye.

Sophie strode to the woman behind the counter. "I have an appointment with Genevieve."

A young woman wearing a white apron smiled. "That's me." She held out her hand. "I'm Gen, the owner."

"I'm Sophie—" she shook the other woman's hand "—and this is my friend and coworker, Cindy James. I'm looking for a unique cake for a unique couple," she explained.

"I just bet you are." Gen glanced at Sophie and winked, as if she were privy to some secret.

Sophie narrowed her gaze. "My uncle and his wife eloped and they never had a wedding reception, so we want this party to be extra special."

Gen leaned forward on her elbows. "Oh, come on. I saw the interview with your uncle. You're marrying Riley Nash, aren't you? You can tell me. Anything you say will be kept strictly confidential."

Behind her, Cindy chuckled.

Sophie rolled her eyes. She was appalled that her uncle had publicly linked her with Riley at a time when she desperately needed distance. She also felt guilty.

Although she was more than used to her uncle's shenanigans, Riley was not. He didn't deserve the unwanted publicity or the crimp this could put in his social life. She ignored the slicing pain in her heart at the thought of him with another woman and concentrated instead on what was fair and right. No matter how good her uncle's intentions, no matter how noble his motives, he stirred up trouble and someone other than him usually took the brunt of the fallout. Riley didn't need the upheaval in his life. Sophie had left a message on his cell phone, calling to apologize.

"I'd like a cake in the shape of two hearts," she told the woman.

Gen took notes. "Pink hard coating?" she asked.

Imagining the look on her uncle's face when he saw the girly cake, Sophie nodded. "Bright pink."

"Wording?" Gen asked, glancing at Cindy.

Obviously the other woman thought Sophie shouldn't choose the wording on her own cake.

Sophie gritted her teeth.

"How about *It took you long enough?*" Cindy suggested lightly.

Sophie grinned. "Two hearts as one," she said, the words suddenly coming to her.

No matter how often they bickered, no two people loved each other more and no two people deserved each other quite as much as Uncle Yank and Lola. As Cindy rightly said, they'd waited for this happiness long enough.

Gen wrote up the order and tallied the bill. Sophie paid with her credit card. "Thanks for everything," she said to Gen.

"My pleasure. It will be delivered as promised on Saturday evening." The other woman smiled. "So this is really a wedding cake for you, isn't it?" she asked, trying again for inside information that didn't exist.

Sophie gave up. Ever since her uncle's retraction, everywhere she went, people asked when she was getting married. They complimented her on snagging such a hot bachelor, and they all refused to believe the truth: that she and Riley were not a couple.

In time, everyone would see it was true.

LIFTING WEIGHTS was Riley's way of blowing off steam. That he needed to stay in shape during the off season was an added bonus. Right now he had to vent angry, frustrated energy or else he'd explode, he thought as he tied his sneaker laces, ready for a workout.

"Sophie called you to apologize?" Mike asked from his seat on the bench in the locker room.

Riley nodded. "For her uncle publicly linking us together. For the fact that—and I'm quoting here— her uncle's display must be cramping my fucking social life." Riley kicked at the floor.

"You added the word *fucking*," Mike said.

Riley nodded. "Sophie Jordan wouldn't curse like

that, especially not when leaving a message. Just like Sophie Jordan wouldn't step out of her comfortable controlled world to take a chance on what might be the greatest thing that ever happened to her." His voice rose to a fevered pitch. "That being me," Riley said, in case Mike wasn't paying attention.

His teammates in the locker room turned and stared.

"Man, you've got it bad. Does she know?" Mike asked.

"Are you kidding?"

Already finished with his workout, Mike rose and began stripping down for a shower. "Hell no, I'm not kidding. Does Sophie know you're in love with her? Did you ever tell her?"

Riley paused. Had he? Had he ever said the words aloud? Or had he turned on the charm and hoped she'd figure out what he was trying to convey? Just as he'd hoped she'd know that the other women he'd flirted with before meant nothing to him while she was the real deal.

"I've been treating her like she was a mind reader," Riley muttered.

Mike grinned. "I'm loving this. The ladies' man needs help." He let out a whoop of laughter.

"I'm so glad you find my life amusing."

Mike wrapped a towel around his waist and started for the showers. He took three steps and turned. "Did I help get your head on straight?"

Riley nodded.

"Glad to help." Still grinning, Mike walked away.

Riley leaned against his locker, preoccupied with thoughts of all he hadn't said and done for Sophie. Something he had to rectify immediately.

To hell with his workout. Riley dressed and was out the door in record time. Unfortunately, the reporters knew his daily routine and accosted him outside on the sidewalk. It was early in the off season for the press to be hounding him, but not unusual for them to cluster where the team worked out.

"Hey," Riley said, pausing for a minute. "Any chance I can catch up with you all later?" he asked in his most affable tone.

"Are you off to see your fiancée?" one of the reporters asked.

Riley laughed. "Real life's so boring you guys need to make up stories?"

"Didn't Yank Morgan say you're involved with his niece?"

"I don't recall him defining that involvement." Riley began to push through them so he could search for a cab on the street.

Another reporter tapped him on the shoulder.

Riley turned. "How about we schedule an interview?" he asked, anxious to see Sophie face-to-face.

A redheaded woman he recognized from eSports Network suddenly appeared in the crowd. "Since you don't want to talk about your social life, would you be willing to discuss your real father instead?"

Riley froze. "What did you just say?"

The woman, whose name was Veronica, shoved a

microphone in front of his face in search of the elusive sound bite. "I asked if you'd sit down with me to talk about your biological father. Spencer Atkins *is* your father, isn't he?"

"Where'd you hear that?" Forcing air into his tight lungs, Riley treated her to his best grin under the circumstances.

"Are you denying it?" she asked.

"I'm questioning your source." Because he couldn't for the life of him imagine how the truth had leaked out.

Whereas normally the reporters shouted out questions, vying for supremacy, the redhead had stunned her fellow reporters into silence. Apparently she had a scoop and he'd bet the revelation had already hit the news on her station.

She cleared her throat. "You know I can't reveal a source. Besides you're the one in the hot seat, Mr. Nash."

Riley's throat burned with pure anger at whoever had violated him and his family this way. "No comment." He stormed through the reporters and hailed a cab.

A yellow taxi approached quickly and he jumped inside. But instead of Sophie's address, Riley headed to his apartment in order to call his parents in private. Damage control had to come before his love life.

RILEY DIDN'T HAVE to call home. As soon as he stepped into the hallway and neared his apartment, he heard his phone ringing. He unlocked the door and ran inside, grabbing the portable receiver right before the answering machine picked up.

"Hello?" he asked breathlessly.

A quick glance at the machine told him he already had five messages. Definitely not a good sign, he thought.

"Riley? It's Dad." His stepfather's voice traveled through the phone lines, barely containing frustration already evident in his tone.

"You heard?"

"Everyone has heard. The question for me is exactly how such a thing got out."

Riley heard the familiar sound of grinding teeth, a habit Harlan had never broken in stressful situations. In his chosen profession, he had many of those.

"I was mobbed leaving the gym," Riley said. "Damn reporter took me off guard. I never saw it coming." He took a deep breath. "How's Mom?"

Harlan let out a prolonged sigh. "As well as can be expected. Her friends here didn't realize she'd been married once before. We didn't hide the fact—it had just never come up. And since we wanted Spencer's name buried, it seemed prudent to just look forward, if that makes sense."

Riley nodded. "It does."

"It's really the fact that Atkins is gay that is causing an uproar."

"Mom didn't know, so that should minimize the impact." Neither had Riley, and now that the news was public, he'd have to deal with the fact on a more personal level. One he had pushed to the back of his mind.

"No matter how you look at it, there's an embarrassment factor for her, but she's a strong woman. She'll survive and do it well," Harlan said with pride.

Riley smiled. "You love her," he said, not realizing he'd spoken aloud.

"Since the day I laid eyes on her."

"She was lucky to have found you. We were lucky." Funny, he thought, how in times of crisis, a person came to appreciate the things he had in life all the more.

A long pause followed. "I feel the same way, son," Harlan said. "Believe it or not, I tried to spare all of us this pain. And not just because of my position and career." Emotion caused Harlan's voice to crack.

Riley's throat filled as well. "I need to make sure Lizzie's doing okay with the fallout, but give Mom a kiss for me and tell her I'll call later."

"I will," his stepfather promised. "I'll also make damn sure I find out who leaked this scandal and see to it that they pay."

"It was bound to come out. Secrets can't stay hidden forever."

"Some can and should," Harlan said.

A click followed. Harlan had disconnected the call.

Knowing the older man, he was already on to other things, handling the crisis in a way only he could.

Riley closed his eyes and thought about his

daughter. Adults handling the news were one thing. A thirteen-year-old being publicly humiliated was quite another.

He grabbed his keys. Next stop Lizzie and Lisa's house.

SPENCER STARED out the window of his expensive penthouse apartment on the Upper East Side of Manhattan. His life had been a jumble of contradictions and clichés.

A gay man marrying to hide his secret. Although at first he hadn't hid his sexual orientation so much as wanted to change who he was. The late 1950s wasn't a time when homosexuality was accepted or even understood. Hell, he thought, it wasn't like his lifestyle was accepted everywhere in this country today. He didn't regret trying to assimilate into the mainstream. He only regretted the hurt he'd caused Anne at the time.

Because if he could have loved any woman in that way, it would have been his son's mother. Anne was his Doris Day, a soft-spoken, sweet-natured woman who would bring any man to his knees. He'd loved her in his way and he'd wanted to make their life together work. Especially when he'd found out she was pregnant.

Unfortunately, that was when things had started to shatter, both in their lives and inside Spencer. It had been difficult enough being with a woman when she couldn't fulfill his emotional and physical needs but once she was pregnant, he had immediately felt himself grow distant. He'd started spending nights out at underground gay bars, stopping for an hour at a sports bar on the way home as his cover.

Anne had hated the barrier he'd erected and he'd hated the lie he was living. The more he'd thought about how unfair he was being to her, the more he'd realized how much worse things would be when his baby was born. The decision to leave her had been the most difficult he'd ever made, but he consoled himself with the belief that she'd be better off without him.

Spencer had come home drunk late one night and told Anne that he hated being tied down in any way. With Yank Morgan as his best friend, Anne hadn't had to look far to see another example of what Spencer claimed to be: a man happier single than married.

She'd moved back with her parents, who'd made it impossible for him to stay in touch with her, not that he blamed them. He'd been torn up inside already and he'd backed off, intending to let some time pass before trying once more to be part of his child's life. But soon after, Anne had met Harlan Nash, a successful man with a law degree and political aspirations, an upstanding man who wanted to marry her and raise her child as his own.

Spencer and Harlan had met one night at the other man's request. In that moment, Spencer had known his wife and child could have a better life, a normal life, without him in it. He'd shaken Harlan Nash's hand and agreed not to contact either one of them again.

However, he hadn't promised not to watch from afar. He hadn't sworn not to pull strings and make sure his son—an athlete as it turned out—had the benefits of having a father in the business. He'd steered the appropriate college coaches toward Riley—not that they wouldn't have recruited the talented young man anyway. And he'd pushed Yank toward representing Riley Nash, making up a bullshit excuse for not going after the Heisman winner himself.

If Yank had known or suspected the truth, he'd never let on. And as the years had passed on, Spencer had come to realize Yank was as much in the dark as everyone else. Keeping his secret had been the only way he knew to live and succeed.

Until Lola had finally left Yank and come to him for a shoulder late one night and discovered him with the man he'd been seeing on and off for the past ten years. Bless Lola, who reminded him so much of Anne, she'd quietly accepted, without passing judgment, and hadn't revealed his secret—until it had slipped out when Yank had broken his hip in an angry tirade, thinking Spencer and Lola were a couple. Then somehow, the news that night had leaked out, though, for whatever reason, the timing of the big reveal had been delayed until a couple of weeks before the draft.

But as much as that news had sent Spencer into a tailspin, it was nothing compared to *this* revelation. This one had the potential to destroy other people's lives. Including the life of the son he'd given up in order to protect him from precisely this secret.

"THE IMPROMPTU MEETING of Athletes Only and The Hot Zone partners will now come to order." Uncle Yank whacked his gavel hard against the table. "Now who the hell's responsible for *this?*" He waved today's paper in his hand.

Sophie took a sip of her coffee. "What's going on?" She hadn't slept well last night and, instead of getting to the office in time to read the morning papers before the meeting, she was about to receive her information from Uncle Yank—when he stopped carrying on, she thought.

"It seems that somebody found out about my connection to Riley," Spencer said.

"What?" The foam cup slipped from Sophie's hand and the dark liquid spilled over the lacquered table, soaking her notepad and spreading outward.

She, her sisters and Lola grabbed their napkins and rushed to wipe up the mess.

"I'm sorry. I'm not usually so clumsy," Sophie said, after they'd cleaned the spill and resettled into their seats.

"You're not usually so upset by the morning news, either," Spencer noted too perceptively.

"Well, it doesn't usually involve people I care about." She caught her words and laughed. "I take that back. Lately it involves people I care about way too often."

After all Riley had gone through after finding out about Spencer being gay, he now had to deal with it publicly as well. She glanced at her watch, wondering how long this meeting would go on.

She wanted to get to the phone and see how Riley was handling the news. She couldn't help worrying about him and she felt certain he needed someone to talk to that he could trust. Heaven knows, she understood what he was going through, Sophie thought.

"So what are we going to do about minimizing the damage for you?" Annabelle asked Spencer.

"I have a meeting this week to find out about that."

"Cryptic," Sophie said.

"Very," Micki muttered.

Spencer nodded. "You're all just going to have to trust that I have this situation under control. Well, as in control as things can be."

Yank slammed his gavel, taking everyone off guard.

"What was that for?" Lola asked.

"You heard the man. He's got everything under control." Yank nodded at Spencer. "Meeting adjourned."

Lola gathered his things and together they strode out the conference room door.

"Remember we're meeting for dinner for last-minute party planning," Annabelle said, gathering her things.

"I'll be there," Micki said.

"So will I," Sophie said.

As her sisters walked out the door, chatting about the upcoming party, Sophie reached for the nearest phone, anxious to call Riley.

He'd come to her the moment Spencer's secret had been revealed and they'd gone through so much together since. He'd confided in her that he was Spencer's son when nobody else had known the truth. She couldn't let him go through the public revelation of that truth alone and she wanted him to know if he needed her, she was here.

"As much as you care about me, I have a hunch that the coffee spill was because you're more upset for Riley," Spencer said, coming up behind her.

Caught, she curled her hand around the telephone. "You shouldn't minimize your role in our family," she scolded Spencer, hoping he'd take the hint and drop any conversation about her feelings for his son.

"Can I give you a piece of advice?" he asked.

"Sure."

"I missed out on a lifetime with Riley because of the misguided choices I made." Spencer placed a fatherly hand on her shoulder. "Don't you do the same thing."

Sophie nodded, unable to speak over the lump in her throat. "Thanks," she finally managed to say.

When Spencer walked out, leaving her alone, she grabbed the phone and dialed Riley at home. When the machine picked up instead of him, she shut her eyes, savoring the sound of his voice.

At the beep, she spoke. "Hi, it's me. Sophie. I just heard about the news in the papers and I wanted to know how you were holding up." Knowing she would soon run out of time, she added a quick, "Call me. Please." Then she hung up.

She dialed his cell phone next and left the same message on his voice mail.

Then she settled in to wait.

CHAPTER SEVENTEEN

RILEY SAT in his ex-wife's kitchen, something that had become a habit this past week.

"Riley, you've been here every night since the story broke. I appreciate it. Ted appreciates it. Lizzie appreciates it. But, frankly, you're driving me insane!" Lisa said, but despite the laughter, the seriousness in her tone spoke volumes.

Riley didn't really want to spend his time here, either, but he had no desire to go home to his empty apartment, and he sure as hell had no desire to head back to the gym and listen to the talk and the snickers behind his back.

Lisa looked around, obviously making sure their daughter wasn't around before speaking. "Has it been that bad for you?" she asked.

"Don't get me wrong. I'm a big boy and I can handle gossip."

"But?" she prodded.

"But it sucks doing it alone," he admitted.

Lisa's eyes opened wide. "It's finally happened, hasn't it?" She pulled out a kitchen chair opposite

Riley's and sat down. Perching her chin in her hands, she developed a huge grin on her face. "You've finally met the one woman who doesn't fall into your lap at the snap of your fingers!"

He winced. "Do you think you could stop looking so damn happy about it?"

"I'm sorry." She wiped the smile from her face. "It's just that I never thought I'd see the day. So what's going wrong?"

He shrugged. "Other than everything?"

"If she isn't standing by you during this mess, you really don't need her in your life, Riley." Lisa spoke bluntly with obvious concern.

"What if she's standing by me *only* during this mess?" He voiced the concern that had been dogging him since the scandal of his parentage had erupted.

Sophie had called him almost immediately after the news hit the papers. He hadn't returned her calls. The problem was, he didn't want her in his life only when there was something wrong. Only because she pitied him or thought he needed her to confide in. He wanted her to come around on her own because she couldn't imagine being without him.

"Before the news hit, I had one foot out the door to see her, literally," Riley explained. "I was finished giving her time and space to miss me. I was going to see her to lay it on the line. To tell her that I loved her and that if she loved me it was time to put away her insecurities and take that leap of faith." He flexed and unflexed his fists, frustration still boiling inside him.

Lisa rose and walked to the refrigerator, pulling out a long-necked bottle. She pried off the top with an opener and slid the bottle over to him. "Have a beer. We keep it around just in case you stop by," she said, laughing. "You seem like you could use one right now."

"Thanks."

"So you changed your mind about seeing Sophie. Why?" Lisa asked.

Although it struck Riley that this was the first serious conversation he and his ex-wife had had in years about anything other than their daughter, he appreciated the insight of someone with a successful marriage.

"At first I had to deal with the fallout of the news. By then, Sophie had left messages for me at home and on my cell. And it dawned on me that I hadn't heard from her since our trip to Mississippi. But as soon as a crisis struck, boom! There she was, calling me."

Lisa wrinkled her nose. "And this is a bad thing?" she asked, obviously confused.

He nodded. "You have to know Sophie. In a crisis, she steams into control mode. She knows exactly what to do, what to say and how to act, in order to take charge and make sure that all's right in her world. As soon as the problem is over, she crawls back into her self-protective shell and won't come out."

"Sounds like she needs you more than you need her. And if you don't mind my saying so, that giving-her-space thing? It's more something a man would appreciate than a woman," Lisa said.

He pinched the bridge of his nose, feeling a headache coming on and treating it with a long swig of beer. "I think she needs to be shaken up a bit," he muttered, not knowing how else to get through to the beautiful, stubborn woman.

He couldn't believe after all the years of women coming easily to him, the one woman he wanted in his life for good, he couldn't figure out how to keep. If this were a damn football game, he'd have a playbook. For all Sophie's rules, there were none on how to reach her.

The doorbell rang and before Lisa could respond, Lizzie's footsteps sounded, padding down the stairs. "I got it, I got it," she called, alerting the neighborhood.

Riley and Lisa shot each other amused glances.

"Grandpa!" Lizzie yelled, surprising them both.

Since Lisa's father had died years ago and Lizzie called Ted's father Poppy, a sinking feeling settled low in Riley's stomach. He rose and followed Lisa out of the kitchen and into the foyer in time to see Harlan hugging his granddaughter.

His eyes caught first Lisa's with a warm smile, then Riley's.

"So what brings you here?" Lisa asked, shutting the door behind him.

Harlan wrapped an arm around Lizzie's shoulder. "I stopped by Riley's straight from the airport. The doorman said he wasn't home, so I figured I'd take my chances and have the car service drop me here. Riley mentioned yesterday that he'd been spending time here this week and I was hoping I could meet up with all of you. At the very least I knew I'd get to see my favorite girl." He hugged Lizzie tight. "Can we all sit and talk?"

Oh, something was up, Riley thought. And it couldn't be good.

"Let me get Ted. He's doing paperwork in his office."

Harlan nodded. "That would be a good idea."

Once they were all seated in the living room, Harlan rose and stood in the center of the room. "I realize nobody in this room has had an easy time of it since Riley's paternity was revealed. Riley?"

He shook his head, uncertain where the hell Harlan was going with this. "It's been tough. Locker-room garbage, reporters hounding me, things like that."

"Lizzie?" Harlan looked at the teenager. "How's it been for you?"

She stared at her bare feet without looking up. "The kids at school think it's funny that my dad's got a gay father. They asked me if Dad's gay, too."

Riley and Lisa nodded. They'd heard the stories over the past few days. It broke Riley's heart that his daughter had to bear the brunt of something that had nothing at all to do with her. After all, being a teenager was hard enough.

"I promised your dad I'd find out who was behind the leak." Harlan knelt down beside his granddaughter. "Is there anything you'd like to tell us?"

Riley stiffened. "Dad…" he said, warning his

father to back off. "Don't go looking for a scapegoat just because you're still angry I told Lizzie the truth about Spencer."

The other man rose slowly, in deference to his age. "I have a hair-trigger temper and I admit I lost it that day, but I can assure you I would never blame my granddaughter unfairly." He turned to Lizzie. "Would I, young lady?"

Lisa jumped up from her seat. "I don't know what's going on here but I don't like it. If you have something to say, just say it. Stop beating around the bush," Lisa said, *her* temper flaring.

Ted placed a hand on her arm, pulling her back down, but staying out of the family squabble at least for now.

"I agree with Lisa," Riley said. "Just spit it out." Riley had to admit his daughter, who was still staring at the ground, looked extremely guilty about something.

"My sources tell me that the person behind leaking the news is a man named Frank Thomas. His daughter, Sara, is a schoolmate of Lizzie's," Harlan said.

Riley groaned.

Lisa leaned back in her seat and sighed aloud.

Lizzie burst into tears.

AN HOUR LATER, Riley drove his father back into the city so he could drop him off at his hotel.

"It isn't easy being a parent, is it?" Harlan asked.

Riley shook his head. "No, it sure isn't." He

paused, knowing he owed Harlan an apology. "I'm sorry I trusted Lizzie with that information. Definitely too much for a thirteen-year-old to keep inside. And now your career is at risk."

Harlan sighed. "As she explained through her hysteria, she just confided in a friend because she was upset about you and your girlfriend being on TV. It never dawned on her that her friend would tell her father or that her father would sell the story to earn a buck. Makes it hard to be angry."

"Well, I still trusted her with sensitive information and she repeated it. She needs to learn that actions have consequences. I suppose now she has." Riley swerved the steering wheel to avoid a taxi who cut him off.

"I hope so," Harlan said.

Riley glanced to the passenger side. "So what happens now?"

"I ride out the scandal and see what the electorate does in November. Nothing else I can do." He set his jaw, grinding his back teeth.

"Are you heading back home in the morning?"

Harlan shifted in his seat. "I have an important meeting at nine. I'll fly out after that."

Riley grinned. "The busy life of a politician."

"Yet sometimes it's your personal life that wears you down," the other man said, laughing despite the circumstances. "So how's that beautiful woman you brought home with you?"

"Fine." Riley wasn't in the mood to discuss Sophie for a second time today. He managed to make small talk and keep his real feelings to himself until they finally pulled up to the curb by the hotel and said their goodbyes.

Exhausted, Riley drove home, parked and took the elevator up to his apartment, ready to fall into bed. Instead as he approached his place, he saw a blonde seated outside his door waiting for him.

Sophie must have heard his approach, because she looked up, then rose to her feet, an embarrassed smile on her face.

His heart sped up at the sight of her in her faded jeans and T-shirt. Her hair was tousled and she wore no makeup.

"Hi there," she greeted him with a wave.

He practically lost his heart all over again, but reminded himself he had good reason to be wary. "Hi, yourself."

"Your doorman recognized me from the interview Uncle Yank did on TV and he said I could come on up and wait."

The interview. Another time she'd seen fit to leave a message because she thought it was the right thing to do, not because she couldn't stay away. She managed to do that too easily.

He put his keys in the door and let them inside. "Been here long?"

"Not really," Sophie lied. More like two hours, she thought. She'd even dozed once.

Once inside, he tossed the keys on the kitchen counter. He turned to face her and she saw how truly tired he looked. She curled her fingers into a fist, resisting the urge to reach out and caress his face.

"I don't mean to be rude, but I've had a really long day. I'm wiped out and just plain not in the mood for company. I'd really appreciate it if you'd get to the point of your visit, so I can get some sleep." As if to back up his claim, his body swayed and he leaned against the counter for support.

She swallowed hard. His curt tone caught her off guard. Though they hadn't been in touch lately, she thought they understood each other and shared a special bond. She thought he'd need her. Wasn't that why she'd come to see him now?

She bit on her lower lip, feeling silly for showing up at all. "This was a mistake. Just forget it." She pivoted fast and started for the door.

"Wait." He caught her arm, stopping her from making a clean escape.

She turned and faced him. Her skin burned where he'd touched her, the desire she always felt in his presence still strong. Stronger though was the humiliation.

"I'm sorry. It's just—"

She waved off his apology. "You don't need to apologize. I shouldn't have just shown up here unannounced."

"Then why did you?" His tone softened and curiosity flashed in his face, along with a warmth she hadn't seen yet tonight.

She spread her hands out in front of her. "The papers,

the gossip, the fact that everyone knows Spencer's your father... I know it can't be easy and I've been worried about you." She paused, then added, "I've left messages, but you haven't returned my calls."

"It's been hectic."

"I'll bet." When had they become like two awkward strangers? Sophie wondered. Even at their most heated, angry moments, words had never failed either one of them. "I figured that since nobody knew about you and Spencer before now, you might want to talk to someone who understood."

"Is that it?" he asked, folding his arms across his chest.

Not a good sign as far as Sophie was concerned. He was obviously blocking her out. She wished she could close her eyes and have the floor swallow her whole.

He remained silent, obviously waiting for her to continue her pathetic explanation.

She might as well oblige or else she wouldn't be getting out of here any time soon and her humiliation would continue. He couldn't make it any clearer that he didn't need or want her compassion or understanding.

She shrugged uselessly. "That's it. I thought you might need a friend. Obviously I was wrong."

"A *friend*." A ruddy stain rose to his cheeks and a muscle ticked in his jaw. "You thought I might need a friend." He repeated her words with complete disgust in his tone. "Well, isn't that special? You know what, Sophie? I have plenty of friends. Dozens, in fact. If I wanted to pour my heart out about my newly revealed gay father, I could turn to any number of people in my life. Hell, I could book an interview on *Access Hollywood* and talk to the goddamn nation!" he said, his voice rising.

She stepped back, away from his anger. "I really should go."

"The hell you will. You came here to offer your friendship and now I'm going to have my say before you leave."

In all the time she'd known him, she'd never seen this side of him. She wasn't afraid of Riley, she never could be. But she'd obviously hit a tender nerve and though she didn't understand, she desperately wanted to.

"Go on." Her words came out more like a croak.

"Do you want to know where I was when I found out that the world knew Spencer Atkins is my father?"

She blinked, waiting.

"I was on my way to see you. Want to know why?" He didn't wait for her to answer. "I'd decided I was finished giving you time and space. I'd decided to lay it on the line and tell you that *I love you.*"

His words hit her like a sucker punch in the stomach, hard and painful, and unexpected and sweet all at the same time. Her chest hurt as emotion and anxiety lodged there and remained.

"I didn't know. You never—"

"Came around or told you." He treated her to a

grim smile. "In the disaster that followed, you left messages checking in on me."

She nodded again. "You never returned my calls."

"Because I realized that you only call or show up when things go wrong. When you can take control and do what Sophie Jordan does best—dig up the facts, tell people how to handle things and generally run the show—you're a great sister and I bet you're an even better friend."

He wasn't exactly listing bad qualities. Confusion raced through her. "I don't understand."

He tipped his head to the side and studied her. "The thing is, I don't need another friend. I love you, Sophie Jordan. But I want the person I love to be by my side in good times and in bad. I don't want someone who shows up to lend a shoulder and who runs away from things that feel too good."

"I don't—"

"You do," he said emphatically. "You most certainly do run away any time you think I've gotten too close." He slowly stepped closer, invading her space.

She couldn't breathe as it was, but now when she inhaled she was overcome by his scent, by all that was Riley, and was forced to admit to herself *she loved him, too.*

She just couldn't say the words out loud, fear pummeling her from all sides. And the more he spoke, the more she realized he knew her better than she knew herself.

He placed an arm against the wall above her head.

"You lost your parents and you cope by controlling things around you, but here's the kicker. You can't control love. And that scares you so badly you're willing to walk away from a damn good thing before I leave you first. Or before, on the off chance, something happens and I die on you. Just as your parents did," he said, his voice softening, melting her defenses and breaking her heart.

Tears filled her eyes and she didn't bother to wipe them away, nor could she summon a reply for Riley. She didn't have an answer that would satisfy him because he was so dead-on accurate it was scary.

Cindy had said much the same things, but coming from a friend, it had sounded like psychobabble. Coming from the man who was causing all the emotional turmoil gave it that much more impact.

"Don't worry. I don't expect you to return the sentiment." His eyes flashed with a mixture of irritation and disappointment at the same time. "But that's my whole point. You can't say the words. Hell, I don't even know if you can feel them." He ran his hand through his hair, leaving it spiked and disheveled.

"That's unfair." Sophie trembled, unable to believe the depths to which this conversation had gone. "I didn't even know how you felt before now."

"Would it have mattered?" He set his jaw, his mind obviously already made up.

She looked inside her heart and asked that same question. Would it have mattered? Could she commit to him even now that she knew he was in love with her? Could she give him the words he wanted to hear, knowing she was in love with him, too?

She swallowed hard and met his gaze, the fear of losing him all-consuming. But the fear of committing to someone and not knowing exactly what would come next was too overwhelming for her to contemplate.

She reached out and touched his cheek, as she answered his question in the most honest way she could. "Probably not," she said, ducking beneath his arm and running from his apartment far and fast. Running from him and everything he made her feel.

SPENCER ARRIVED at The Waldorf Astoria hotel for his meeting with Senator Harlan Nash. He wasn't early. He wasn't fashionably late. He was exactly on time. He didn't know if he should be thanking Yank or wanting to murder him for encouraging—or more like forcing him—to set up this appointment.

He knocked on the door and the other man promptly answered and let him inside. There was no need for a formal "hello" or "how are you."

Spencer settled into a seat in the spacious outer room of the suite.

"Drink?" Senator Nash asked.

"Whiskey," Spencer said.

"I think I'll join you." The senator poured them each a shot and then sat, sliding Spencer's glass toward him on the table by the couch.

When they both had their drinks in hand, they stared each other down until, finally, Spencer had had enough. "Can we agree on one thing? That we both have Riley's best interest at heart?"

Harlan nodded. "We always have."

"And for all these years, you've done my job," Spencer admitted. "You raised my son to be a damn fine man and for that I owe you." The words didn't come easily, but they were long overdue.

"Before you go on, there's something you should know." Harlan rose and paced the carpeted floor. "This news leak was the last thing I needed in my career. And public humiliation is the last thing I wanted for my family."

Spencer nodded. "It's been no picnic for me, either," he muttered. "And if you think I stayed out of my son's life all these years only to have him find out anyway, you'd be sadly mistaken."

The senator paused and turned to face Spencer. "Then you'd understand if I told you I would have done almost anything to ensure the news never came out."

Spencer allowed himself to enjoy the burn of the whiskey as it traveled down his throat before replying. "Your point?" Spencer finally asked, unwilling to let this powerful man think he was rattled or thrown by either their meeting or whatever the senator had to say.

Although Spencer had called for this meeting, the other man had agreed readily and obviously had an agenda of his own. Which was fine with Spencer, since he hadn't let the other man in on what *he* wanted out of this talk. Not yet, anyway.

"What we say tonight never leaves this room," Harlan said, his words more a command than a question.

Spencer nodded. "Agreed, although I have to wonder why you'd take me at my word."

The other man downed his drink and poured himself another. "Because you're Riley's flesh and blood and anything said here tonight can only hurt him. Since you spent a lifetime making certain that never happened, I have no choice but to trust you now."

"You mean since I spent a lifetime staying away from him?"

Harlan nodded. "I can't imagine you'd waste all those years of doing the right thing just to get back at me."

Spencer exhaled hard. "No more games, Senator."

"In November I have an election against a tough opponent. I needed every edge I could find against a man who isn't afraid to fight dirty," Harlan said, beginning to explain at last. "When the news broke about your lifestyle," he said choosing a diplomatic term, "the last thing I needed was someone making the connection between you and my family."

Spencer nodded. "So far I'm following you."

"I also knew Riley had tracked you down and extracted a promise that you wouldn't suddenly decide that with one secret revealed it was time to let the rest of the skeletons out of the closet and admit he was your son." The senator shoved his hands into his front pants pockets and stared vacantly, his mind obviously preoccupied with telling his tale.

He'd certainly captured Spencer's interest. "Something tells me my word wasn't enough."

Harlan let out a harsh laugh. "Not in that particular case. I needed you too preoccupied to even think about bonding with your son or talking to the media."

Spencer narrowed his gaze. "So you…"

"Paid someone to sabotage you. Nothing that would destroy your business for good. Just a little something to keep you busy."

Realization dawned at once, anger surging up like bile in his throat. "The computer crash? The break-in? The *camera in Sophie's bathroom?*"

"The camera was a dud, but you must admit all those things gave you little time to think about your personal life or any desire to reconcile with Riley." The senator raised an eyebrow, obviously pleased with his success.

Spencer clenched his hands around the glass. "You have brass balls, Senator."

"I do what I need to in order to survive."

"Tell me something. After the draft, things quieted down. Weren't you worried that maybe I'd have time then to think about renewing my connection to my only child?"

Harlan nodded slowly. "I certainly did. I also knew I was out of options since there was nothing else I could do to stop it, should that be what you desired— nothing except talk to you man-to-man, which I had every intention of doing. Unfortunately the story broke anyway, thanks to Lizzie, and so here we are." He tipped his glass, tapping it against Spencer's.

Spencer pinched the bridge of his nose. He'd come here to make a demand of the senator, one he'd thought would cause a war between them. Instead he'd been handed the keys to his own personal kingdom, Spencer thought.

"Do you realize that you're behind a felony?" Spencer asked.

"Only if you can prove it. And so far the NYPD has been unable to find any leads."

The man's smugness turned Spencer's stomach, but he forced himself to remain calm.

"Sophie's been petrified," Spencer said through clenched teeth, unable to hide his anger. "Her uncle walks the floor at night on his bad hip, concern for her eating him alive." He leaned forward in his seat. "And Riley's been worried sick about her."

Guilt etched Harlan's features for the first time this evening. "I'm sure you can see why you wouldn't want Riley to know I was behind these things." The sound of the senator grinding his teeth sounded loudly in the room.

"Just why did you reveal your role to me?" Spencer asked.

Harlan splayed his hands outward. "Because the guilt was getting to me," he admitted. "And because I want you to convince the police to drop the investigation."

Spencer eyed the other man warily. As a politician, Harlan was obviously skilled at hiding his emotions when dictating his will. So Spencer was glad to see that the man who'd raised his son had some remorse for his actions.

He was also glad to be handed the opportunity for a little quid pro quo. "I want something in return for my silence," Spencer said.

Harlan didn't need to know that Spencer would never hurt Riley by filling him in on his stepfather's actions. Riley admired the man and loved him like a real father. He deserved nothing less.

"What do you want?" the senator asked.

Spencer rose from his seat, going toe-to-toe with the senator for the first time. "I want you to give me free rein to mend the rift with my son." He spoke past the emotion lodged in his throat. "I can never be the parent you've been, nor would I ever try. And I would not undermine your role in his life. You've been everything to the boy and that's as it should be even now."

The senator eyed him with a mixture of admiration and wariness. "Anything else?"

Spencer nodded. "Should Riley come to you or to Anne, I want you to voice your approval aloud. He values your judgment and he wouldn't want to do anything to hurt you. If he thinks getting to know me will bother you, he'll back off."

"Riley's his own man. He makes his own choices," Harlan warned. "I won't sway him if he wants to maintain his distance."

"All I ask is that you not discourage him."

Harlan slowly nodded. "You've got yourself a deal." He extended his hand and Spencer shook it, feeling lighter than he had in years.

Despite Harlan's underhanded dealings, Spencer would walk away with a weight lifted off his shoulders, because before him now lay the potential for a reconciliation with his son.

"Atkins?" Harlan's voice stopped him just as Spencer reached the hotel-room door.

"Yes?"

"This Sophie Jordan woman, is she any good for my—for our son?" Harlan asked.

Spencer turned around, a smile on his face for the first time all night. "There's no better," he assured the senator.

He neglected to mention that she was as stubborn as they came with walls a mile high and pain buried deep. Spencer had his doubts even Riley could get through to her.

CHAPTER EIGHTEEN

RILEY STRAIGHTENED his bow tie and held the door open for his date. Together they walked through the ballroom doors leading to Lola and Yank Morgan's belated wedding reception. Riley had thought long and hard about whether or not to attend. He had more reasons to bail than to show up—from being in the same room with Atkins to facing Sophie for the first time since she ran out on him. But he had one major reason to come. Riley Nash had never run from a confrontation or situation in his life and he wasn't about to do so now.

But he'd opted not to arrive alone. "You ready, beautiful?"

"As I'll ever be."

Riley glanced into his daughter's eyes. Despite all the turmoil of the past few weeks—or maybe because of it—he'd never been as proud of Lizzie as he was lately. First, she'd owned up to her mistake and seemed to really understand how widespread the repercussions of her actions were. She hadn't just betrayed a confidence, she'd potentially affected her grandfather's career. Although she couldn't undo the telling of the secret, she was trying to behave in a more mature way.

She'd also agreed to therapy. Weekly sessions with a psychologist to help her deal with her anger and her issues. There was the occasional family session thrown in for good measure, which didn't thrill Riley, but he'd do anything for his daughter.

They walked inside arm in arm. Riley didn't immediately see the guests of honor, nor did he catch a glimpse of the Jordan sisters or his errant father.

He breathed a silent sigh of relief. "How about a drink?" he asked Lizzie. "Want a Shirley Temple?"

"Da-a-a-d!" she said, appalled.

He winked and refrained from ruffling her professionally blow-dried hair. "Can't blame a father for trying to keep his best girl a little girl."

He leaned against the bar and when the attendant looked his way, Riley said, "Two Cokes, please." No reason to drink with Lizzie around and every reason to keep his wits about him tonight.

"I wasn't sure whether you'd make it tonight," a familiar voice said.

Riley waited for the drinks, handed one to Lizzie and turned slowly to face his real father. "I wasn't sure myself," he admitted.

Considering this was the first time the two men had been in the same room together since being publicly outed as father and son, Riley tried not to squirm under the other man's obvious scrutiny.

"May I say that I'm glad you're here?" Spencer asked.

"You can say whatever you want." Riley had been about to add, *It's a free country,* when he noticed Lizzie's wide-eyed stare.

She'd obviously caught the undercurrents between the two men and Riley knew she'd seen the pictures in the newspaper of Riley and Spencer side by side. No question, Lizzie was aware that this man was Riley's real father.

At that moment, Riley realized he had a choice. He could walk away, as his gut instinct told him to do, or he could stay and talk to Spencer Atkins, as his rapidly beating heart was asking him to do. He could show his daughter that the solution to difficult situations was to run away or he could teach her to stand tall and face her fears.

"Can I order you a drink?" Riley asked the older man. As an olive branch, it wasn't much, but it was the best Riley could do under the circumstances.

"No, thank you." Spencer shook his head, but relief flickered in his eyes. He'd probably been expecting something along the lines of a brush-off and cold shoulder, Riley thought.

But then Riley would lose the chance of getting to know his real father, even for a few brief minutes. Now that their connection was known, no more harm could come to Harlan's career.

He was forced to acknowledge the fact that he had many questions to ask Spencer and little time. Unless he took a step toward opening up to his father. Then perhaps the other man would meet him halfway. Stranger things had happened lately, Riley thought. And he had just the icebreaker with which to begin.

Riley cleared his throat. "Elizabeth, there's someone I'd like you to meet." He wrapped his arm around Lizzie's waist, pulling her close. "Spencer Atkins, this is your granddaughter, Elizabeth. We call her Lizzie." Riley smiled, unable to contain his pride in the young woman she was becoming. "Lizzie, this is…" He stammered over his choice of words.

"I'm Spencer Atkins," the other man said, helping Riley out. "I'm—"

"My grandfather," Lizzie said. "Well, one of my grandfathers. I already have Grandpa Harlan."

"I'm hoping you have room for one more."

"Sure," Lizzie said, and shrugged, as if all this blended, extended family stuff was commonplace.

In her life, Riley supposed it was.

"Well, good. But a beautiful girl like you can call me whatever you like," Spencer said, grinning.

"Watch out," Riley warned. "Give her an opening like that and you just might hang yourself." Riley couldn't help but laugh.

"Hey! I'm not that bad. Give me some credit!" Lizzie said, blushing.

"This from the girl who's just now working her way back into everyone's good graces? I think there's someone else you should apologize to for spilling the beans." Suddenly he was no longer thirsty. Riley placed his untouched glass back on the bar and waited for his daughter's defiant outburst.

But to his never-ending shock, Lizzie didn't argue. Instead, she nodded. "I'm sorry," she said to Spencer. "It wasn't my secret to tell." She glanced down and away.

Spencer's eyes opened wide, stunned at her admission. "That's a very mature thing for you to admit," he said at last.

"My shrink says taking responsibility is important." She glanced around the room, suddenly distracted. "Hey, Dad, isn't that Brandon Vaughn?" She pointed to the retired football player who'd married Sophie's sister Annabelle.

Riley felt certain the middle sister couldn't be far away and he stiffened in preparation for that meeting, as well.

"It sure is Brandon Vaughn," Spencer said, before Riley could respond. "Would you like me to introduce you?" Spencer asked.

Lizzie's head bobbed up and down. "Can I go with him, Dad? Please?"

Riley didn't hesitate. "Of course you can go."

Over Lizzie's head and eager bouncing, Spencer met Riley's gaze—gratitude, appreciation and more in his solemn expression.

A silent understanding had just passed between them, Riley realized. The first awkward bridge had been crossed.

As he watched his daughter, his pride and joy,

walk off with her grandfather, an unfamiliar emotion swelled in his throat. Lizzie would have another adult to look up to in her life.

It came at an important juncture, when she was impressionable and vulnerable all at the same time. There had been a time when Riley wouldn't have envisioned Spencer Atkins as any kind of role model, especially not for Lizzie. But so much had changed in such a short time.

Nothing could alter the fact that the other man had ignored Riley for the first part of his life. But Riley had also learned that Spencer hadn't lived a carefree existence during these past years. He'd suffered plenty, too. Riley admitted to being curious about the details, and he'd always had a burning desire to understand the father he'd never really known. He finally had his chance.

There was nothing except his pride to prevent them from going forward from here and he wasn't about to let it get in the way of what he'd wanted his entire life.

SOPHIE WAS RUNNING LATE. Unintentionally, but she was still going to end up making an obvious entrance. That was something she'd have preferred to avoid, but not even her uncle's wedding reception could change the fact that she had an upset client who'd demanded her attention.

But she was here now, and though she'd spent hours planning the details of this event, tonight she was simply a guest. Lola had hired a staff to see that the night ran smoothly. Sophie would rather be preoccupied with the details, but Lola had insisted she relax and enjoy the evening.

She smoothed the beading on her long gown, drew a deep breath and walked inside the ballroom of the beautiful hotel.

"You're late!" Annabelle grabbed Sophie's arm the moment she set foot inside the room.

"I had a work-related emergency."

"Nothing serious, I hope?" Annabelle asked.

Sophie shook her head.

Annabelle exhaled with relief. "It's just that the break-in and other problems are still fresh in my mind."

"Mine, too," Sophie admitted. "Spencer said he'd taken care of things. He won't say what he did or who was responsible, but he swears it's over. And you know Spencer—when he holds on to a secret, nobody finds out."

"Not for decades anyway," Annabelle said wryly. "Okay, on to other things. You look beautiful," she said, kissing Sophie's cheek.

"Thanks." Sophie stepped back and took in her sister's formfitting light blue gown that set off the color of her eyes.

Annabelle's pregnancy was over but its effects remained, her already voluptuous curves even more pronounced. As always, Annabelle looked statuesque and gorgeous, Sophie thought. "You look fabulous yourself."

"I second that." Annabelle's husband, ex-pro football player Brandon Vaughn, came up beside his wife, linking his arm through hers. He turned to Sophie and grinned. "You're looking pretty damn good, too, little sister." Vaughn treated her to a brotherly wink.

Sophie laughed. "Thanks. You clean up pretty nicely yourself," she said, taking in his black European-cut tuxedo.

Annabelle rolled her eyes. "Oh, don't boost his ego. He already thinks he's the stud of the night." But it was obvious by the way she devoured her husband with her eyes that Annabelle agreed with Sophie's assessment.

Vaughn tipped his head to one side. "You mean I'm not?"

Sophie chuckled once more. "Where's my sweet little niece?" she asked.

"You didn't really think I'd turn down a kid-free night out on the town, did you?" Annabelle asked, grinning.

Sophie shook her head. "No, you're a normal mother who needs a break."

"But who's called home every hour on the hour," Vaughn said.

Annabelle shrugged off her husband's words. "Like you're any better? The sitter told me you've been calling in between my check-ins."

He flushed guiltily.

"Hi, guys." Micki joined them, rescuing Vaughn from further embarrassment. "What are you doing huddling in a corner? We should be mingling!"

"My wife, the people person." Micki's husband, Damian, stepped up behind her and slid his arms around her waist, pulling her close.

Vaughn glanced at the two. "Newlyweds," he said, and groaned.

"Don't tell me you have a problem with public displays of affection?" Micki teased as her brother-in-law absently rubbed his own wife's back with one hand.

"None at all when I'm the one involved. It's watching other people do it that turns my stomach." Vaughn laughed.

Damian glanced at the women in the family, his attention lingering for a moment on each. "You ladies are looking gorgeous tonight." He nodded approvingly, his stare settling on Sophie. "You're looking particularly hot."

"Oh, brother." Micki laughed.

So did Sophie. "You always forget there's no more need to charm me, Fuller. I finally decided I like you even if you are a ballplayer."

Micki patted her husband's arm. "He can't help himself. He sees a beautiful woman and he has to react."

Damian shook his head. "Not since I met you, babe." He pulled Micki tighter against him.

Sophie sighed and tried *not* to focus on the fact that she was the odd woman out in this sea of couples. They only needed Uncle Yank and Lola to make the unit complete, but those two were due to have their own special entrance in a few minutes.

Looking past her sisters, she scanned the room and she caught sight of Riley. Even surrounded by other men in formal attire, Riley Nash stood out. He was devastatingly handsome in a tuxedo—as well as out of it, as she remembered all too well.

He appeared happy and relaxed, flanked on one side by his daughter, Lizzie, and on the other by his father. His real father. Riley and Spencer appeared to be having a civil conversation near the bar. An actual smile lifted Riley's lips into his trademark heart-stopping grin.

She felt her stomach flip, unnerved at seeing him for the first time since their conversation in his apartment. She recalled that moment as more like a monologue than a conversation, and she still hadn't mentally recovered from all he'd had to say to her that night.

Yet here he was, apparently over the scandal of his real parent being revealed, and making inroads with the man, whom he'd sworn he would keep at arm's length. My, how things had changed, she thought. Riley was clearly giving Spencer a chance.

Something she hadn't been willing to do for Riley, himself. He'd said that she was so afraid of the things she couldn't control that she would risk walking away from him first, before he walked away or left her. When she'd run away, she'd backed up his claim. By being here tonight and socializing with Spencer, Riley was, in sports terms, one-upping her.

He was showing her up by being brave. He was

the ultimate risk taker and the one person Sophie couldn't predict or control. Just like she couldn't control her love for him, and that love still surrounded her, making the air she breathed so heavy and thick that she couldn't inhale easily.

She needed space, not just from Riley but from the happy couples surrounding her. "Excuse me," she said to her sisters, who were already involved in other conversations.

Sophie lifted the hem of her dress and headed for the ladies' room located outside the ballroom doors. No sooner had she entered the empty powder-room area and begun to rummage through her purse for lip gloss, than the door opened wide and someone stepped through.

Sophie glanced into the mirror and saw Riley's daughter staring back. "Hi, Lizzie," Sophie said immediately, hoping to break the ice that had still remained between them since last time they were together.

"Hi." A tentative smile curled the girl's lips, surprising Sophie.

"Beautiful dress," Sophie said, admiring the lilac gown the teenager wore.

Lizzie's smile grew wider. "Isn't it cool? My mom took me to buy it."

Where was the hostility? Sophie wondered. The sullenness? The anger? And then she realized the cause for the young girl's friendly attitude: Sophie was no longer dating her father.

Sophie had achieved Lizzie's good favor at the

expense of Riley's. Pushing that thought aside, she refocused on the teen. "Well, you can tell your mother for me you both have great taste. Of course, I bet anything you put on would look stunning on you."

Perhaps Lizzie was encouraged by their civil tone, because she slowly edged closer to the mirror where Sophie stood.

"Can I talk to you about something?" Lizzie asked.

Sophie nodded. "Of course."

The girl bit down on her lower lip, her nerves showing. "I…um…I wanted to say I'm sorry for…you know, being such a brat back in Mississippi."

Another shock, Sophie thought. "You already apologized at the airport. You don't need to do it again," she said softly. "But I appreciate it."

"I hope so, because I mean it this time."

Sophie tried not to laugh and failed. She wanted to explain that she wasn't laughing *at* Lizzie but the teenager spoke first.

"I know why you're not seeing my dad anymore."

Sophie blinked, stunned into utter silence. Lizzie claimed to know what Sophie couldn't even explain to herself. "You do?" she asked, buying herself time to come up with another, more appropriate response.

Lizzie nodded. "It's because of me. Because you think I'd be miserable if he was still with you and because you think I'm too horrible for words."

This time Sophie managed not to laugh at the teen's over-dramatic words. "You're wrong," she assured the young girl. "You have nothing to do with it."

"But—"

Sophie held up a hand, forestalling an argument. "I'm willing to bet that whatever you believe I think of you is one-hundred-percent wrong." Sophie drew a deep breath. "Because I happen to think you're a teenager going through normal teenage stuff," she said. "Added to that, you have parents who love you but are divorced, so you have to share your mom with her husband, but you've never had to share your dad. Right?"

Lizzie nodded, still not looking up.

"So you copped an attitude with me. Big deal. I'm an adult, I can handle it. Especially since you apologized."

"You mean it? Because I told my shrink that it's my fault that you left and my dad's been a major grump ever since."

Lizzie waited for her to respond, finally meeting Sophie's gaze with wide, hopeful eyes.

"I mean it," she assured Lizzie. Though Sophie wasn't sure what shocked her more. That Lizzie was seeing a therapist or that Riley had been miserable ever since they'd been apart.

But she had to focus on his daughter now. "I have two sisters, one older and one younger, so I know girls," Sophie told Lizzie. "I also deal with star athletes and, trust me, many of them throw bigger tantrums than a teenager with attitude." She grinned, liking her analogy a lot. "Do you believe me?"

"Yeah." Lizzie nodded. "You know what?"

Sophie tipped her head to one side. "What?"

"You're not so bad."

Sophie had to laugh at that. "But would you say that if your father and I were together?"

"You know what? I know that I would." Lizzie's eyes shone bright with approval.

Sophie didn't kid herself that if she and Riley were a couple, there wouldn't be rough patches with this kid, but for now, she had Lizzie's seal of approval. But what was she going to do with that acceptance?

"You're not so bad yourself." Sophie smiled at the teenager and winked.

"I have to go to the bathroom," Lizzie said, and headed for the other room.

Sophie reached into her bag and swiped some gloss over her lips. Her heart raced a mile a minute and she was uncertain as to why. Then again, all the unexpected developments tonight were enough to bring on a case of full-blown anxiety. With that in mind, she stepped back out to the ballroom, uncertain of what awaited her next.

CHAPTER NINETEEN

THE BALLROOM LIGHTS had been dimmed, making it more difficult to locate people inside. Sophie hoped she could use the cover of darkness to gather her thoughts.

"There you are!" Cindy made a beeline for Sophie, pulling her aside. "I've been looking all over for you."

Sophie smiled. Despite the chaos she was feeling, she was happy to see her friend. "Well, here I am."

"Looking fabulous," Cindy said. "Gosh, I envy you that silky blond hair."

Sophie had had her hair blow-dried straight for tonight's party. Meanwhile her friend had a headful of glorious red curls falling over her shoulders and striking a perfect contrast with her emerald-green dress.

Sophie shook her head. "Why is it we always want what we don't have?" she asked lightly.

"I have it now!" Cindy said, her words not making any sense but her excitement tangible anyway.

"I don't understand."

Cindy drew a long, deep breath. "I always spent my life witnessing other people's happiness. You know, the beautiful girl gets the gorgeous guy. I never thought it would happen to me."

Realization began to dawn. "I see now. This is about Miguel, isn't it?" Sophie asked.

"Yes! That's what I've been trying to tell you," Cindy said. "Miguel and I both agree it's too soon to talk marriage or engagement, only because he's a traditional man and he hasn't met my family—well, the people from the restaurant back home that I call family. And I haven't met his parents and relatives. They're in the Dominican Republic, but he booked us a trip. First to L.A. and then to the Caribbean!" she explained in a long-winded rush, her eyes glittering with joy. "And just so that I don't think he isn't serious, he gave me this." Cindy held her right hand out to reveal a huge emerald ring.

"It's gorgeous," Sophie said, finally able to get a word in. "And so are you. Gorgeous and glowing with happiness. I couldn't be happier for you." She pulled her friend into an embrace before stepping back.

She no longer believed Miguel Cambias was anything other than a rival agent, despite them never having solved the mystery behind the sabotage at the office. Without another incident to go on, the police had pretty much stopped searching for more clues. The NYPD had more important things to do than investigate a dead end. And in her heart of hearts, Sophie refused to believe that a man who made her friend this happy could be the culprit.

"You deserve all good things," Sophie said, squeezing Cindy's hand once more.

"No more than you do." Cindy's meaningful gaze bore into Sophie's, as if she could transmit the message and make Sophie believe it, too.

Sophie swallowed hard, the lump in her throat as painful as the hole in her heart. "Don't you have a Latin hunk waiting for you in the other room?" she asked, forcing a light laugh.

Cindy nodded. "You can't control everything, but you *can* control your own choices. Think about it, please. Before it's too late."

Sophie opened her mouth to speak, but words wouldn't come. Just then, a loud drumroll sounded into the hall. "Would everyone please gather around?" Spencer's voice reverberated from the microphone.

"Saved," Sophie said, too low for anyone to hear. Then she turned and followed Cindy back into the ballroom.

The next few minutes passed in a hazy blur. Spencer introduced the newlyweds and Uncle Yank blustered about how lucky he was that he hadn't lost Lola long before now. Many of his reminiscences had Sophie laughing aloud. Some nearly had her in tears.

But one thing became clear as she stood in a room surrounded by Uncle Yank, Lola, her sisters and her new brothers-in-law. All of her life, she'd told herself that as long as she had her family, she would be fine. But tonight, for the first time, she was surrounded by every single family member she adored, and yet she was still *completely alone*. As alone as she was in her apartment night after night. As alone as she'd be for the rest of her life if she didn't do something about it.

She didn't have to look far for the courage to act, either. All around her were examples of people who'd fought their inner demons and won. Bravery surrounded her. From Annabelle and Vaughn to Micki and Damian, from Uncle Yank to Spencer, she was faced with people who'd confronted their fears and let themselves trust—in both love and in a future.

She could be like them, like the brave woman who'd gone parasailing with no fear, or she could remain alone wondering what might have been. She could walk out of here tonight without taking a chance on Riley, and accept a future of being alone and lonely. Or she could take that leap of faith and trust that Riley would catch her.

"Well, Sophie?" she asked herself. "Which one will it be?"

RILEY HAD HAD ENOUGH socializing and making nice, talking to everyone except for Sophie. He hadn't seen her since she'd entered the room, talked to her sisters and walked out again. By ignoring him, she'd made her feelings and intentions perfectly clear.

He might have chased Spencer around for years before catching on to the fact that the man hadn't wanted anything to do with him, but he was older and wiser now. He wouldn't make the same mistake twice. He'd give Sophie the space she so desired. Permanently.

He'd sent Lizzie to say goodbye to whomever she wanted to before they left and he had a hunch she'd made a beeline for the ladies' room because his daughter was nowhere to be found.

He had to admit the evening wasn't a total bust. He found a surprising satisfaction in having made a tentative peace with his biological father after all these years. He didn't know what the future held for them, but he had a positive feeling where before he'd felt only anger and disappointment. Not bad for a party he hadn't wanted to attend.

He glanced around but he didn't see Lizzie and wondered if she'd decided to meet him by the entrance. He'd turned and started for the door, when a light touch on the shoulder stopped him.

Having had his share of people and small talk for the evening, he jerked around with every intention of abruptly excusing himself without a long explanation. And then he saw Sophie.

"Care to dance?" She spoke boldly, but in her eyes he saw vulnerability.

She obviously wasn't sure what to expect of him. And damned if a part of him didn't want to just turn and walk away to make her feel as rejected as she'd made him feel all night long.

Instead he placed his hand in hers and led the way to the dance floor. Although he tried to keep an emotional distance, he found it difficult when holding her in his arms, inhaling her unique scent and knowing how her soft curves fit so perfectly against him.

"Enjoying yourself?" he asked, his voice gruff.

She drew a trembling breath. "Not really."

Her words surprised him. "I'd have thought you'd be thrilled to celebrate your uncle and Lola's marriage."

"I am."

"But?" He swung her around and eased them away from the prying eyes of her family, who stood too close to where they danced.

She tipped her head back. Moisture fringed her lashes, making her blue eyes glassy. "I'm…lonely."

He blinked, certain he'd heard her wrong. "I don't understand. Your entire family is here. How could you feel alone?"

She treated him to a grim smile. "I've been asking myself that same question. All my life, I told myself that family is all that matters. First we needed to stay together after my parents died and later we just needed each other."

By her serious tone of voice, he sensed things had shifted for her in a way that had affected her deeply.

"But now…" Her voice trailed off. Her eyes grew even more glazed and unfocused.

She was obviously thinking about what to say next. It was difficult not to make suggestions to lead her to the conclusions he wanted to hear, but he refrained. "Go on," he said, not wanting her to think he wasn't listening.

She nodded. "Have you ever been surrounded by people you loved and yet been completely alone?

That's such a surreal thought and yet that's exactly what happened tonight."

He understood her, because being here tonight with his daughter and the man whose approval and love he had always sought hadn't been enough for him, either. Not with Sophie little more than an arm's distance away physically but emotionally on the other side of the earth.

"I realized tonight that the family I hold so precious isn't enough anymore," Sophie whispered. "I need more."

Despite their slow and easy dancing, Riley nearly tripped on his own feet, because her words gave him a shot of hope for a future between them for the first time.

"It's confusing," she said, obviously talking things through for both herself and for him.

"What is?" He switched his grip, lacing his fingers through hers.

"All the rules in my life have shifted. It's like I've done a one-eighty and now I can't find firm ground."

"I can relate," he muttered. The way Riley's stomach was bouncing around inside him, he couldn't settle down, either. She was giving him explanations with no firm conclusions and his nerves were shot waiting to see what exactly she was trying to say to him.

She smiled. "I know I'm talking in circles, but I need to do this my way."

And their ways were never quite the same, which was what had given her pause to begin with, Riley knew. So he shut up and let her continue. Otherwise he might lose this one last chance—at what, he hadn't a clue.

He could only hope.

"So I looked around the room and realized that I had half-a-dozen examples in front of me of people who had conquered their fears, and I could either do the same or end up alone." She grinned at him, her smile too bright, too forced, her fear of rejection palpable.

He hated to do this to her, but he had no choice. "Sophie?"

"Yes?"

"I have no freaking clue what you're trying to tell me. Okay, I take that back. I have an idea, but if I'm wrong, I don't think I could handle it." *It* being having his heart squashed by her again. He didn't see a reason to define it graphically for her.

He stopped in his tracks in the middle of the dance floor. He already held her hands in his and he brought them up to his chest, near his heart. "I get all the why's about how you're feeling. Now you have to tell me *what* you're feeling. You have to say it and mean it."

Her eyes opened wide and she nodded.

He took a risk and continued. "Fear's okay. I'm afraid before every game I play. Just don't tell anyone," he said, forcing a laugh when he felt anything but light-hearted. "So fear's okay, but giving in to it isn't." He squeezed her hands tighter, hoping to instill her with the courage he already sensed she possessed.

"My family isn't enough for me anymore. They're married and happy and settled…and I'm not." She bit down on her glossed lips. "My sisters faced their fear of losing someone they loved and took the ultimate risk. What I'm saying is, I'm ready to take that risk, too."

He gave her an encouraging nod. Meanwhile his heart pounded hard in his chest and a pain gnawed at his gut while he waited. For her.

Slowly, she pulled her hands out of his and cupped her palms around his face. "I know I've put you through hell and that you've been a major grump, to use Lizzie's words." A smile tugged at her lips. "And I'm sorry for that. But I can't fit you into any mold and that scares me."

"You can't control me by reading a book. You can't guarantee that I won't get sick or injured or worse one day. Life is a risk."

She nodded. "I realize that now. And I want to take that risk with you because I love you."

"Say that again," he said, the pain in his chest and stomach slowly easing.

"I love you," she said on a hoarse whisper. "And I want to spend my life with you."

He knew the courage she'd needed to take this step and he planned to make sure she never regretted it. He reacted on instinct, picking her up and twirling her around.

"Now I'm going to make you a promise you *can* count on, because it's within my control," he said, letting her down onto her feet.

"What's that?" she asked, grinning from ear to ear. Obviously she approved of his reaction.

"I will never leave you and I will never consciously do anything to hurt you."

Sophie nodded, her throat full, unable to believe this rebel man was hers and hers alone. "I'm sorry it took me so long to come around."

"Who am I to criticize someone doing something their own way?" he asked, laughing.

"Hey, I found this girlie hangin' around outside." Uncle Yank strode up to them, Lizzie in tow. "I know she belongs to you," he said, poking Riley in the chest. "What kind of parent leaves his kid alone while he hits on a woman in the other room?"

Lizzie's eyes grew wider. "Is that what you were doing?" she asked.

Sophie rolled her eyes. "Uncle Yank—" *Not in front of the child*, she almost said before catching herself and shutting up.

Riley grasped Sophie's hand in his. "Let me handle him."

"By all means." Smiling, Sophie stepped back so the two men could tangle.

Riley looked at Lizzie and winked before turning to the older man. "Yank, you've been my agent for my entire career and we've always gotten along well," Riley began.

Uncle Yank raised one bushy eyebrow. "Your point?" he asked gruffly, still in protective guardian mode.

"I'm hoping we can get along equally well if you're my uncle-in-law," Riley said.

The older man's mouth opened then shut again. Apparently he'd rendered Yank Morgan speechless—not an easy feat. Considering Sophie was stunned at the comment herself, she could understand her uncle's reaction.

"In-law?" Sophie asked, wanting to make sure she understood exactly what Riley was saying.

"That's what I want to know," Yank said. "Are you askin' for—"

"Your niece's hand in marriage."

"You want to *marry* me?" Sophie asked, stunned. It was one thing to talk in generalities, another to know he wanted the entire commitment.

"You want to *marry* her?" Lizzie parroted, sounding equally surprised.

"What the hell is wrong with everyone?" Riley asked. "I love her. Of course I want to marry her," he shouted, silencing the entire room.

"Yes!" Lizzie said, recovering first.

"Well, I guess I can't argue with that," Yank said gruffly, beaming with happiness and obvious approval.

Without warning, the crowd reacted next. Her sisters, and then Uncle Yank and Lola, who now stood beside him, broke into a round of applause.

"You aren't upset?" Sophie asked Lizzie quietly when the clapping had died down.

She noticed that Riley leaned in closer, waiting for his daughter's answer.

"Hell, no. Now Dad'll be in a good mood all the time and he'll start saying *yes* to things again," Lizzie said, grinning.

"Miss Mouth," Riley said, warning her.

But even Sophie noticed the twitch in his lips. His happiness shone through his disapproval and warmed Sophie straight through to her toes. "You're quite the little schemer," Sophie said, laughing.

"What can I say? It's part of my charm."

"She inherited it from me," Riley said. "And now I'd like a word alone with my future bride." Instead of telling everyone else to scram as Sophie expected him to do, he turned to Yank. "As your first official duty, you can keep an eye on your soon-to-be...whatever you want to call her," he said, laughing.

Lizzie narrowed her gaze in a way that said, *I'm gonna get you for that.* But her eyes were dancing with happiness. Apparently she wasn't kidding; Lizzie did approve of Riley and Sophie at last.

Riley grabbed Sophie's hand and pulled her through the ballroom, out the large doors and into the unoccupied coatroom closet, slamming the door behind them. A dim light glowed from overhead.

Riley bracketed his hands against the wall over her head. "I cannot believe I finally have you alone," he said, his eyes glittering with desire.

She was way ahead of him. Every pore in her body craved his touch.

"Did I tell you how gorgeous you look tonight?"

She shook her head. "No, but something tells me you're going to."

A slow, wicked smile spread across his lips as he settled his mouth on hers. It was a long, sensual while before he lifted his head and met her gaze. "You look spectacular," he said in a husky voice.

"Tell me again," she said.

"You're brave, beautiful and mine." Then he dipped his head and he told her in other ways. Over and over and over again.

EPILOGUE

SENATOR HARLAN NASH and his wife had insisted on having Sophie and Riley's wedding at their Mississippi estate, and Sophie, God love her, Yank thought, had agreed.

What the hell would have been wrong with the Plaza or another of the old New York City hotels? Yank wondered. He was paying for the shindig anyway. At least he thought he was. Between all the arguing going on, he could never be sure.

Annabelle and Micki had made gorgeous matrons of honor while Lizzie had been the only bridesmaid, and the cute kid had reveled in the attention. As she'd walked down the aisle, she'd waved to everyone like the Queen of England. With her spunk and attitude, she actually reminded him a little of Micki as a kid, he thought, grinning.

Then Yank had walked Sophie down the aisle— without his cane, he thought proudly. He didn't need a walking stick when he had a dog as smart as

Noodle. Never mind that she'd sniffed something and taken off for the other side of the bushes, wedding rings hooked into her collar. A waitress had retrieved them, crawling out of the greenery with leaves poking from her head in time for the *I do's*.

The best part of the day had come when Spencer had walked his son halfway down the aisle. The senator had taken over midway. It seemed like a fair compromise to all involved. Everybody had ignored the protestors out back. Harlan had announced his intention to let the voters have their say come November and if retirement was in his future, he had plenty of other pursuits, he'd said. Yank hadn't a clue what those were, but the man seemed resigned to Spencer's orientation and place in Riley's life. Nothing else mattered as far as Yank was concerned.

Now he stood in the backyard, the party tapering down. Many of the senator's Southern guests had *taken leave,* as they called it, which was just fine with Yank. The women and their umbrellas and finery, the old men and their fine talk. He'd been like a goddamn fish out of water, is what he'd been. Even with his friends here—like Curly and, of course, Spencer— Yank had kept getting nudged in the ribs by Lola.

Minding his manners and his p's and q's wasn't his way. Never had been.

The only good thing was that Spencer's fruitcake sisters had behaved worse than Yank ever had. Rose and Darla had both dived for the bridal bouquet, pushing the younger women out of the way, ending up fighting each other smack dab in the middle of the dance floor. In the end, they'd split the bouquet in half, though Yank couldn't see what kind of man would have either of the nut jobs. He had to admit Spencer's niece, Amy, seemed nice enough, but she had her hands full keeping her mother and aunt in line.

The day was almost over and Yank shook his head in disbelief. He'd raised and married off all three of his girls. Hell, he'd even gone and gotten married himself. How the heck had *that* happened? he wondered.

Well, at least he still had his Cubans, he thought, patting his breast pocket. He'd hand the suckers out when Lola's back was turned. The woman had eyes like a hawk.

God how he loved her.

"What are you thinking about?" Lola asked, coming up beside him and linking her arm through his.

"Just admiring my handiwork."

She looked up at him, confused. "What handiwork?"

"Well, the girls and their men, of course!" He pointed to their family gathered beneath the large white tent.

"The girls all found themselves perfect mates, which as far as I can see, had nothing whatsoever to do with you." Lola patted his shoulder. "But you tell yourself whatever makes you happy, honey."

Now he knew she was goading him on purpose. Probably because she liked kissing and making up so much. "Now, Lola, give me due credit. I was the one who made sure Annabelle went up to Greenlawn to work on Vaughn's resort PR, wasn't I?"

"You were," she agreed. "You were also the one who showed up unannounced, stayed and drove them insane."

"Surveying the lay of the land, so to speak. Checkin' up on them."

Lola frowned. "You were running away from me and you know it. Annabelle and Vaughn found their way to each other on their own, no thanks to you."

"I sent him after her," he insisted. "Now take Micki and Damian. Who arranged it so Micki had to be the one to go on down to Florida to handle the Renegades' publicity?"

Lola nodded. "You did. Where she was set up and ended up in a strip joint. Admit it, Micki and

Damian had some real issues standing between them. That they came together is a credit to them not you."

Yank groaned at her stubbornness. He opened his mouth to speak but she cut him off.

"And before you go saying you're responsible for Sophie and Riley being together, that had everything to do with Spencer running off to Florida and nothing to do with you."

The woman wouldn't give him credit for a dang thing.

"But there is something you get one-hundred-percent credit for," she said, her voice softening as she leaned in close.

He inhaled, enjoying having her near. He might not be able to see her so well, but he knew every last thing about her and that was all that mattered.

"Is that a new perfume you're wearing?" he asked, enjoying the sexy scent.

"Why yes, it is," she said, her voice rising with pleasure.

He nodded with satisfaction. Women liked it if a man noticed the little things, he'd learned. It had only taken him almost thirty years to get that through his thick skull, not that he'd admit what a slow learner he was to Lola.

Besides tonight his attentiveness might get him some action with his loving wife.

"Now pay attention," Lola chided. "Don't you want to know what I'm giving you credit for?" she asked.

"Yes, yes, I certainly do."

"You raised three absolutely wonderful young women. Caring, kind, smart, strong, beautiful and, most importantly, brave." Lola lovingly caressed his cheek with her soft hand.

His stomach flipped like a kid's at Christmas. Instead of her impact on him diluting since they'd been married, it had only grown stronger. Her approval meant so much to him, but he no longer let it scare him. Instead he accepted it as the way things were.

"Go on," he said gruffly.

She laughed. "You need more compliments? Seriously, Yank. You raised them to be strong and independent. They may have had issues from losing their parents, but all three were brave enough to overcome them in the end and go after what they wanted. It's a credit to you."

"She's right, Uncle Yank," Sophie said, joining them.

"She's always right," Micki said.

"Always has been," Annabelle added.

His whole family surrounded him. Could he get any luckier than he'd been in his life? Yes, yes, he could, Yank thought, an idea coming to him and he laughed aloud.

"What's so funny?" Sophie asked.

Yank smiled. "I'm just wonderin', where are all your men at?"

"Why?" all three sisters asked warily, as if they didn't trust him.

"Because I wanted to ask 'em when you're all gonna give me a bunch of grandchildren to bounce on my knee. Now that my hip is working better, and all."

Sophie groaned. "I'm out of here," she said, blowing him a kiss as she made her way across the grass.

"Ditto," Micki said. "I love you, but you've got to find yourself a hobby." She took off, too, leaving him with Lola and Annabelle.

"Don't you even look my way, Uncle Yank. I've done my duty," Annabelle said and she, too, disappeared.

He shook his head. "Now what'd I do to make 'em run off that way?"

Nobody answered. "Lola?"

"I'm gone," she called, her voice sounding distant.

He hadn't even realized she'd taken off along with the girls.

Yank laughed and glanced up, letting the sun warm his face the way all his women warmed him.

They might grouse and complain at his meddling ways, but he just knew he'd have grandchildren on the way from each of them by year's end.

Family, he thought, grinning like a fool. A lucky man like him didn't need one single thing more.

HQN™

We *are* romance™

USA TODAY BESTSELLING AUTHOR
Sue Civil-Brown

An emergency landing on an island full of lunatics,
an approaching hurricane and Buck Shanahan are
DEFINITELY not in Hannah's plan. The sassy pilot has no
time for island bumpkins like Buck and his buddies—until
a hurricane bears down, grounding her on tiny Treasure
Island. But as Hannah throws her chips in with Buck to
save the place from destruction, the stakes may be higher
than she ever dreamed….

HURRICANE HANNAH

Flying into bookstores this June.

77001	HOT STUFF	___ $6.99 U.S.	___ $8.50 CAN.
77055	HOT NUMBER	___ $7.50 U.S.	___ $8.99 CAN.
77080	BRAZEN	___ $6.99 U.S.	___ $8.50 CAN.
77143	BODY HEAT	___ $6.99 U.S.	___ $8.50 CAN.

(limited quantities available)

TOTAL AMOUNT $ _____
POSTAGE & HANDLING $ _____
($1.00 for 1 book, 50¢ for each additional)
APPLICABLE TAXES* $ _____
TOT $

To
o
3

P.O.

BAKER & TAYLOR

WWW.HQNBOOKS.